when we were monsters

◆·· ALSO BY JENNIFER NIVEN ··◆

All the Bright Places

Breathless

Holding Up the Universe

when we were monsters

JENNIFER NIVEN

Alfred A. Knopf
New York

A Borzoi Book published by Alfred A. Knopf
An imprint of Random House Children's Books
A division of Penguin Random House LLC
1745 Broadway, New York, NY 10019
penguinrandomhouse.com
rhcbooks.com

Text copyright © 2025 by Jennifer Niven
Jacket art copyright © 2025 by Alexis Franklin
Interior art used under license from Adobe Stock

Penguin Random House values and supports copyright. Copyright fuels creativity, encourages diverse voices, promotes free speech, and creates a vibrant culture. Thank you for buying an authorized edition of this book and for complying with copyright laws by not reproducing, scanning, or distributing any part of it in any form without permission. You are supporting writers and allowing Penguin Random House to continue to publish books for every reader. Please note that no part of this book may be used or reproduced in any manner for the purpose of training artificial intelligence technologies or systems.

Knopf, Borzoi Books, and the colophon are registered trademarks
of Penguin Random House LLC.

Excerpt from "Mad Girl's Love Song" from *The Bell Jar* © copyright 1971
by Harper & Row

"The Dreamer" by Penelope Niven reproduced by permission
from Jennifer Niven, her daughter.

Ness's poetry within these pages reproduced by permission
from the author of these poems, Vanessa Cato aka VCPoetry.

Editor: Katherine Harrison
Cover Designer: Trisha Previte
Interior Designer: Michelle Canoni
Production Editor: Melinda Ackell
Managing Editor: Jake Eldred
Production Manager: Natalia Dextre

Library of Congress Cataloging-in-Publication Data
Names: Niven, Jennifer, author.
Title: When we were monsters / Jennifer Niven.
Description: First edition. | New York : Alfred A. Knopf, 2025. | Audience term: Teenagers | Audience: Ages 14 and up. | Summary: "A group of boarding school students attend a winter program where they experience a series of disturbing and bizarre lessons from their teacher" —Provided by publisher.
Identifiers: LCCN 2024049030 (print) | LCCN 2024049031 (ebook) | ISBN 978-1-5247-1302-7 (hardcover) | ISBN 978-1-5247-1304-1 (ebook)
Subjects: CYAC: Boarding schools—Fiction. | Schools—Fiction. | Dead—Fiction. | Secrets—Fiction. | LCGFT: Thrillers (Fiction) | Novels.
Classification: LCC PZ7.N6434 Wh 2025 (print) | LCC PZ7.N6434 (ebook) | DDC [Fic]—dc23

ISBN 979-8-217-12281-3 (int'l ed.)

The text of this book is set in 11.5-point Adobe Caslon Pro.

Manufactured in the United States of America
10 9 8 7 6 5 4 3 2 1

The authorized representative in the EU for product safety and compliance is Penguin Random House Ireland, Morrison Chambers, 32 Nassau Street, Dublin D02 YH68, Ireland, https://eu-contact.penguin.ie.

Random House Children's Books supports the First Amendment
and celebrates the right to read.

For James Earl Jones,
who taught me about bone memory
and soul stamina

Van Shank,
my sixth-grade teacher,
whose wisdom, humor,
and belief in my big imagination
transcended the walls of Westview Elementary
and accompanied me into the world

Lucy Kroll,
who told thirteen-year-old me that
I was destined to be a writer

Will Schwalbe,
my very first editor, whose voice
I hear as I write every word

For my mother, most of all

And for the teachers
everywhere who nurture
our wild and enormous dreams

It is true, we shall be monsters,
cut off from all the world; but on that
account we shall be more attached to
one another.

—*Mary Shelley, Frankenstein*

The day before we kill Meredith Graffam is calm and blue. Like Massachusetts in summer after the rain. The scent of earth and flowers and fresh, clean air. Just a perfect sunlit day.

None of us will walk into the forest that night planning to commit murder. It's easy when you're surrounded by beauty and opulence and acres of privilege, when you're young and filled with possibility, to convince yourself that life will always be as rose-colored as this and nothing can go wrong.

At the end of a long, sweeping drive, lined by the tallest trees, surrounded by forest and the sea just beyond, lies the campus of Brighton and Hove. The student body is, for the most part—present company excluded—comprised of the offspring of the very rich and the highly accomplished who can afford to send them anywhere but choose to send them here, to the woods of northeastern Massachusetts.

But like every too-bright place, darkness lingers at its

edges. The wizard behind the curtain. The painting in the attic. Hyde. It's there in the hazing of first-years that occurs each fall. In the ruthless competition among students. In the surrounding forest, where, each January for sixteen days, eight of the school's best and brightest are handpicked to live and study with someone world-famous and world-renowned at the Moss, the rambling old home of Moss Hove, our founder.

We don't have secret societies at Brighton and Hove. Instead we have Jan Term, its own elite, slightly nerdier organization of students past and present—our equivalent of being tapped. Everyone eager for the *illustrious, powerful connections* it promises outside these halls. In our *real* lives. In our *future* lives.

Built in 1916, the Moss sits surrounded by ten thousand acres of pristine forestland—formally known as Murton Wood, informally as Murder Wood—with whole swaths of primeval trees and miles of unpaved roads, all of it owned by the school. Unless they're lucky enough to be chosen for Jan Term, most students don't wander too deep into Murton. A seventeen-year-old student was killed there in 1995, a tragedy—a blemish—the school has never forgotten.

Proving that bad things can happen anywhere, even on a campus as beautiful as Brighton and Hove. Even on a crisp, star-filled January evening. Even to the four of us.

Effy, the orphan, who doesn't believe in ghosts but is haunted by them.

Isaac, the legacy, who carries the world on his shoulders.

Vanessa, the wallflower, who never thought she belonged.

And Arlo, the prodigal son, who returned to the school he walked away from two years earlier.

We were just four individual people before Meredith Graffam, *the* Meredith Graffam, arrived at Brighton and Hove. She was the one who brought us together. And the one who tried to tear us apart.

Tomorrow she will die.

I will wish for today, the day *before*, this bright, calm, blue day, like Massachusetts in summer after the rain. Or better yet, three weeks before. The beginning of the new year, back when Graffam was still alive and I couldn't think of anything to write because the only thing that had ever happened to me was too painful. I was anxious for material, for a story of my own. And now I have one.

Here it is.

BRIGHTON AND HOVE
PREPARATORY ACADEMY
Parkerton, Massachusetts

December 15

Dear Effy Green:

Congratulations on being selected for B&H's annual Jan Term Visiting Artist series. With only eight spaces available, competition for those slots was fierce, and you should be immensely proud of your hard work and talent.

This year's theme will be Immersive Storytelling. During this sixteen-day experience, you will be living in the Moss with our Visiting Artist, #1 *New York Times* bestselling author, Oscar-winning actor, director, and screenwriter, and Tony Award–winning playwright Meredith Graffam.

On completion of the class, one of you will be awarded a scholarship in the amount of $15,000 and the chance to have your work produced and/or published in your field or genre.

Jan Term begins Wednesday, January 7, and ends Thursday, January 22. Please arrive January 7. Pickup information will be emailed to you.

Please note that the attached nondisclosure agreement and waiver must be signed, notarized, and returned before your arrival. This is to protect your work and the work of our Visiting Artist, and to grant permission to be filmed or recorded should the opportunity arise. If you have any questions regarding either document or your upcoming experience, please don't hesitate to reach out.

We look forward to seeing you on January 7!

Sincerely,

Scott Booker
Dean of Students

week one

Immersive Storytelling

Wednesday, January 7 – Sunday, January 11

SESSION ONE

- Cast fears and inhibitions aside.
- Do whatever is needed to stand out.
- Lean into your strengths.
- Keep your eye on the end credits—what will you do to be the last one standing?
- If you don't have a story, create one.

Everybody steals in commerce and industry. I've stolen a lot myself. But I know how to steal.
—**Thomas Edison**

Effy

WEDNESDAY, JANUARY 7

I glance behind us, through the back window of the van, no longer able to make out the distant gleam of campus. Even with the brights on, Murton Wood is the darkest place on earth.

By contrast, the Moss looks warm and welcoming silhouetted against the sky, perched on a cliff overlooking the sea. At forty rooms and over fourteen thousand square feet, its aging beauty makes me think of all the best houses in literature. Manderley. Thornfield Hall. Wuthering Heights.

The seven of us have spent the van ride huddled over our phone screens, making the most of cell service while we still have it. Dean Booker pulls into the drive, gravel crunching beneath the wheels, and silences the engine.

For a moment, we sit there, phones forgotten, staring up at the house. Like every good Brighton and Hover worth their salt, I've heard the stories of Jan Term, that coveted experience enjoyed by only a choice few. Jan Term, which says to us—and everybody else—that we are the visionaries of our class, the ones poised to change the world through our art.

"We're here," someone says, and I feel the words more than hear them.

The van door opens, letting in a rush of cold air. Ness begins to gather her things, which have, in true Ness fashion, exploded across the seat. "This is what I don't like about winter," she's saying. "The in and out. Heat. Cold. Heat. Cold. The swaddling up head to toe like a penguin." Even when she complains, Ness sounds cheerful. It's one of the things I love most about her. Her lightness. Her joy.

One by one, my classmates spill out. I continue to sit there, suddenly wondering why I came, wishing I was home with Gran, a thousand things running through my head:

This is your last year at Brighton and Hove.

You only have five more months left of school.

What if you and Ness go to separate colleges and don't stay friends?

Why is life so full of endings?

A rap on the window and I jump. A face presses against it, wild coils of black hair, glasses, breath fogging me in. Ness rubs at the fog. Mists it up again. Rubs at it. Mists it up again. Then writes *Open!* backward. Everyone else stands in the drive, loosely assembled around Dean Booker, better known as Books, a bear of a guy, affable and folksy.

I join them outside in the night, my breath creating clouds. Ness, Isaac Williams, Ramon Santos, Joey Fiske, Peter Tobin, and Leela Kim. Seven, including me.

"You may not know," Books is saying, "that the tradition of

Jan Term began in 1926. But it wasn't until after Hove's death in 1942 that students were invited to stay here."

"I thought there were eight of us," I whisper to Ness, but she isn't listening because a woman, barely older than we are, is making her way toward us from the house. She has a round, pretty face framed by a waterfall of coppery hair and wears overalls speckled with splashes of paint.

"Drea Garcia," she says, shaking hands. She speaks with a faint Spanish accent. "I'm Meredith's assistant."

Meredith. As in Meredith Graffam. One of the hottest talents in books, theater, and film. And one of the most controversial. I would have traveled to another continent to study with her, but instead she has come to us.

We follow Books and Drea along a path between the house and the cliffs. Below us, the ocean pounds against the rocks, and I can almost feel the spray of water on my skin. I make the mistake of looking down. The drop is sheer—no bottom, just darkness.

I hurry after the others, across the brick courtyard, onto a sweeping veranda, and then finally through the wide, arched doors of the house.

We wind our way to a large room, papered in gold. At the far end is a gilded balcony, a grand piano in the alcove beneath it. The ceilings soar upward like a cathedral. A lone portrait of a man hangs above the fireplace. This would be Moss Hove, the school's cofounder, who fled California and his conservative oil baron family. Who fell in love with his friend Zachary Brighton. And who—two decades after they established Brighton and Hove—accidentally drowned offshore.

"Housekeeping will come once a week," Books tells us. "Wesley, our caretaker, will remain on-site. Ms. Graffam has brought her own chef, who will provide your meals. If you need anything, let Wesley know. He has the master key to the gates that let you in or out of the property."

Drea starts handing out index cards. Our names, numbers, and emails are printed there, as well as room assignments and Wi-Fi info.

"Aren't there supposed to be eight of us?" Ramon asks.

"Our missing student had a flight delay," Drea says. Then she holds up another card. "Each night, you'll receive one of these under your door, giving you the schedule for the following morning."

She and Books go over the rules then, including no sharing of beds. No leaving the house after dark. If we're going outside, be sure to prop the door or unlock it because—as we will see—all doors leading out of the house are kept locked at all times, with the keys inside them. No roughhousing, as most of the items in the house were collected by Moss Hove himself. Jan Term is a privilege, blah, blah, blah. If the tradition is to continue, we need to behave, blah, blah.

"The house is"—Books squints into the distance—"well, it's a bit of a maze. They call it the house with no hallways. As you've already seen, the rooms feed into one another, so that you never have to return to the main entryway. The ceilings vary in height. The floors too—there's a lot of stepping up and down, short staircases and long staircases. Treat the Moss as if it's your own."

We follow him to the front door. Dean Booker twists the

key that sits in the lock and steps through into the courtyard. "One more thing," he says, holding up a finger. "Just like on campus, the forest is off-limits."

Even though Lara Leonard was murdered decades ago, it's a sensitive topic for the school. We murmur our understanding. Then Books is off, with a wave and a wink, swallowed by the darkness outside.

MY ROOM IS the Belfry, a turret with windows looking out over the sea. I drop onto the bed and pull the envelope from my coat pocket, smoothing the edges. I have carried it with me ever since it arrived. It looks thumbed and worn, as if it was mailed a decade ago. The handwriting is innocuous. Short, fat letters all in caps. The envelope addressed to OPHELIA GREEN. If I had known who it was from, I wouldn't have opened it. But he must have realized that because the return address is simply BOSTON, MASSACHUSETTS.

I open the letter and read in the soft glow of the uranium glass that edges the windowpanes.

DEAR EFFY,

YOU MIGHT HAVE BEEN TOO YOUNG TO REMEMBER THIS, BUT THE SUMMER YOU WERE SIX WE TOOK YOU TO NEW YORK CITY. EVERYONE SAID TO LEAVE YOU AT HOME, AND MAYBE WE SHOULD HAVE BECAUSE YOU HATED IT ON SIGHT. HATED THE NOISE AND THE TRAFFIC AND THE CROWDS. BUT IT WAS WHERE YOUR MOM AND I MET, AND SHE WANTED

YOU TO SEE IT, TO BE PART OF THE US BACK THEN THE WAY YOU WERE PART OF THE US THAT SUMMER. THE FUNNY THING IS, DISASTER THAT IT WAS, I CAME AWAY FROM IT WITH ONLY HAPPY MEMORIES. YOUR MOM'S SMILE. YOUR HAND IN MINE. THE WAY WE WOULD SWING YOU BETWEEN US.

YOUR HEAD HEAVY ON MY SHOULDER, SLEEPING AS I CARRIED YOU BACK TO THE HOTEL. I'VE THOUGHT A LOT ABOUT THAT TRIP OVER THE PAST 4,017 DAYS. I GUESS I'M HOPING THAT NO MATTER HOW MUCH YOU HATE ME, ONE OR TWO HAPPY MEMORIES MIGHT HAVE SURVIVED . . .

Eleven years ago, my father was sentenced to fifteen years in prison. After his conviction, he told me goodbye, and just like that, all contact stopped. He decided he wasn't fit to be a dad, so I not only lost my mom, I lost him too. This past September—on the 29th, to be exact—he was released early for "good behavior." Three weeks later, I received the letter. The first I've heard from him since I was six.

For the past eleven years, while he was in prison, I was able to tell myself that he died too. I didn't have to think about him because he was locked away like a memory. But I don't know what the fuck to do with this.

I slide the letter under my pillow. The day after it arrived, Gran received one of her own. I watched as she fed it, unread, to the shredder, as the ribbons of paper dropped into the trash, which she bagged and immediately took to the curb. She wanted to shred mine too, but I lied and told her I'd destroyed it already.

The Wi-Fi doesn't connect right away, but once it does, I

text Gran to let her know I won't have reliable service while I'm here, and I give her the number for the landline.

And then I pull out the books I brought with me to read over the next three weeks. A dog-eared copy of *Frankenstein* that once belonged to my mother, her notes and highlights filling the margins. *The Hunt*, Meredith Graffam's first book. And *The Lie*, her second.

The Hunt was an overnight literary sensation, hailed as one of the most bloodcurdling true crime books since Truman Capote's *In Cold Blood*. Graffam was lauded with awards and accolades around the world for her account of her best friend's murder and her personal crusade to put the killer behind bars. The acclaim turned to blame when, six years after publication, new evidence exonerated the man Graffam helped convict for the murder of Lara Leonard. By then he'd already served eight years for a crime he didn't commit. The public went after her with their proverbial torches as if she had personally betrayed them. She issued an apology to the man and then disappeared from the public eye.

Ten years later, she reemerged with another memoir—this one titled *The Lie*, in which she came clean about her past. Not only documenting every lie she'd ever told, but the shame of putting an innocent man in prison. *The Lie* was turned into an off-off-Broadway show, which became an off-Broadway show, which became a film, which led to other films and other books, and by the time she was forty-five, Meredith Graffam's career was bigger than ever.

As much as she fascinates me though, Graffam is not the only reason I'm here. I'm here because I have a story to tell. A story of lives changing in a single moment. The way mine did when my father drove his truck into a tree and killed his only passenger—my mom. She was twenty-eight years old.

As Victor Frankenstein says, *Nothing is so painful to the human mind as a great and sudden change.*

Something scratches against the window, and I start. Gran and I live in an old house, so I understand their creaks and groans. There's always an explanation—old pipes, tree limbs that need pruning, changes in temperature that can make wooden floors and doorframes contract, a general settling of the foundation over time. Gran says houses have aches and pains like we do. The Moss has stood on these cliffs for over a hundred years accumulating aches and pains of its own.

I lean into the window, my eyes adjusting to the night. There aren't curtains because I'm high above everyone else, too high for anyone to see in. If I wanted to, I could step right into the trees.

Have you ever stood on the edge of a rooftop or bridge—someplace high up—and thought about jumping? I'm not talking about suicidal ideation. I'm talking about a primal instinct, a what-if response. As in *What if I hurled myself into the abyss?* And the more you think about it, the more worried you are that you'll actually do it.

There's a name for it. L'appel du vide. *The call of the void.* You technically don't want to jump, but the impulse to jump remains. Scientists have concluded that the call of the void stems from a deep desire to live. And this is true, at least for me. It's a reminder. *I could crash my car into the guardrail. I could leap onto those train tracks. I could dive off this cliff.* I imagine my body crumpled at the base of the rocks before being carried out to sea.

I turn away, catching sight of my face in the old mirror above the mantel. The glass is wavy and speckled, as if I'm seeing myself through a dusty field. *Do I look as empty as I feel?*

I smile. Not with teeth. That's not my thing. But enough so that people can tell it's a smile. Corners of my mouth lifted. Catlike, Gran says. The smile doesn't reach my eyes or light them up, as if my mouth and my eyes aren't connected at all. As if they belong to two separate people.

Arlo

WEDNESDAY, JANUARY 7

Since Boston, I've been talking nonstop to my Uber driver, Barry. We've covered everything from Jack Kerouac to my favorite cryptids to the epidemic of strange blue sea creatures that washed up on our beaches last summer.

"Picture it, Barry. These blobby blue discs as far as the eye could see. *Velella velella*, they're called, like tiny Frisbees with a clear sail on top."

Barry appears unmoved.

"They spend most of their lives surfing around the Pacific Ocean. But the really cool thing is that each sailor is actually a colony of animals working together. You've got one for feeding, one for reproduction, another for defense. But they can't survive alone, they have to rely on each—"

"School starting a little early this year?" Barry asks, eyeing me in the rearview like I'm up to something.

I don't bother explaining the concept of Jan Term to him, or the fact that my being here isn't exactly a choice. That, truth be told, my academic livelihood depends on it. That's what happens when you miss the first five weeks of senior year due to crippling grief. You end up short of credits to graduate and your parents and brother decide the only solution is to ship you off across the country to your old alma mater. Thankfully for me, I'm a skilled enough bullshitter to have landed a spot in Bullshit Prep's most coveted course.

Instead I say, "You can't keep me away, Barry. I'm that guy who just lives for school."

Barry pulls into the drive, the Moss rising up and around us, windows lit, looking almost friendly. He tells me to get out, happy to be rid of me. I pick up my hat and put it back on, even though my hair refuses to be contained. It's a vintage Lakers baseball cap that I've been wearing since summer. I unfold myself from the car and stand there as Barry roars off. Jesus, there are a lot of trees.

For the past few weeks, I've been planning my return to Brighton and Hove. My comeback, if you will. Now that it's here, now that I'm here, I feel awash in loneliness. It's the product of being a military brat, of having parents who are almost always overseas. Of having an unreasonably perfect older brother who represents everything I'll never live up to.

But it's also the product of the past year. Of last summer. Of you. Jonah. My best friend. Dying as I watched.

I DELAY GOING inside, reveling in my aloneness a little longer. I stand on the cliffs, where I can breathe, drinking in the sight of the great and powerful Atlantic, the world's second-largest ocean. Nothing but a fathomless black void stretching across the horizon. The only thing disrupting it is a small expanse of rock several hundred meters offshore and the lonesome beam of the lighthouse, searching. The tide seems to be going out, but the waves still rush in, and in the dark it's hard to tell if there's a beach at all.

I dig through my bag till I find the joint, the one I've been carrying around for months. It's not actual marijuana. Weed*s*, yeah. Weed, no. It's just a bunch of grass, dandelions, and dirt we rolled together, Jonah and me, one night when we were bored.

My hand is shaking as I reach for a lighter. The stars are bright overhead. I search, as always, for Ophiuchus, my favorite celestial dude.

Look up, I hear you say.

Your voice is so real that for a second I'm back in the sea cave on a hot July day. You were always saying things like that. *Look up. Look around. Be here now.* So when you said it that day in the sea cave—*Just look up*—I didn't think twice. I see your head bobbing above the water and we're laughing and in that moment I'm thinking how it feels like you've always been there, all my life. And then. *And then.* It's the *and then* that will always be right here lodged in my chest like a bullet they can't dig out.

Just look up.

I light the joint, take a long, deep inhale—and start to cough. I cough and hack and hack and cough and there are these alarming croaking sounds coming from somewhere, and it's me. I'm the one making the croaking sounds.

I glance back at the Moss, where a shadow stands at one of the windows. Is someone watching me cough my lungs out like an idiot? Is it *her*, the one and only Meredith Graffam? I double over as another series of hacks overtakes me. And when I look up again, the shadow is gone.

Bullshit Prep never was the most welcoming place. While I didn't expect a parade—not even close—the sad truth is that I don't have anywhere else to go. It's not like I can join my parents in Kuwait. It's not like I can stay with Aaron and his boyfriend and their dog in their cramped Tribeca studio. All I have is the next sixteen days here at the Moss and this last semester at school. After that, beyond that, I've got nowhere.

Effy

Thursday, January 8

I feel it before I hear it—the deep, resounding toll of a bell. The vibration reaches into my bones as it rings and rings and rings. I force myself out of bed, warm feet hitting the cold floor. The room is drafty, the windowpanes vibrating from the wind and the power of the ocean below.

A woman stands in the courtyard. I recognize her immediately. Meredith Graffam.

I'm dressed in minutes, but Ness is already gone. As I race down the hall from my room, I collide with another body and go sprawling onto the floor.

"Shit," he says.

He holds out a hand to me. The hand is attached to an arm that's attached to a body dressed in jeans and a Bigfoot T-shirt that reads *Leave No Trace*. His voice is lower and huskier than it was at fifteen. He's still lanky, but more man, less boy. Beneath a baseball cap, his hair is windswept and disorderly, wild and dark. Eyes that seem to be laughing at some private joke that only he finds funny. A generous mouth that might be called sensuous if it wasn't always yammering away. Good-looking—objectively speaking. Unless you know him. Which I do.

Arlo.

Arlo, who left at the end of sophomore year without a word, as if—like the rest of us—he'd be back in the fall. Arlo, who never told anyone where he'd gone or why.

I stare up at him and he stares down at me, and for a long, excruciating moment it's as if we are frozen.

"Hey," he says finally. "Elsie, right?"

Elsie.

Suddenly all I can hear is the furious thump of my heart. I push myself to my feet, ignoring his hand, which falls to his side, rejected. And that little motion, that hand dangling there empty, makes me feel like somehow I've won. Or at least recaptured a scrap of my dignity.

"I'm back," he says, opening his arms wide.

"Well," I reply.

And then, because there's too much to say and none of it is nice, I turn and walk away.

MINUTES LATER, THE eight of us assemble outside on the cliff. The air smells of salt and a pale dankness of leaves. The wind whips our hair and stings our cheeks.

Here in the daylight I can see the jaggedness of the descent. No sand, no beach, just these enormous slabs of rock, sloping down, down, like steps, cascading into the sea. The cliffs are fractured by a narrow gap, no more than ten or twelve feet wide, an open wound in the landscape.

Drea appears at my side, red hair bright against her jacket. "Stray's Chasm," she says cheerfully. "The name of it. A sixty-foot drop from here to the ocean. You always want to watch where you walk, especially at night."

My eyes find Arlo. When he catches me looking, he tilts his head back and winks, and I imagine shoving him off into the abyss.

Fucking Arlo Ellis-Noon.

The last time I saw him, we were sophomores. And we were naked. I wish I didn't remember his mouth. His lips soft but electric. The way he leaned in and I leaned in and we both leaned until we were falling through the ground below, through the outer ring of damp, cool earth to the core of fire at its center. So much possibility and maybe and might have been.

"I should probably warn you," a voice booms, jolting me back to the present, "that your time here is going to be unconventional in ways you might not expect."

Meredith Graffam stands, looking like a great and powerful witch, between us and the water. If she feels the chill, she doesn't show it. She wears her dark hair long, as in her earliest author photo. It swirls around her now like smoke. Beneath it, her face is colorless except for the arched brows, the large eyes, the pink shine of her mouth. Very little makeup, skin clear and luminous, as if she washed her face in a cool mountain stream.

"I believe you can't teach writing," she says. "You simply

have to write. It's the only way to learn. As storytellers, we need to be able to excavate. Starting with ourselves. Go places no one else has gone, not even us. Get uncomfortable, be afraid. That's when and where you write. I haven't won two Oscars and a Tony Award because I played it safe. As a student at this school, you expect the world to be handed to you, to come out on top. But here, with me, you'll have to fight for it. If you want to be a storyteller, in whatever form, in whatever space, you need to be willing to do anything for the story, no matter how uncomfortable it makes you. No matter the cost."

In person, she's a presence, the molecular energy of the air charged around her. Her voice is a furnace, articulate and impassioned.

"How many of you didn't have a say in ending up at Brighton and Hove? How many of you don't have a say in your own lives? How many of you would be somewhere else if you could?"

Isaac raises his hand, followed—one by one—by the others. I'm not sure whether to raise my hand or not, and so I don't. I want to stand apart. It seems to work because Graffam's eyes linger on me.

"The power of choice," she continues, to me. "The challenge is to live outside the box. To live and then to create."

Peter coughs loudly, drawing her attention back to the group.

To all of us, she says, "I can make you into real storytellers. I can help you distinguish yourselves from the thousands and thousands of writers and creators trying to make it in their industry. But you have to trust me. This won't work if you don't. You should assume everything is part of class, even if I'm not present. And that you are always being graded. In each exercise, there will only be one winner. I promise there's a method to my madness. Effy." She smiles, and it's as if the sun has chosen me, out of everyone, to shine on. "Hold this."

She hands me her phone. I stare down at the case, which is a blinding fluorescent yellow—the poster for *Whittier*, one of her more recent films. Then she sheds her coat, letting it drop onto the ground.

"Metaphorically, you have to jump into that deep end. Once you leave the Moss, you can choose to stay inside, where it's warm and dry. You can choose to be safe—or not. Joan Didion said, 'You have to pick the places you don't walk away from.' Let this be one of those places."

And then, Stray's Chasm to the left of her, she glides down the natural staircase formed by those enormous rock slabs. She comes to a ledge maybe twenty feet above the water. And steps right off. Into the ocean. The eight of us draw a collective breath.

We descend quickly to the ledge where she stood just a moment ago, salt spray hitting our faces. From up here, there is only a sheer drop into the sea, and my heart knocks against my chest. To the left of us, the chasm. To the right of us, the giant's staircase continuing until the lowest level of rock disappears beneath the water. Ness accidentally bumps me, and I grab on to Arlo to keep from plunging over the edge.

He looks at me. I look at him. I immediately let go and move away.

Suddenly—a pool of black appears just below the surface of the waves. We leave our perch and clamber downward as

Meredith Graffam rises from the water like Aphrodite, hair and clothes plastered to her skin. She pulls herself out of the water and stands.

"Now you," she says as we reach her. "Each of you. No more safe. Safe gets you nowhere."

We stare at her, at the ocean, back and forth as if we don't understand.

"In fifteen days, I'm going to choose one of you to have your work produced, filmed, or published. Not eight of you. *One* of you. I have the power to make that happen. A film. A TV series. A book deal. A play. Whatever it is, just imagine. One of your greatest wishes coming true. Like *that*." She snaps her fingers. "But I can also send you home right now. There's no reason to waste my time."

Ness and I exchange a look. I can hear her teeth chattering over the sound of my own.

"Whoever is still on these rocks by the time I count to ten will vacate the Moss today. One . . . Two . . ." Graffam's mouth wears a half smile. Her eyes are glittering.

Because I, Effy Green, have decided to stand apart, because I want to win and because I have nothing to lose, I hand Meredith Graffam her phone, shed my own coat, walk to the edge of the rock, and jump.

My heart explodes with the shock of the cold. Everything stops—breath, heartbeat, pulse. Time slows down, the world in slow motion. I feel heavy. I feel light. My eyes close against the freezing water. Body suspended.

A memory. Winter in Maine. Gran and me on the beach. Me dodging waves as the tide came in, Gran wading right through it in bare feet.

"Don't catch pneumonia," I said because I didn't want Gran leaving me too.

Her response: "I don't plan to."

She was wearing all white and had this scarf around her neck that blew away in the wind. I reached out to catch it and nearly pitched headfirst into the sea, but just in time she grabbed hold of me and said, "It doesn't matter, it's only a scarf." As I watched it float away, I imagined a girl my age finding it on the shore of some far-off land—Ireland, Wales.

Now I burst through to the surface, to the wind and the blue above, and I am gasping from the cold and trying desperately to fill my lungs with air. I look up as Isaac executes a perfect swan dive. As he sputters to the surface shouting expletives, I start to laugh, the skin of my face threatening to crack. He sends a wave of water at me, and I send one back.

Leela cannonballs in, followed by Peter, who starts to scream as soon as he hits the water. Joey shrieks and then leaps, weightless for a second before hitting the ocean like a slap.

"Come on in," I shout at Ness, teeth chattering. I splash water in her direction, sending her skittering backward.

The others join me in chanting, "Come on in, come on in . . ."

"Ahhh." Ness glances at Graffam, at the water, at me, at Graffam again.

"Six . . ."

Ness sets her glasses on the ground, and then she is running toward me across the rock and launching herself into the air, arms wide. At the last minute, she wraps them around herself and hits the water hard. A few seconds later, she reappears, hair curling around her face. I throw my arms around her, and we bob like buoys, the waves catching us and pulling us forward, pushing us back, so that we lose our footing. The water is shallow here, but the current is powerful and it keeps trying to yank us under. I imagine it dragging Moss Hove out to sea. How terrified he must have been when he knew he couldn't fight any longer.

"Seven..."

Ramon lumbers forward, and I expect him to take flight. Instead he sits on the edge of the rock, where he removes his shoes and socks, rolls up the legs of his jeans, and—bitching the entire time—drops his feet in, first the left, then the right. We tread water, waiting for him to submerge himself, but he only sits there.

"For the record," he says to Graffam, "I don't see what this 'exercise' has to do with storytelling." He makes air quotes around *exercise*. "Or even creativity. Me not wanting to catch hypothermia during school hours is just good common sense."

Graffam counts, "Eight... Nine..."

As Ness and I hoist ourselves back onto the rocks, I sneak a glance at Arlo. He stands with hands in coat pockets, head turtled into his collar.

The moment Graffam utters "Ten," Isaac grabs Arlo by the arm and yanks him in and dunks him like it's a baptism. The water starts to churn around him and over him, and I watch as, like that, he is gone. *Don't come back up*, I think. *Stay down there so I don't ever have to think about you again.*

Arlo disappears completely, consumed by the tide. Waves roll in and out. Now I'm the one counting to ten. By the time I get to fifteen, he's still gone.

Isaac shouts, "Noon!" He glances up at Graffam, at me,

and then he dives below the surface. As quickly as I've been wishing for Arlo's imminent death, I think, *Don't ghost me again, asshole. Not like this.*

A body materializes from the deep, and it's Isaac. And then Arlo's head breaks through to the surface and he is pulling himself up to standing, the waves rushing around him. He wheels on Isaac and shoves him hard, sending him under, and then he starts spinning, digging through the water like he's looking for something. He leans down and swipes up a hat.

He doesn't wait for Isaac to come back up, doesn't check that he's okay. There is fury in his face and in the way he moves, climbing out of the water and up, up, up to the top of the cliffs.

Arlo

Thursday, January 8

Inside it is warm and quiet except for the pounding of my heart. In here there's no wind or cold or ocean closing over my head, filling my lungs, trying to hold me under. I wring out the Lakers cap, water pooling on the floor, and watch Graffam and the others through the window.

The moment I saw her, it all came rushing back. Effy Green. Her defiant, slightly off-kilter beauty. Her colossal, churning brain. The vast ocean of feeling tucked away behind impassive green eyes. Dark hair in waves and a dusting of freckles, like stars, across her nose and cheeks.

Of course I remember her. I remember every fucking moment. I don't know why I acted like I didn't. Maybe because I'm a shitbag. Or maybe because I thought it would be easier somehow.

Effy was my first. I was hers. And then I went away.

They are heading for the house now, trailing after Graffam like ducklings. Isaac bursts through the door, taller and broader and better-looking than he was two years ago, and still the world's most confident person, even soaking wet.

"You always were a dick, Noon," he says to me.

Right back atcha, I think.

Thankfully, the others appear. Graffam, then Ness, Peter, Ramon, Leela, Joey. And then Effy. I squint up at the ceiling to avoid meeting her eyes.

Coats are hung, boots are removed, scarves and hats are flung into a bin. Once our outer layers are shed, Graffam leads us onward to the Octagon Room—which is, true to its name, eight-sided. The walls are black, but everything else is red—rugs, artwork, décor. There is a roaring fire in the hearth. An antique birdcage is suspended in one corner, an enormous stuffed crow—as in an actual dead, taxidermy bird—perched on a swing, and an octagonal table, nine chairs pulled up to it, sits in the exact center of the room.

Drea brings a tray with hot tea, and I warm my hands on the mug. Effy is seated as far from me as possible, clutching a faded old book to her chest like it's a life raft that will carry her away from here. I read the title—*Frankenstein*—before she sees me looking and drops the book onto the table with a bang.

Graffam says, "Before we begin, I want to apologize." She turns to me. "That"—she waves toward the window, toward the ocean—"was thoughtless of me, and I'm sorry."

The others glance at one another, trying to figure out how and why such a thing has come to be—the one and only Meredith Graffam apologizing to Arlo Ellis-Noon.

"I'm okay. I'm good," I say, my voice tight. I stare up at the bird and it stares back at me with dead, beady eyes.

Isaac mutters something under his breath, and then quiet encircles us except for the popping and crackling of the fire.

Graffam opens her hands as if she is holding something—the air, the room, us. She says, "I want us each to tell a personal story. Writing can be solitary. It can also be about collaboration. About learning to listen and to respect someone else's point of view."

Her voice inside is different from her voice out there. She has changed it to suit the atmosphere.

"And it's about being honest. Revealing things about yourself that you'd rather not. The creative process is the most intimate thing I've ever experienced. It can be more intimate than sex. That said, I believe competition is a good thing." Her expression shifts. Her eyes brighten. "It gives you an edge. It keeps you from getting lazy. There's always someone waiting in the wings, ready to take your place. The people in this room are the people you're competing against. *Never* forget that they want what you want and that only one of you can win."

"So who won that exercise?" Isaac asks. "Out there?" Like Graffam, he waves at the window, at the cliffs beyond, an expectant smile on his face.

"Effy," she says simply.

Isaac's smile evaporates. All eyes, including mine, go to Effy.

"Once upon a time"—Graffam's voice is suddenly hushed—"there was a girl who wanted to tell stories. But no one believed she had anything to say."

At first I think she's talking about Effy, but then I realize this is her personal story. She stares down at her hands, then up at us, and the look on her face is so—naked.

"You know the feeling you get when you're in a large crowd of strangers, when you're by yourself and everyone walks past without a second look? That's how it feels to be disregarded and underestimated. Because no one believed in her, the girl who wanted to tell stories had no choice but to believe in herself. She became rich and famous and successful. She achieved everything she'd dreamed of. More, actually. The lengths she went to. Her tenacity. None of it was acknowledged by the people who dismissed her. Every night when she puts her head on the pillow, she thinks of them. And as much as it hurts, as much as the pain of it—this sharp stab of pain right here"—she taps at the spot below her heart—"as much as it sometimes takes her breath away, the girl still wants their approval."

She looks up, and we are silent, her words reverberating through us. We sit for twenty seconds, maybe longer, before Ness clears her throat. That small sound in this moment, in this quiet room, is like a *crack*. I'm not the only one to jump. Nervous laughter follows, breaking the tension.

And then Ness tells us about her parents, who adopted her after they lost their biological baby. Her parents, who love and support Ness in everything she does. But who can never erase the fact that she is with them because another child died. It's due to this that Ness feels the need to measure up, be more, be perfect, be enough, be someone she's not.

Isaac's story is, naturally, about how his parents expect him to work for their Fortune 500 company as soon as he graduates from Duke or Harvard. Duke because that's where Dad earned his degree. Harvard because that's where Mom went. As far as they're concerned, there are no other options for school or career, not as long as they're paying for it.

Ramon tells us about the first boy he loved, about how, at the age of twelve, when he confided that love, the boy kissed him and told him he loved him too. And then outed him to their Catholic school class. Ramon was bullied for years because of it, and it took him a long time to trust anyone, much less men. This is why he breaks up with his current boyfriend, David, again and again as a way of testing his love. He worries that one day David won't come back.

Then Leela: *My twin brother didn't tell me until the night before I first came here to Bullshit Prep that he was staying in Puget Sound to go to public school. It felt like someone amputated my leg, until I discovered that—3,111 miles apart—we came out as pansexual on the same day.*

Then Peter, who, after a lengthy, name-dropping soliloquy, revealed: *My parents wanted a girl.*

Then Effy.

"This is a story about Clay Reynolds," she begins. "Age forty. Eleven years ago, he plowed his Ford F-150 into a tree on a curve of road between Kittery and Portsmouth. He walked away with a concussion, but his passenger was killed. Clay and his wife, Charlotte, were on their way back from the movies. It was their first date night in months because they had a six-year-old daughter at home. Clay was found guilty of first-degree manslaughter—he'd been drinking. They both had. What's more, he said something to the police about an argument the two of them had, about the whole thing being his fault. Enough to make everyone wonder and whisper, *What if he did it on purpose?*"

For the first time in my life, I go perfectly still. Effy never told me any of this. Not that we did much talking sophomore year, but you'd think I would have heard the story from someone at school.

"He served eleven years of a fifteen-year sentence," she continues. "Eleven years without any communication with his daughter. Three months and two weeks later, he was paroled. One week after his release, he wrote that daughter—now seventeen—a letter telling her that he wants to be in her life again." She looks up, green eyes dark and solemn. "The world is terrifying without parents. When one of them is dead and the other might as well be. Like being lost in a foreign country on your own, one where you don't speak the language."

She stops talking abruptly—just stops. My hand has gone cold around the mug as I sit thinking about this girl whose mom died and whose dad left her. And then I came along and left her too.

After a long moment, Graffam says, "We are all alone in this life. In these bodies of ours. But right now, for the next fifteen days, inside these walls"—she glances up and around—"we are not alone."

A smile blooms on her face, and I'm surprised to see Effy smile back. I focus my eyes on the fire. Secrets seem to hover in the air. No matter what happens, no matter where we go when we leave here, I will be one of the few souls in the world who knows the things I do about these people.

Effy

Thursday, January 8

My mind fizzes and crackles and I feel strangely alive. My hair still smells like the ocean. But the cliffs are already a distant memory, eclipsed by the words I've just spoken.

It's what I left unsaid that cuts the deepest. The unforgivable part where my father saved himself from the wreckage instead of helping to free my mom. She died minutes after first responders arrived, still trapped in the car, still breathing, still conscious, while my father sat on the side of the road.

I've studied photos of the car after the accident. I've visited the crime scene—that fucking tree—again and again, searching for clues as to what happened and why. Had he meant to do it, to leave her there? Did he have a choice? Could he have gotten her out if he'd tried? But each time it's only made me feel further away from that night and the moment of impact. I've dug up police reports. Researched statistics regarding alcohol regulations. Delved into the effect of weather, road surfaces, traffic, and even night blindness on fatal collisions. Gone deep into Clay Reynolds's medical history and the medical history of the entire Reynolds family, looking for signs of seizures or blackouts or depression or mental illness, anything that might explain where he was in that moment he lost control of the truck.

When asked why he hadn't tried to rescue his wife, my father blamed it on shock. The most I could come up with was that it was an accident. The road was slick from a recent storm. He had been drinking. He never should have gotten behind the wheel. There was clear evidence that he slammed on the brakes and tried in vain to stop. But instead of giving me answers, the picture of that night remained foggy and out of reach, just like my father.

"Talk about a fun act to follow," Arlo quips.

When no one smiles, he forges ahead. "Okay. What can I tell you? How about when I was fifteen, I was an asshole. This went beyond your normal teenage assholery. Because I was a scared little boy who didn't know better, who felt out of his element here. And basically everywhere else in the world. And so, you know, better to be the hunter than the hunted, right? So—yeah, that's it. That's my excuse. Anyway. I met a girl. Not just any girl." He shakes his head at a private thought or memory. "She was something else. She still is. Equal parts hypnotic and terrifying."

I glance at him and then away. *Do not say my name. If you say my name, so help me God, I will drag you back to the sea and throw you in.*

Beside me, I hear the moment Ness puts two and two

together—a subtle creak of the floor as she shifts her body, head swiveling back and forth between Arlo and me.

"No one tells you when you're fifteen—at least no one ever told me—how not to fuck up a good thing. I think it's easy for people to discount how you feel, like your feelings aren't as big or real because you're not an adult. But I had real feelings for this girl, and I fucked it up. I know it's hard to imagine."

He tries a smile. Graffam shakes her head. *Don't worry about us. Worry about the story.*

It takes him a minute, and finally he says, "She was my first. I was hers. And then I left. I knew I was leaving. She didn't. No one knew. That was my little secret. Because if she had known, maybe she wouldn't have slept with me, and at the time that was the most important thing I could imagine. Getting laid."

"Jesus," says Leela.

Jesus, I think.

"Not because it was sex, although I'm not going to lie—that also made it appealing. But because getting laid meant validation of me and my poor scared little-boy ego."

I want to walk out. I actually try moving my feet, but my limbs have gone as numb as my heart, which suddenly feels like a cold, dead weight in my chest.

"I found out in April of sophomore year that my parents were coming back to the States, which meant I could live with them and we could be a family. My whole life, they've been in and out of the country. We've moved a lot. I've learned how to disappear. *Don't memorize names. Don't get close. Don't say goodbye.* These are the rules that make it easier. In a way.

But then I met a girl. As I said, not just any girl. So I wish I could say I'm sorry. But not just to her. To me too. The me of back then."

He looks up, his face lit by the glow of the fire. I'm the only one who doesn't comment, who doesn't congratulate him on coming clean and being honest about what an asshole he was. Is. *You knew*, I think. *You. Knew.*

Which leaves Joey. I barely hear what she says—something about her love for all God's creatures, about her parents' company doing animal testing, about her escaping home to live with an aunt. Her words are fuzzy, just like the mildewy scent of the room, as if the ocean has forced its way in and swallowed us.

"Do you know why I chose you?" Graffam asks when Joey is done, and the sound of her voice brings me back. "All of you? Because you're not afraid to take risks."

She gets to her feet, fracturing our little circle. We watch as she moves to the bench beneath the window, where eight black bags sit in a row.

"I want you to leave your phones on the table." Over the groaning that ensues, she says, "In return, I'm issuing you each a camera. Please take good care of it. This is your lifeline for the next fifteen days. You will use this to film short projects. To record notes for your work. You will use it to film your daily video journals. Yes, journals. They are a requirement. It's all in the title—Immersive Story*telling*. You need to be able to *tell* as well as write. And it's just as important to know your own narrative because *your* narrative is what drives the narratives of your stories. So have one. Find it. Know it.

Explore it. And if you don't have anything interesting to say, make something up."

She hands out the cameras one by one, and we dive in like it's Christmas Day. The camera is beautiful. Light but substantial, and most definitely expensive.

"There's a new memory card in each one. Theoretically, if by some miracle we can get the Wi-Fi to work, your material should automatically back up to the cloud to a private account that only you can access. Drea will get you set up."

"Speaking of Wi-Fi." This from Isaac. "I couldn't get on this morning. Like, at all. Last night it took me maybe three tries, but today nothing."

"Drea's looking into it, but in a house this old and this far out from everything else . . ." She shakes her head. "We'll do what we can. Meanwhile, if you have any questions and you can't find Drea or me, I've got these." From nowhere, she pulls out packs of sticky notes in various colors and passes one to each of us. Ness automatically holds out her green Post-its, and I trade her my pink. "Leave any questions, thoughts, musings—where?" She glances around at the windows, the walls thick with art, portraits, books.

"The kitchen," Arlo says. "Because we'll all be able to find it. If nothing else, our stomachs will lead us there."

"Perfect. That's our storyboard." She smiles. "Now. It's our first full day, and it's been—exhilarating?" She cocks her head. "Weird?"

Laughter.

"I want you to think of this class as a dialogue. If you have an issue, come to me." She tilts her chin, giving the impression that she's gazing down from a great height, and her eyes land on my copy of *Frankenstein*. "Is that the 1831 edition or 1818?"

"The original version. 1818. Before Percy Shelley got his hands on it." Graffam nods with approval, so I add, "It was my mom's favorite book."

I don't mention that I've read it over and over again countless times, trying to know Charlotte Green better, to understand who she was and how she thought and felt. Her notes in the margins lend me some insight—she admired Mary Shelley's genius, was entranced by the Arctic setting because an ancestor had once ventured north on a whaling ship, and she hated the persecution of the creature the way she hated the mistreatment of animals and children. But this still doesn't tell me enough.

"Which raises the question," Graffam says, tapping her chin. "Free will." She picks up my book. "Shelley famously writes about it in here. But do you believe in it? Is fate avoidable? Or are our lives decided for us?" At first she seems to ask it of me specifically, but then her gaze finds the others, one by one. The look on her face is one of genuine curiosity, as if whatever we have to say on the matter is important.

We glance around at each other, at Meredith Graffam, at the room itself. I stare past her for a moment at the vast blue of the ocean and the sky. I know it's cold outside, but I have this urge to wander the shoreline and put my feet in the water again.

Without thinking, I say, "I can't believe that somewhere someone is pulling the strings, that no matter what I do, I'll end up in the same place. I have to have a say in what happens."

Even though I wouldn't be at Brighton and Hove if my

mother hadn't gone here. For me, there was never any choice. I would go anywhere to be close to her.

"And how do we make sure we get a say?"

Arlo's mouth opens, but I get there first. "By picking the places you don't walk away from. By leaping into the void. By jumping into the frigid ocean in the middle of winter."

I look at Arlo. Smile. An almost-imperceptible shake of his head before he looks away. The meanest part of me—the part that will hate him forever—feels like I've won.

Graffam nods. "And by taking opportunities when they come. Or if they don't come, by making them." Uttered by anyone else, these words would seem trite, but from her they feel profound.

She hands the book back to me. The eight of us watch as she walks away, turning when she reaches the doorway.

"By the way, congratulations, Arlo. Judging stories can be subjective. But yours resonated with me."

Then she flashes all of us a blinding, beautiful smile. I catch a whiff of her perfume as she exits the room—something earthy yet feminine. Instinctively, I want to follow it, to follow her.

Instead I turn back and set my phone on the table as the others crowd Arlo like runners-up in a beauty pageant.

I make my escape, trying and failing to find my way back upstairs, one room spilling into another—a kitchen I've never seen before, a wallpapered study with a writing desk, a room dedicated to crystal vases and pitchers in a rainbow of colors—when someone calls my name.

Suddenly Arlo is there, and it's just the two of us, surrounded by acres of glass. Before I can run away, he starts talking. "I don't know if you're aware, but according to the *Journal of Personality and Social Psychology*, the average person keeps at least thirteen secrets. Now, personally? I've got five. But really good ones? Three."

Things are coming back to me. The way he talks too much and all the time. The way the dimples fade when he isn't smiling, but not completely. The way he messes with his hair, brushing it out of his eyes with his right hand—never the left. The way his eyes darken like a bruise when he's angry.

"That's a long way of saying—"

"Don't worry about it. We're good. This—us—doesn't have to be awkward or interfere with our time here."

"Let me just—"

"Arlo. Stop."

It comes out louder and harsher than I meant for it to. Arlo stares at me, dark pupils engulfed by all that gray.

I draw an invisible line with my shoe, right between us. A border between two hostile countries. I tap one side. "This is me." Tap the other. "This is you. There is nothing you can say to me that will make me want to cross this line."

Arlo

Thursday, January 8

Everyone chooses a corner of the house to write in. If you walk into a room and someone's already there, it means they've claimed it as their own. I wander the first floor, opening doors, restless. I reach for my phone, forgetting I've turned it over to Graffam. I used to be halfway decent at having alone time. Never great at it, sure, but better than I am now.

The game room is flooded with light, its dark wooden walls polished to a shine. Stuffed birds perch on shelves, staring down at me. There's a pool table, a card table, a chess table, and a long window seat with a cushion. A bookcase is stuffed with board games and old tin toys, and the walls are covered in framed photographs. In some, Moss Hove and his ragtag group of friends—they called themselves The Odds—play checkers, cards, pool, and charades in various rooms of the house. In others, they pose outside in the shadow of the Moss with croquet mallets, badminton rackets, or swim costumes.

There is an entire wall of photos, each one dated—THE WILD HUNT: RULER OF THE FOREST, reads a plaque at the very top. The earliest picture is from 1926, the latest from last year. Each of them a photograph of someone who stares directly at the camera and wears a crown of leaves.

I browse the games—the boxes dusty, the contents dustier—and then I browse the books. The stack on the mantel in my room is a stuffy array of classics, from *Hamlet* to *The Hound of the Baskervilles*. Now I pull a title at random and open it—*Byron's Poetical Works*—reading the first page I turn to.

> *I had a dream, which was not all a dream.*
> *The bright sun was extinguish'd, and the stars*
> *Did wander darkling in the eternal space . . .*

I skim to the end, to the last line. *She was the Universe.*
And of course I think of Effy.

Effy, who hates me with good reason. Because what I did was so completely shitastically shitty. Why should she ever forgive me? I wouldn't forgive me either.

I pick up the camera Graffam gave me. I spend a few minutes going over it, playing with the different settings. I walk to the window and aim the lens at the outside world. I zoom in on trees and clouds and snap a burst of photos of a bird flying past.

Then I drop onto the window seat, find the video button, and turn the camera on myself. Here, bathed in sunlight, I don't look half bad, which is to say I don't look like me. I shake out my hair and run my fingers through it so it's the right amount of messy, then position the Lakers cap on my head at a jaunty angle, the way you used to wear it. I smile, showing dimples. I hit record. Sit there. Say the first thing that comes to mind.

"'She was the Universe.'"

Feeling ridiculous, I set the camera aside. My creativity goes largely dormant during daylight hours. I do better at night, when the world is still and everyone else is sleeping. Only then can I let it in—the dark, the summer, your death. I basically just open a vein and bleed, a remote part of my brain thinking as I do: *Is there such a thing as bleeding too much?* When the words run out, I draw. This means the novel isn't really a novel—more a jumble with no structure, a mess of prose and art. Chapters that start and stop, comic book figures and pencil sketches, but nothing digital—all hand-drawn.

The cold is seeping through the glass. I open the window seat, thinking I'll discover more games, but instead I find a narrow staircase descending into darkness.

For maybe a minute, I stand there, one hand holding up the seat. I stare down into the abyss and then it occurs to me to search for a light. I mean, if there's a staircase inside the window seat, why not a light too? My fingers fumble across the wood just inside the compartment until I feel an indentation, small and round. I give it a push, and the space below goes bright.

The room at the bottom is barely larger than a walk-in closet. The walls are hand-painted, a mural of what must be

Murton Wood—more fondly known as Murder Wood—wrapping all the way around. Rough whitewashed floors and a built-in daybed strewn with cushions. On it, a set of playing cards lies face up and scattered, as if the players have just walked away for a minute. Next to it, an old Scrabble board, letter tiles spilling out of a velvet pouch. The air is dusty, as if no one's set foot in here since Moss Hove.

I stand in the middle of the space, taking it in and thinking, *Eat your heart out, Isaac Williams. This is mine.*

AT BRIGHTON AND Hove we dress for dinner, and the Moss is no exception. Everyone spit-shined and gussied up. The dining room is formal, and we are formal in it. The windows arched, the ceiling high, the walls a deep, cadaverous plum. A heavy chandelier is suspended over the table. The centerpiece is an actual candelabra. The Roaring Twenties music, with its vigorous, feverish energy, floods the room through invisible speakers. I can feel our morning confessions surrounding us like shadows, like eight additional people.

Because it's never far from me, I hang the Lakers cap on the back of my chair. Across the table, Effy wears dark blue, reminding me of the night sky. In the glow of the candlelight, I stare at her a little too long, the velvety notes of a song springing into my head.

Hello?
Is it me you're looking for . . . ?

"What's wrong with you?" she snaps.

"Don't mind him," Isaac says. "He's probably high."

"Where's Graffam?" asks Peter.

It's then I notice that the place opposite Drea is set but the chair is vacant. Joey Fiske is also absent.

Instead of answering Peter, Drea talks about how at home Moss Hove was in a world of oddities. Which is why he collected them. He himself felt like an oddity until he was befriended by a group of scandalous, disreputable, bohemian artists and intellectuals who lived on the fringes of respectable society.

"It's why he built the perimeter walls around the forest and the house," Drea says. "So he and Zachary Brighton and their friends could live freely."

As she says it, I think of how safe my life had been up until last summer. All my rebellions existing within a world that seemed certain and fixed. Until it wasn't.

The chef and her staff serve the meal, and we begin to eat. For a few minutes, I give myself over to this food. This fucking miraculous food, which is somehow more than mere pasta pomodoro with a side of roasted artichokes. Something much more akin to heaven.

"Where's Joey?" asks Isaac.

The reverie broken, we all look up.

"She left," Peter says, mouth full. "Graffam kicked her ass out." A note of triumph in his voice, so happy to get to deliver this news to the rest of us.

Drea says, "It was more civil than you're making it sound, Peter—"

"Not from what I saw."

I have this desire to knock the grin off his face, not that I've ever punched anyone or would even know how. What kind of force to use, what kind of aim—the jaw? the nose? the stomach?

I laugh at the image just as Peter goes, "She was bawling." Which is unfortunate timing. Effy's not the only one who glares at me. Undaunted, Peter charges on. "I mean, it's literally been one day." He pats his mouth with his napkin. "I'd feel almost bad for her if, you know, she wasn't the competition. But I guess Graffam said she didn't have it in her. She's smart, but not smart enough."

"That wasn't exactly—" Drea begins.

This time it's Ramon who cuts her off. "Wait, so she can really send us home anytime she wants? Just like that?"

"Yes. But always with good reas—"

Ramon cuts her off again. "Nowhere in the acceptance letter does it say that. If that's really the case, they should make it clear coming in."

"Easy, tiger," says Isaac. He turns to Drea. "So where's Graffam, then? Why isn't she here?"

"She's working." Drea doesn't volunteer *on what*.

The kitchen staff appears again to replenish drinks and remove the plates.

Drea takes advantage of the interruption to ask about our projects. To break the ice, she goes first, telling us about her activism in the body positive movement, including her own current project—something she calls the Petunias. She's setting out to create one hundred small sculptures of one hundred female figures of all different shapes and sizes. "Goddesses of self-love," she says. When she's finished, she's going to invite one hundred different women to choose a Petunia and paint their insecurities. "Now your turn." She looks around the table. "Isaac?"

As usual, he doesn't hesitate to launch into his favorite topic—himself. "Yeah, so mine is a dark comedy with political overtones written for the screen." According to him, the script will give him his big break, and then he plans to slide right into directing.

Ness is writing a book of poetry that tackles themes of self-love and acceptance. Leela is a stand-up comic who's writing feminist monologues "with a '90s slant," a series of them that she can perform. Peter wants to be a "journalist," which surprises no one—he's one of the biggest gossips at school—and is planning on creating "both scripted and unscripted" online content.

Ramon refuses to tell us the exact nature of what he's working on, other than the fact that it's a novella that he will then turn into a play that he will then turn into a screenplay. Effy is writing short stories, which may become a book. Like Ramon, she is cagey, only offering, "I'm interested in lives changing in a single instant."

When I feel their eyes on me, I say, "I too am writing a book. A very long, very clever book about a super-hot guy who returns to his East Coast boarding school after living in California for two years and then, well, hijinks ensue."

Maybe it's just me, but I swear Effy's mouth twitches. Not a smile exactly, but an extremely tiny hint of one that comes and goes in the blink of an eye. Still—progress. As soon as I smile back, she lifts her chin and looks away.

Dessert arrives, and as the rest of us devour it, Peter turns beady, greedy eyes on Drea. "So do you know the reason Graffam's here? After all these years? I mean, she was, like, persona non grata, not just at Brighton and Hove but everywhere. So why in the hell would she agree to teach Jan Term?" He nods at us like, *I got this*, as if we're with him.

Peter Tobin is, on his best days, insufferable. His parents are media moguls—they own newspapers, magazines, a small but powerful publishing company, and one famously vicious gossip site. The need to know runs in his family.

Drea studies him. Peter shifts under her gaze. Finally she says, her voice quiet but firm, "Remember that she's human like the rest of us. I think people forget that sometimes." She excuses herself then, and we listen to her footsteps go tapping away.

"Good job," Effy says to Peter. "You've just reinforced every horrible private school stereotype she's ever heard."

But he's out of his chair and bounding from the room with the energy of a frenzied leprechaun.

"Where's he going?" Leela says, in her usual flat tone.

"Probably to kiss Graffam's ass. Like, literally kiss it." Isaac drops his napkin onto his plate. "I miss my phone."

"I miss mine too," echoes Leela. "Dude, all my music is on there."

"So now imagine being me and not having it." He sighs.

"Why, because you're popular in a way none of us can possibly comprehend?" Ramon rolls his eyes and then, to make it clear just how disgusted he is, rolls them again.

"Did you know," I volunteer quickly, "that pasta was first eaten in China? They can trace it back to as early as 5000 BC."

This is, unfortunately, the extent of my pasta knowledge.

"Who?" asks Isaac. "Who is tracing the origins of pasta? Like, who fucking cares?"

"I don't know. Historians."

"Meanwhile," Ramon says, "in Syria." He pushes his plate away.

Isaac goes, "What's that supposed to mean?"

"It means that here we sit in all our privilege talking about useless facts when there are people in the world who are less fortunate."

"And?" Isaac says. "I don't see you over in Syria helping out right now. I see you across the table from me in this big-ass mansion with a mostly empty plate of food paid for by your rich senator mom, who's putting you through private school."

Ramon opens his mouth to reply just as Peter returns, carrying a bottle of wine. "A 2009 Château Lafite," he croons. He pours some of the liquid—a deep plum like the walls—into his empty glass and takes a sip. "Meh. Not bad." He drops into Graffam's vacant chair, which somehow feels like blasphemy, and waves the bottle, a wicked smile on his wicked face. "Come on, you pussies."

One by one, we help ourselves. All but Ramon.

In the candlelight, Peter has the small, gleaming eyes of an animal. He raises his glass. "To Graffam," he says.

"To her devoted students," I say.

"May the best person win," Isaac adds.

We all clink glasses and drink.

The Château Lafite tastes like every other wine I've ever sampled—bitter, sour—but in spite of that, in spite of Isaac hating Ramon and Ramon hating Isaac and Effy hating me and me hating me, this is nice.

"Here's my question," Old Peter the Instigator says. "Did she deserve a second chance after getting that guy locked up and blaming it on the school?"

Leela leans in. "In a world where people are canceled and then never heard from again, she managed to remake herself."

I have a flash of memory. Ninth-grade history. Leela perpetually slouched in the front row, until the last day of the semester, when she straightened in her seat and embarked on a diatribe about the lack of women's history taught in schools.

"Her husband published his own version of *The Lie* nine months after hers—*Confessions of a Galway Fraud*." Peter kicks back in his chair, a little too comfortable. "He accused her of stealing his idea, said he had to change his entire premise at the last minute—"

"Her husband," interrupts Effy, "also publicly cheated on her with Britt Toms."

Britt Toms is an Irish author, a good fifteen years Graffam's junior.

"How could she steal his idea"—Leela practically spits the words—"if her book was based on what she went through?"

Effy overlaps her. "She didn't lie. She believed Timothy Hugh Martin was guilty."

"Maybe she was pulling the strings to make it look that way," sniffs Ramon. "Graffam doesn't impress me. My mom is a senator. I've been around powerful people my entire life . . ."

"Ah, politics," I say. "So you're used to liars, then."

Effy glares at me, and I'm enjoying this—the way she's taking it personally, as if we're discussing her and not Meredith Graffam. She goes off then, on the establishment, the patriarchy, us close-minded males, and I settle back to listen. I love her voice, the heat of it, the rise and fall of it, the raspiness of it, especially the more she talks. And talks. And talks.

Wesley appears. His eyes flick to the bottle, nearly empty, and the glasses glazed with wine, but he doesn't say anything. Silently, he pours us each a cup of coffee, and as he walks out again, Ness leans forward, hands curled around the stem of her glass.

"Imagine you're The Odds." Her eyes shine as they rest briefly on each of us. She seems looser than she did earlier, less on edge. "Allowed to be your truest self, but only within this secret group of other outcasts." She sounds almost wistful.

"Try being a gay Catholic," Ramon says.

"Or a triple legacy with zero interest in the family business," adds Isaac.

"Or a nepo baby," says Peter.

"Or stuck in the wrong era," Leela offers.

"Or the biggest girl in the room," sighs Ness. "Impossible to ignore but always on the outside."

"Or an orphan."

I look at Effy. Her face is hard to read.

The air feels suddenly heavy, but also close and friendly. Safe.

"Or me," I add.

Thankfully, they laugh. Leela says, "Isn't that the crux of life? We can never see ourselves clearly." In spite of the formal dress code, she still wears her signature black beanie. "Mirrors, film, photos—they aren't the real us. They're reverse images. And the people who look at us, who can physically see us as we actually appear, only see what they want. So are we ever really seen for who we are?" She lets the question hang there. "Or are we ghosts?"

At this exact moment, the lamps go out, submerging us in gloom.

For a moment, there's no sound except for the waves outside.

I whisper, "The call is coming from inside the house."

Something or someone smacks me in the arm. Wesley appears through the doorway, brandishing a lighter.

"Does this happen a lot?" Isaac asks him.

"Pretty much." He relights the candles on the table, then moves to light the sconces. "Especially this time of year. It can get cold in here pretty fast."

"Sorry for hitting you," Ness whispers to me. "I hate the dark."

"You should have been here over Christmas," Wesley says to her. "It got below freezing, and the electricity was out for three days. But we couldn't leave because of the snow."

He departs, and in the flickering light, there is a general feeling of the evening winding down. Somewhere, a clock chimes ten, and I realize I'm not ready for it to end.

Leela pushes her chair away from the table and raises her

empty glass. "'Life is a waste of time and time is a waste of life, so let's all get wasted and have the time of our lives.'" She bows her head as she holds her glass higher. "To the late, the great Kurt Cobain."

A clamor as the rest of us get to our feet.

"And to us," Effy adds. "A new generation of Odds."

THE KITCHEN IS lit by lanterns and the glow of the unseen moon through the skylights. Beneath them, Wesley moves efficiently and methodically as he cleans up the dinner mess. Given the power outage, I expect rain or snow or clouds, but instead I can make out pinpricks of light where the stars shine through. I say, "Do you usually lose power when there's no storm?"

"Oh yeah. But you never lose your power."

"What?"

"One of my mom's platitudes." He grins, shakes his head, says in this hard Boston accent, "'You may lose electricity, but you never lose your power.'"

"I dig it." I grab myself a soda and offer to help him clean up, but he waves me off. I watch as he stacks dishes and puts away silverware. He's on the short side but built like a tank, and he moves expertly through the work. I feel weird not helping, and I want to tell him I'm not one of them—your typical Bullshit Prep kid who needs a staff picking up after him.

"How long have you been working here?" I ask. "It seems like a cool gig."

"Almost a year. I'm saving for med school next fall. Before I took the job, I was never much into history, but my wife says I'm, like, Mr. History now. They basically make you learn everything, not just about Moss Hove and Zachary Brighton but about all the things in the house. Artwork, artifacts, renovations, wallpaper, paint colors, right down to the smallest detail."

"What's with the birds?"

"Hove said he wanted to give them another life, like all the discarded relics in the house. He wasn't a hunter like his brothers. If you ask me, I think he felt a connection to them. The birds, not his brothers. Even though he left his family, I'm pretty sure he felt discarded by them. He flew away, if you will." He grins.

"Booker mentioned house staff, but I haven't seen anyone else."

"Yeah, Graffam sent most of them home. I get the sense she likes to be in control of her surroundings, and that means people too. Usually there are five of us, including my wife. We split time between here and her parents' house in Parkerton."

"Have you ever seen the Gloucester Sea Serpent?" I'm speaking, of course, of the Loch Ness Monster's American cousin, rumored to live in these waters. Sightings began just off Brighton's Woe in 1817, and there was a two-year period where crowds used to gather on the shore here and watch the creature frolic in the waves.

Wesley laughs. "No."

"Hey, don't laugh. The gorilla, the Komodo dragon, the

giant squid, and the duck-billed platypus were once mythical creatures until their existence was proven."

"Yeah, well, I don't see that happening with old Glossy."

We shoot the shit for another minute, and it's refreshing talking to him. He's only a few years older than I am, and I get the feeling that, like me, he doesn't come from extreme wealth.

"So I have to ask." He glances at my Lakers hat, which is back on my head. "Is that . . . ?"

"Authentic? Yeah. It belonged to a friend."

"Oh man. Magic Johnson. Kareem—who was *forty*, by the way. Lakers versus Celtics, the defending champs—107 to 106 in overtime in game four of six. When my dad's in a shit mood and wants to feel worse, he watches footage of that game all over again because it was the one that turned the tide. If you ever tell anyone this, I'll deny it. You don't root against the Celtics here and live to tell it, but the '87 Lakers? They're my team."

"Yeah." I don't have the heart to tell him that you, Jonah, were the Lakers fan, not me. That your parents gave this hat to me after you died because they knew you'd want me to have it. "So, hey, what's the deal with The Wild Hunt? Ruler of the Forest?"

He freezes for a split second, then crosses to the fridge and helps himself to a soda.

"How do you know about The Wild Hunt?"

"I saw the portraits of the winners in the game room."

He nods, his expression hard to read. "It's this game they invented. The Odds. Based on some European legend where the dead hunt the living and the door between worlds opens wide."

"A kind of Skull and Bones free-for-all?"

"Like a creepier hide-and-seek, but for rich people with too much time on their hands. No offense."

"None taken. Believe me."

"It's a last-night-of-Jan-Term tradition. They go all out. Capes. Masks."

"I've heard rumors."

He sets the can on the counter and folds his arms over his chest. "You know about that girl who was killed? Back in the nineties? They were playing the game that night. Kaya, that's my wife, she always makes sure she's nowhere near here when they play, but then, she hates anything remotely scary. I can't even get her to watch those old black-and-white horror movies—you know, back from the 1930s."

"Kaya and me both," I say.

"It's harmless, though. The game. Creepy but harmless."

I want to know more, but he yawns, apologizes, and then yawns again. He bids me good night, his footsteps fading away under the *rattle rattle* of the windows. Outside, something scrapes against the wood siding. There's a creak of floorboards somewhere overhead. The house is stirring to life. Waking up for three weeks every January, then drifting back into slumber the other forty-nine.

I gaze up at the portrait of Zachary Brighton, standing on the island known as Brighton's Woe, his gaze fixed across the water on the Moss. I think about what he must have felt when the man he loved drowned. And maybe I wasn't in love with Jonah, but I know what it's like to lose your best friend and not be able to do anything to bring him back. If I were Brighton, if I were Hove, I'd haunt the fuck out of this place.

"I'm sorry he died," I say to Brighton now. "But if you could do me a favor, please don't haunt me."

Effy

Thursday, January 8

The bedroom Ness and Leela share is twice as large as mine, the floor painted black, the wallpaper pink with roses. Ness and I sit on her bed discussing the day, a tradition we've had since we were fourteen. Across the room, Leela is dead asleep, eye mask on, snoring loudly.

"It felt significant," I say. "Inclusive. Momentous in a way I can't describe."

Being an only child raised by her grandmother, I've spent most of my life around adults. Gran's friends have always treated me with respect, like one of them. And then I came to Brighton and Hove, where I've had good teachers and bad teachers, and learned that adults don't always care what you have to say.

Unlike Moss Hove or Gran, I've never found my people, at least not as a group. But today I felt like part of something. For a little while, I forgot about my father and Arlo Ellis-Noon, even though he was sitting across from me, talking too much, being too flip, messing with that dark chaos of hair. *Look at me, I'm so adorable, I'm so funny, I'm so charming.*

"I just feel bad for Joey." Ness takes off her glasses and sets them on the bedside table. "I mean, I don't understand it. Why did Graffam send her home? And if *she* got sent home . . . I don't know. How long will *I* be here?"

Despite the good grades that got her early admission to Sarah Lawrence, UMass, and Brown, Ness is going to need some major financial aid to afford college. For the past two years, my best friend has joined every academic and creative club, edited the school newspaper, volunteered for Habitat for Humanity, and held down two part-time jobs in her frantic mission to impress scholarship committees.

She picks at a loose thread on the comforter. "I just don't know why Graffam chose me."

I feel a flicker of irritation. I want to talk about leaping into the water and spilling our souls to *Meredith Graffam*. I want Ness to feel as excited as I do.

"She chose you because you have something to say."

"Do I?" she asks. "Sometimes I wonder whether my words are actually interesting to anyone. Part of me wishes she'd sent me home instead."

I hate it when she gets down on herself like this. Ness has never been the most confident person, but the longer she's at Brighton and Hove, the more self-doubt attaches itself to her like a barnacle. All she wants is to earn a seat at the table, but at a school like this, she's always coming up short—middle of the class, middle of the crowd, sidelined to the edges of the room.

"It's not a competition," I say. "I mean, it *is*, but not in the sense of who's the most wounded or who's got the wildest stories. It's not about anyone else."

Except for the fact, of course, that each of us believes our story *is* the most deserving. And as much as Ness needs to win here, I need it more. For me it's about my own survival. A kind of reckoning with what happened to my mom, my dad, me. The short stories I'm writing are from the perspectives of six people whose lives change overnight. The worst thing that will ever happen to them is about to happen. It's not the aftermath I'm writing about. It's the leading-up-to. The sweet unawareness of what's coming.

"You're here because you're Vanessa effing Cato." I nudge her with my foot. "Why don't you ever believe me?"

"Because I feel like an impostor."

"Everyone feels like that."

"Isaac doesn't."

"He probably does in ways we don't know. And besides, Isaac is Isaac." When she gets quiet, I nudge her again, doing my best to appear light and easy, even though I no longer feel light and easy. "Am I not wise? Am I not all-knowing?"

"You're my best friend. You have to think I'm amazing, no matter what."

"No. I'm your best friend *because* you're amazing."

She smiles. Just a little.

"I love you," I tell her.

"I love you too." A beat and then she goes, "Are you okay, you know, with Arlo being here?"

"Am I glad to see him? No. Am I okay? I think so."

"I'm sorry he came back. But you need to remember that

you're Effy effing Green." She giggles at the sound of it. "And you're amazing too."

I nudge her with my foot, and she nudges me back.

Then she crawls under the covers and closes her eyes. "Has the card come with tomorrow's schedule?"

"Not yet."

For a second, I think she doesn't hear me. But then, from somewhere inside the blankets, she says, "Oh my God. This bed is like a cloud." And a few minutes later, she starts to snore as loud as Leela.

THE WALLPAPER IN my room is a soft green with flowers and vines, birds and butterflies, so that it feels like being in a garden. I pick up the camera Graffam gave me earlier and sit on my bed under the eaves, blinking into the lens. I press record and begin to talk:

We were at a party at the end of sophomore year. With three weeks left of school. I'd known Arlo for a while but not well. He was just this nerdy guy who was always talking. His hair wasn't as long then. He wasn't as broad through the shoulders. But his smile was the same.

The party was behind the field house on a warm, starlit night. There was music and drinking, only I wasn't drinking and neither was he. He was off by himself, on the outskirts of the party, lying on the ground, staring at the sky.

He was so still, which was weird because the Arlo Ellis-Noon I knew was never still. He had this look on his face—like whatever it was he saw up there was filling him with wonder.

And that was weird too because Arlo was always so sarcastic, so quick to push people's buttons.

I lay down beside him so I could see what he was seeing because suddenly I wanted to glimpse something wonderful too.

"There." He pointed. "Ophiuchus, the Serpent Bearer. It's one of the largest constellations, but it's usually hard to spot. Which is why it's so forgotten. The thing I love about this guy? He's equally visible everywhere. Like, it doesn't matter where you are. He's always there."

In that moment, it felt profound. It was hard to be fifteen years old and miles away from everything you knew. But the loneliness went beyond that. I'd been lonely maybe all my life.

"I'm lonely too sometimes," he said, reading my mind. "I love my family, but we're so different. The things I want in this world are different."

I knew exactly what he meant when he said it. It was possible to love the family you were raised with and still yearn for something else, some answer to why you're you.

The night had a heartbeat, loud and throbbing. I watched him as he watched the sky. Finally, he said, "That's why it helps to have things like the stars and, you know, someone to wrestle the serpents for you."

This was not the Arlo I thought I knew. In that moment, he seemed new and profound, and like someone who was going to be important to me in a way I couldn't yet see.

"I like Polaris. The North Star," I said, wanting to join in and be profound too. "All the other stars travel these great distances, but the North Star stays pretty much rooted in the sky. It's not the brightest but it's the most reliable, and it shows you your direction."

I raised an arm, pointed.

"Technically," he said, "*it's the earth that's moving. Which makes a lot of the stars seem like they're moving too. But Polaris is aligned closer to our North Pole, so it looks like it stays still. Also, it's not one star. It's five. Two of them orbit the main star, which is the brightest . . .*"

On and on as I blinked at him. This was the Arlo I knew.

"*Seriously?*" *I said. Like that, the moment was gone. He'd chased it away.*

But then he turned to look at me. And he said, "*Effy Green,*" *without any of the usual jokey charm. His eyes were the palest gray that changed with his mood.*

"*Yes, Arlo Ellis-Noon?*"

And then he asked if he could kiss me and I said sure.

It wasn't my first kiss, but it felt like the only one that mattered. The kiss held all this promise. It said, I get you. You aren't alone after all, not just because I'm here and you're here, but because I see you. I'm like you.

That wasn't the night it happened. For the next three weeks, we were always together. On that last night, we talked about the summer. I knew he was from California. He knew I was from Maine. Miles between us: 3,046. Driving time: nearly forty-four hours. An entire country between us. We promised we'd meet in the middle, in Omaha, Nebraska. And, of course, there was always junior year. We'd both be back at Brighton and Hove in the fall. Then we had sex.

The next day, I texted him as soon as I arrived at Gran's house in Ogunquit. He never texted back.

No one wants their heart broken. But Arlo was the first time I'd ever risked mine. And even though he didn't exactly break my heart, there's the finest hairline fracture right down the center. Arlo, *it says. It's why I like old places and ruins and shells of houses—because I feel like an abandoned place too.*

There's a sound on the back stairs, and I freeze, goose bumps rising on my skin. I watch as a card slides through the crack beneath the door.

When you know that ghosts don't exist and things that go bump in the night are nothing to be afraid of, you can let yourself enjoy creaky old houses. But still a shiver runs up my spine. As if looking for a ghost, I scan the angles and gables, the glowing green glass that outlines the windowpanes, the mirror above the mantel.

I stop recording and kind of hop-skip across the cold floor to collect the schedule card. Then hop-skip back to bed. Outside, the wind is picking up. The tower seems to sway. I read the card, turn off the light, and close my eyes.

Sometime later, I wake up to music so loud it fills my room.

Arlo

Thursday, January 8

(the wee hours)

In my stupor, I click on the bedside lamp, which casts an orange glow across the floor. The power is back on. Not the power. The electricity. Because we never lose our power. Except when we do.

I stumble out of my room, and Effy is there, barefoot, hair loose around her shoulders, wearing a red-and-green Christmas nightshirt. I've dreamed of this moment or one like it, only in that dream there was no nightshirt and we weren't in a strange old house filled with strange pulsing music.

"What the hell?" Effy hisses at me, as if I'm responsible.

"I don't know."

"What is that song?"

"I. Don't. Know," I say again.

If the others hear it—and they *must* hear it—they're nowhere to be seen.

"You don't think they're sleeping through this?" She sets

off down the hall, which yawns endlessly before us, then looks back at me. "You might want to put on some clothes."

I realize with a flush that I'm in my boxers. I grab a shirt from my room and catch up with her on the stairs, my heart ticking too fast. There's no such thing as walking silently through an old house. With every creak and groan of the floorboards, Effy shoots me a death look.

"What?" I can't resist saying. "Like anyone can hear me over the music?" The walls of the Moss are practically vibrating from the speakers in every room.

The lights are low, with red embers glowing drowsily in the fireplaces, as if the house itself drank more than its share of wine at dinner and now needs to sleep it off. Every piece of furniture becomes a creature waiting in the shadows. Every painting comes alive, the eyes of the people in them following us as we move. Doorframes gape into darkness like mouths opened in a scream.

I had this psychology class once where we talked about fear of the dark. Fear, like pain, is there to protect us from danger. It's normal to be afraid of the dark because we're afraid of what we can't see. Our cave-people ancestors would have struggled to spot predators after nightfall, so the fear has evolved along with us. I remind myself of this now. *It's normal. It's ingrained in you from a different time and place.*

Effy and I quickly lose our way in the labyrinthine house, passing through multiple dining rooms and parlors, a study, a guest room, another guest room, on and on. We follow dark passageways that dead-end, then we turn around and feel our way back.

It's like that old game: Now we're hotter; now we're colder. We move through the kitchen, the laundry, the dining room, the Octagon Room. Outside, a flash of lightning. A crack of thunder. It's night out there and it's night in here. And still we don't find where the music's coming from.

A voice behind me: "What the fuck is that racket?" It's Leela in her beanie, followed by Ness, bundled in a blanket.

By now I know the words of the song by heart:

The twelvemonth and a day being up,
The dead began to speak:
"Oh who sits weeping on my grave,
And will not let me sleep?"

The three of them are not amused when I start singing along. The song, like the house, is distorted, a fun-house mirror, warped and uneven. The words conjure images of overgrown cemeteries and crumbling gravestones, of a bloodless hand rising from the earth.

Together, the four of us press onward, uranium glass lighting our way, painted eyes watching us from gold frames, stuffed birds with wings spread and beaks open wide.

Lights blaze in the theater, where we find Isaac, Ramon, and Peter. No Graffam. No Drea.

"You crave one kiss of my clay-cold lips,
But my breath smells earthy strong;
If you have one kiss of my clay-cold lips,
Your time will not be long."

"Is this you?" Leela says to the three of them, waving her arms at—presumably—the music.

"Nah, dude," says Peter, sounding like Isaac. "We just got here."

Then, suddenly, the music bumps to a stop. Effy emerges from the alcove behind the piano, holding up a flat black disc. "There's a record player back there," she says.

I take the album from her. *The Unquiet Grave.* Artist: *Unknown.*

"The same song," I say. "Over and over."

"What the actual hell." Leela snatches it out of my hands.

"Uh. There's more."

We turn. Ramon stands beside the piano, his head bent over something. He holds up a piece of paper and reads out loud:

> *Now that I have your attention. In order to improve the creative dynamic of the group, someone else must go. You decide who it should be.*

One by one, we gather around him, as if he's all-knowing. There on the piano is a stack of index cards, a cup of freshly sharpened pencils, and a wooden box with a slot in the top.

Ness reads over Ramon's shoulder:

> *After voting, return to your rooms and pack your bags. Set them outside your door. One of you will be gone by morning.*
>
>   *x MG*

"Oh!" She looks up, eyes sparkling with excitement. "This is like *The Bachelor*, when they do the two-on-one dates, and one of them will get sent home at the end of the night." Her brow furrows as it hits her. "Wait, no. This is terrible. We shouldn't be . . . It shouldn't be up to us to say, *You don't belong here* . . ."

"We're not *really* going to do this." I search the faces of my fellow students, my colleagues, my comrades-in-arms.

But Peter is already passing around the cards and pencils, and the others are spreading themselves across the room, scribbling away. I look at Effy and she looks at me. And then she smiles, a terrifying display of teeth.

Afterward we find the stairs to our private wing, all of us quieter than usual. One by one, everyone vanishes into their rooms, no *Good night*, no *Sweet dreams*, no *Farewell to you if I'm whisked away from this house and these woods before morning*, just the soft clicking of doors opening and closing.

Before Effy can vanish too, I say, "Wait."

The last door clicks shut, and now it's just the two of us.

I gaze at her in the twilight. Her lips, just inches away, suddenly real and tangible after all the time I've thought about them. I want to touch the ends of her hair. I want to brush her cheek with my fingers. I want to lean in and kiss her. Because what if I never get the chance again? What if this, right here, right now, is it?

"What?" she says, impatient.

I'd forgotten how long her lashes are, black against the vivid green of her eyes. The way she can look like she's smiling and frowning at the same time, her mouth doing one thing, her eyebrows another. I count the freckles on her cheeks. One. Five. Ten. Twenty.

"Nothing. I just . . . I wish I hadn't screwed everything up with you sophomore year."

"If you're hoping to change my mind about the voting, you're too late."

"I don't care about the voting. Well, maybe a little, but that's not why . . . This is me trying to apologize so you won't hate me forever." I attempt a charming smile, as if to say, *See what you'd miss if you hate me forever? All this.*

Her eyebrows shoot skyward, consumed by her fringe. "You lied to me so I would sleep with you." She drags each word out so that the whole sentence has, like, a thousand syllables.

"I mean," I say, "more like I failed to mention a pertinent piece of information."

"That's lying. You knew you were leaving. And you knew I thought you were staying. Because that's what you wanted me to believe. All that talk about *when we come back junior year* and *when we do this* and *when we do that*. It was all bullshit."

"It's more complicated than that."

"Is it?"

"I wanted to stay," I tell her. "And I wanted to go. I wanted to be in two places. Here with you. There with my parents. By the time I knew I was going, I didn't plan on you. And then—you. But I was already leaving. I just wanted to pretend I wasn't."

She shakes her head. She's half smiling, half frowning, and I don't know which to believe.

"I can't do this, Arlo. I have, like, zero interest in being friends with you. Besides. You got what you wanted, right?

Wasn't that the whole point?" She tilts her head in a way that reminds me of Graffam. "Do you know why I never told anyone about you after we slept together? Because it was a mistake."

I try to swallow the bitter lump that's lodged in my throat. It doesn't move, not even a fraction, and I won't be surprised if it stays there forever.

"Got it," I say.

"Do you?"

"Yeah. I'm pretty sure I do."

And then, without looking back, I go to my room.

TEN MINUTES LATER, I've packed my earthly belongings—something I've gotten depressingly good at over the years. I set my duffel outside the door and then drop onto the bed, pulling the Lakers cap low over my face.

I am thousands of miles from home. Thousands of miles from family. Jonah is dead.

Once again, I am solidly, eternally awake. I do what I've been doing since summer, since I stopped sleeping—I pick up my sketchbook and draw. Green eyes fringed with black lashes. Freckles like stars.

I don't want to leave this place as long as Effy is here. Part of it is wanting to make things right, to make amends. And part of it is still wanting her. Not just the first girl I ever slept with. The first girl I ever loved.

Effy

Friday, January 9

I wake to the ringing of the courtyard bell. Gran will tell you that I'm not someone who just springs into action in the morning. It takes me a while to get started. The clock on the wall tells me it's eight a.m., and I feel strangely guilty that I slept at all.

In a rush, it comes back to me—the night before. The song. Graffam's instructions on the piano. *Someone else must go. You decide who it should be.*

And then the realization: *I'm still here.*

I throw the covers back and race across the cold floor. The hallway is empty except for the bags that sit in front of each door. So maybe not yet. I count one, two, three, four, five, six, seven, eight. Not including mine. Three of them belong to Ness, which means one of the suitcases is missing. At first I think it's Arlo's, and I feel this strange mix of relief and something else I can't place. But no, his is the room with the red door, and there's an army duffel planted outside it.

Then I see there's only one bag outside the large bedroom, the one Isaac and Peter share. Which means she actually went through with it. Graffam sent someone home.

TODAY'S SCHEDULE CARD tells us to meet in the Octagon Room at nine o'clock. I get there early, as does Ness, as does Leela, all of us wanting to see who left. I'm not sure who Leela voted to send home, but I know Ness voted for Isaac.

The boys take their time showing up, arriving just as the clock strikes nine. Ramon walks in, followed by Arlo, and then—finally—Isaac, as if he wanted to make us wait. He strolls in, hands clasped above his head in victory. He does a little dance just like the one he does in the end zone every time he scores a touchdown.

Arlo says, "And then there were six."

"So Peter's gone?" Leela makes it sound like a question.

"Yeah." Isaac drops into a chair. "They came to get him around five a.m. And booted his ass out." For someone who just scored the largest room to himself, his tone is pretty somber.

But then we're all a little quiet this morning. The air feels weighted as we look at one another, wondering who voted for us, wondering who might be next.

When I meet Arlo's eyes, his expression is unreadable. *I didn't pick you*, I think. *I was going to, but for some reason I couldn't.*

He breaks our gaze first and reaches for something in the middle of the table. Another index card. "'Come outside,'" he reads. Then flips the card around and holds it up for the rest of us to see.

* * *

MEREDITH GRAFFAM STARES down at us from the rooftop. With her dark hair pulled back, she's just a pale face in a billowing white coat, a ghostly apparition. Except that she's real, and she's very high up, and the roof is slick with ice and snow and precarious in its angles and peaks and slopes. She is balanced on the edge as if she's planning to take flight.

"What the actual . . ." Arlo's voice trails off as he follows my gaze skyward.

"Fear," Graffam says. We stand below, mouths agape, eyes fixed on her. "It doesn't belong in storytelling. You cannot be afraid and write. Because if you're afraid, the writing will be dishonest. A false note on a piano in the middle of what could be a beautiful melody. No one will remember the tune. If they remember anything at all, it will be the fear."

A gust of wind loosens her hair from its tie, and my heart knocks against my chest as I picture Graffam herself hurtling through space. But she remains planted like she's part of the roof, a weather vane or a chimney.

"Writing is one of the scariest things you can do. It means accessing ourselves. Excavating our deepest, darkest feelings. Then exposing those feelings to readers and viewers who will tear them apart. An assault. That's what it feels like if you excavate enough. But so much better to suffer for something that is true and honest and real than for something that is small and tentative—or aims to please some unknown audience."

"You said before that we need to get uncomfortable and be afraid," Isaac calls to her.

"I did. You need to be afraid but *not* afraid at the same time.

Be afraid to go where you don't want to go. But be fearless when writing what you find there. Everything is fair game."

It's hard to explain how it feels on the ground looking up at her. At no point in the history of ever has a teacher of mine balanced on a snow-slicked roof or told me to jump into a frigid ocean or forced me to sacrifice one of my classmates. I have this dizzy, too-warm feeling, like I'm standing on a roof too.

An arm links through mine. Ness, her breath coming out in small white puffs. I pull her closer to me, a human security blanket. *This is all I have in the world*, I think. *Ness and Gran.* The two people who know me best and love me most.

"Now is your chance," Graffam booms. "To reveal that fear and free yourself. Let the wind blow it away. Let the waves drown it. I'll start. My biggest fear—well, aside from heights . . ."

Nervous laughter from those of us on the ground.

"My biggest fear is being ordinary and commonplace, of having nothing of my own to say. Of being sent home from the party. Of never being invited to begin with. Of being forgotten."

Another gust of wind. Her hair unleashes itself fully, dark strands whipping across her face.

"Now you," she cries.

The six of us exchange glances, furtive, like, *What the fuck do we do?* I'm not about to stand here and shout what I'm afraid of in front of Meredith Graffam and Arlo and the others. Not even Ness. There's a reason I try to hide the things that scare me most. No one wants to walk around in this world like an exposed nerve.

Isaac goes, "Yeah, pass." He grins at us, at her. "If it's all the same."

"Isn't it enough to just tell *ourselves* what we're afraid of?" Arlo asks. And then he looks at Ness and me and murmurs, "You know this is fucked up, right?" He nods at Graffam, three stories above us. "Like, seriously fucked up." I search for some trace of a smile to let me know he's entranced in spite of it, just like the rest of us. But he looks as serious as I've ever seen him.

Graffam calls out, "If you don't reveal your fears, how do you expect to make an impact? Your words matter, even if you don't think so. By nature, we doubt ourselves, whether it's what we've been taught or just who we are. *Why would anyone want to hear what I have to say?* I'm telling you now, if you don't have a story, invent one. And if you don't reveal your biggest fear, I will jump off this roof."

When no one speaks, she moves closer to the edge, loosening an avalanche of snow. Her foot slips, and she holds out her arms like wings. We watch as she fights for her balance, Ness's arm clenching mine, my jaw tight, my heart pounding like the surf. *This*, I think. *You falling off that roof is my biggest fear.*

Leela cups her mouth with her hands and shouts, "I love my brother, but I don't want to become him. He plays it too safe. I'm afraid of playing it safe. Of being old before I'm old." She glances at us. Shrugs.

"I'm afraid of being sent home," Ness says.

"Louder," Graffam calls. "I can't hear you."

"I'm afraid of being sent home," Ness yells. "From here. I'm afraid you'll realize I don't deserve my place and that I'm just taking up space that belongs to someone else."

"Good." Graffam stares down at the rest of us. "All or nothing. I can still jump."

"I'm scared of being left." Ramon keeps his eyes trained on Graffam, as if it's just the two of them there. "I don't want to be left. Especially if it's my fault for pushing someone away or for believing they'll go." His eyes drop to the snow at our feet. I look at the way his head is bowed. There's something vulnerable about the bare skin on the back of his neck.

"I don't want to live someone else's life," says Isaac.

"Good," she says again. "Arlo. Effy."

I can feel him waiting for me to go first, just as I'm waiting for him.

A shower of snow comes crashing down around us, and my head jerks upward to where Graffam balances on the very edge now, arms splayed, eyes closed.

"I'm going to count to three," she says to the sky. And I know she means it. She will jump off this roof. I imagine calling Books, who will call 911, who will send an ambulance, which will whisk her off to the nearest hospital, and the six of us will be sent home, forever known as the kids who broke Meredith Graffam.

We speak at once, Arlo and me, shouting over each other. His is something about not wanting to survive and fail, while mine is "I am afraid of cutting my dad out of my life forever, and I'm afraid of letting him back in."

"No," she cries. "No." She is looking at me. "You're not listening. You don't get it. That's not what I mean. You will never get anywhere if that's as far as you're willing to go."

And then she jumps.

As I watch her fall—body suspended in midair, dark hair

streaming like ribbons—my blood goes cold in my veins. My throat ices over and my limbs ice over and I no longer feel my heart. I can only stand there frozen.

She lands in a snowbank below the roof, one we somehow failed to notice because we were too busy looking up. We watch as she dusts herself off and gets to her feet, once more—like the rest of us—on solid, regular earth. She sounds almost victorious when she tells us she enlisted Wesley to build the snowbank for her.

She was probably always planning to jump, Ness says afterward. *It wasn't because of you.*

But it was because of me. Because, as usual, I wasn't able to go where I needed to go, which in this case was deep into myself.

AFTER LUNCH I gather my laptop and books and search for a place to work. Graffam has given us the assignment of writing a paragraph pinpointing our fear and dissecting where it comes from. A single paragraph, which we will hand in by evening.

I pass through the theater, with its gilded balcony. Just beyond, in a shadowy corner—so dusky I almost don't see it—is a staircase with a banister carved into a serpent, its head at the base, its jaws open wide. I place my hand inside its mouth, letting it rest there. Ness would tell me not to. She would be afraid that somehow the jaws would snap shut, trapping my hand. I lean in close, staring the snake in the eyes, and hiss.

Then I gaze upward. These stairs must go to Graffam's

wing, a back entrance. I stroke the head of the serpent and place my foot on the first step.

Suddenly I'm distracted by a scent in the air, heady and sweet. I follow it past the stairs into another room.

It's a solarium with sky-high glass ceilings and walls of glass. At first I think I'm outside. But then I notice the half-moon sofa, a deep velvet green, hidden among blooming plants and trees. Enormous pillows are strewn about. The vines that climb the walls are as much a part of the Moss's structure as the chimneys.

I drop onto the couch and listen to the trickling of an unseen waterfall. I don't know much about plants. Enough to recognize ferns and palm trees, wisteria and English ivy. Camellias maybe. Beyond that, I don't have a clue.

The house tells me a lot about Moss Hove. He liked to entertain. He loved to read. He enjoyed music and games. He was intrigued by the supernatural. The bright colors of every room and the treasures he collected reinforce what I know about his love of beauty. Yet he appears to have been equally drawn to the dark and the monstrous. And he loved nature. I can feel him everywhere. As if he just stepped out for a minute and might return anytime.

This room is mine, I think. I shut the doors so that the others know not to come in here, and return to the sofa, where I tip my head back and stare up at the sky. The weather outside changes from cloudy to sunny to cloudy again. I hear the distant strains of music.

I breathe the sweet air, and for a while I write. The first short story is the most personal, about a teen who loses her parents in a single night. Unlike in life, both the fictional parents are killed. It's the story that got me accepted to Jan Term and the only one I've been able to finish. The others have so far been a struggle. As if my imagination dried up the minute I came to the Moss.

Creativity is fickle. It can arrive full force, all cylinders firing and ready to go. It can elude you, like a butterfly fluttering off just before you catch hold of it. It can abandon you altogether, leaving you dry and empty and wondering if you'll ever write again. There's nothing like knowing you *have* to produce something to render you unable to produce it.

I still can't access the Wi-Fi, which means I don't get to obsessively google *Clay Reynolds. Charlotte Reynolds. Woman killed on impact when truck hits tree. Man sentenced to fifteen years in prison for death of wife.* I tell myself it's probably for the best. There won't be anything anyway because there's never anything. Only a ten-line announcement about his release on the front page of *The Weekly Sentinel*, an article I've read so many times I've memorized it.

For the first few years after my mom died, I would talk to her. It didn't matter where I was or what I was doing, I just talked anytime there was something I wanted her to know. And then one day I stopped, because having these one-sided conversations was only making me miss her more.

"He called it the Sky Room."

I look up to find Graffam standing in the now-open doorway.

"The Sky Room," I repeat. "I like that."

It's intoxicating being around powerful people. Over the years, Gran has introduced me to friends and colleagues—artists, musicians, playwrights, photographers like her. Icons she photographed who later became like family.

But the magnetic pull of Meredith Graffam—at such close range—is dizzying. She is one of those people who comes with her own thermosphere, as if she could channel the sun itself. She's been through hell. She has battle scars. She's powerful and fierce and intensely human. She does her part to shatter the glass ceiling for women, and she's not above giving young writers a chance. In many ways, she's who I want to be.

When she doesn't leave right away, I make room for her on the couch. She sits, angling her body toward me. "I thought you might have something to say to me."

"I feel like I made you jump."

"You didn't make me do anything. You're not responsible for me. Just like you're not responsible for Ness or any of the others."

"I know. It's just—I'm not the best at looking inward. I can do it, but I don't like to."

"None of us do. It's something that, with enough work, you can get better at. There are parts of my life I still don't like to talk about. But sometimes talking about them is the only thing that exorcises the ghosts." She settles back. "I had a Ness once. She was named Lara. Only, I was the scholarship student. She was the pedigree." I flinch at the word. "You have to understand that I wasn't happy here. Not at first. It didn't matter that I'd gotten in on my own merits—I was treated like I was nothing. But then I met Lara. We were like sisters, so much so that the lines became blurred. Where she ended and I began. I don't think I fully realized what I could do though, until . . ." She clears her throat. When she speaks again, her voice is froggy with emotion. "Until much later."

A lull as I take this in.

She squints at the ceiling, glances around at the room. Then her eyes are on me again. "So tell me why you're here. I want to know the actual reason."

I don't even have to think about it. I tell her how I used to go along on Gran's photo shoots when I was little. I was amazed at the way she could photograph the ordinary, everyday world and make it look interesting or magical. Capturing the truth of it but also—even in her grittiest photos—the beauty. I grew up wanting to do that too, not with a camera but with words. And then my dad got out of prison and wrote me a letter and I didn't know what to do with that. So I thought I could write about it, or write *around* it, to make sense of the feeling.

I pick up *Frankenstein*, set it down.

"This book," I say. But don't finish because how do I say, *This book talks about free will and choice, good and bad. About what makes a monster, human or otherwise. And maybe somewhere in its pages is why and how, a way to understand. Or maybe the answer is here at the Moss in the project that I'm working on.*

Graffam interrupts my inner monologue. "So how can I, Meredith, help you, Effy, capture the truth?"

I feel myself relax a little. Shadows play across her face, and she is suddenly striking. Wise. Sphinxlike.

Because I don't know where to start, because I have so many things I want to ask her, I say, "The video journals. I recorded my first one last night, but it felt so, I don't know, unnatural, just sitting there talking to myself. I've never kept a journal before, unless you count the letters I've written to my father . . . I started writing to him years ago. Telling him about my life." This was after I stopped talking to my mother. "At first it was like, *Look how shitty it is, look how broken I am, look what you've done to me.* But then, after a while, there was some good mixed in. I've never mailed them. But it helped. It helps."

Graffam is the first person I've told about this. Gran doesn't even know.

"So why not address your video journals to him?"

A part of me balks at the idea of inviting him into the Moss like this, in such a personal way. But then, haven't I already brought him in?

She says, "Your journals are whatever you want them to be, and you've already been doing this in some form. If it feels more natural to you, direct them to him. That doesn't mean he gets to guide your story. Not any more than you let him." Then she smiles. "You can use it, you know."

"What?"

"Your father. And whatever else is on your mind. Whoever else is on your mind. Put it into your work. That's what I'm supposed to tell you. The truth is, sometimes you're too close. You're in it and you don't want to be in it, especially when your work is supposed to be a refuge. Sometimes I just want to burn it all to the fucking ground."

"God, me too."

"But here's a secret. You can embellish. Lie. Whatever you want to call it. Take the truth and twist it. Improve it. Give it a better ending. Everything that's ever happened to me is material for my work. Even as I'm going through it, I know

I'll write about it. Maybe not today, maybe not tomorrow, but eventually."

I feel the urge to type her words into my laptop, but this is a conversation, not a class. So I just nod, trying to memorize all she's saying.

"So," she says. "Your biggest fear?"

"Losing. Losing this. As in Jan Term. Losing people. Like my gran." The death of my mother is proof that it doesn't matter how invincible you seem, how watchful and prepared. Life still finds a way to upend you. "Just . . . losing."

Graffam takes in a breath, then huffs it out. I wait for her to congratulate me on my honesty, for finally digging deep, but instead she says, "I can relate. More than you know."

She studies the ends of her hair, loose around her shoulders, then deftly begins working it into a braid.

"I never wanted kids," she says. "I knew when I was your age that I wasn't meant to be a mom. But what I don't get is being villainized because I'm a woman. If I were a man, it would be different. And in Hollywood—in any business, really—you're not allowed to fail if you're female. If you do fail, you're not allowed to fail more than once."

She pauses, and I follow her eyes out the window, where I imagine she's watching her younger self.

I say, "And if you sleep with someone you shouldn't, they don't forgive you, not even when it's a stupid mistake. You get slut-shamed. You're also not allowed to sleep with someone because you like them and they make you laugh. Especially when they leave without a word, heading to this whole new life, and you have to stay in the old one."

As soon as the words leave my mouth, I want to stuff them back in.

"After lying to you so they can 'get laid'?"

I must look surprised because she says, "It wasn't hard to figure out. And I'm sorry you have that distraction here. I love men, but they can get in the way. It's up to us not to let them. Whether you're seventeen or almost fifty, the same rules apply. As women, we are not allowed to be human or fallible."

She smiles, and I feel myself smiling in return. I think of the NDA I signed before coming here, of the fact that her secrets and mine are safe in this room.

"Clearly I believe in second chances. In certain circumstances. But a word of advice? Always watch your own back. A few years ago—this is before Me Too—there was this producer. He made it plain that if I slept with him, he'd help me get ahead. I really wanted to work on his film. It was a good film. Such a good film that I didn't want to walk away, even though he was a prodigious prick."

"What did you do?"

"I told him no. And I stayed because—well, this was after *The Hunt* came out and all that ensued. I felt desperate, like I had to take whatever they gave me. I was grateful to even be working at that point. I was second AD—assistant director—but he had me fetching him coffee and these disgusting kale grass smoothies he liked. I can't remember how I got the idea, but I guess I just noticed the Visine in my bag one day. And I started adding a few drops to his smoothies, just enough to make him feel like he had food poisoning for a couple of weeks. Pretty unoriginal but oddly satisfying."

She smiles and I feel myself smile too.

"Also pretty terrible, but I was young and angry. And then one day I added too much and he collapsed on set. They rushed him to Cedars-Sinai and replaced him on the film while doctors ran diagnostics. They never did find out what was wrong. It sounds bad but it's not like anyone died, and trust me, he deserved it. I think he knew it was me, so no police were involved and, like magic, it all just went away."

She seems lost in the memory. A bittersweet memory by the look on her face, but more sweet than bitter. It makes me wonder if that's the worst thing she's done. I think of her first book. Just what was it she'd been guilty of? Mistakenly picking someone out of a lineup. Fighting to make sure this man—a man she believed to be guilty—got locked up. She didn't do it to be malicious. She did it because she thought he killed her friend. Yet she was vilified for it.

"As women," she says, "we need to be careful. What we give of ourselves and how much we give, especially to people who don't deserve it. If I could give my younger self a piece of advice, it would be to keep my eyes wide open, no matter what the situation. Barring that, it would be to carry Visine at all times."

The moment feels strange and surprisingly heavy. I say, "I kind of wish I'd brought some with me. I could've used it."

She laughs, and then she rises off the sofa. "I should let you get back to it. I'm looking forward to reading more of your work, Effy Green." She smiles at me. "And if you don't mind? Don't tell the others you saw me."

As she leaves, I sit there with the scene playing in my

mind—the asshole producer brought to his knees, literally, by the scorned young writer. I imagine doing the same to Arlo. Slowly poisoning him until he ends up in the hospital.

For a long while, I don't move, lost in thought. Not until the clocks chime and I realize it's time to get ready for dinner.

Arlo

Friday, January 9

The house is alive and feverish with singing and laughter and lit candles in every window. Isaac and I follow the noise to the theater, where Meredith Graffam, dressed in white, holds court with several dozen strangers. They mill about, drinks in hand, laughing and chattering. The middle of the room has been cleared to make space for frenzied dancing, and men in tuxedos weave through expertly, trays balanced overhead.

A bald woman, maybe early thirties, sits on the piano bench pounding away at the keys, while an octogenarian in a ball gown stands above us on the balcony warbling something loud and bawdy, eyes closed, swaying so violently I'm afraid she'll go plunging over the railing. People sing along or shout over the music in order to be heard. The whole mood gives frantic Prohibition-era vibes, and for a moment I feel like I've fallen into a wormhole and spun back in time.

At my side, Isaac is nodding in approval. "Okay, then. All right." Isaac Williams loves a party.

Across the crowd, Graffam catches sight of us and waves before letting herself be twirled away by a man in a hot pink feather boa. The energy in the room is infectious, and I feel myself absorbing it. I wonder if it's like this wherever she goes—leaving a trail of electrified people in her wake.

A waiter thrusts drinks into our hands—martinis, I think. I wait for some responsible adult to swoop in and pluck them away, but when no one does, I look at Isaac and he looks at me and we chug them down.

Someone calls hello, and I see that it's Drea, sparkling in red, hair swept up off her neck. "Meredith's giving a party," she shouts over the music.

"We can see that," I shout back.

"Who are these people?" Isaac sets his empty glass on a passing tray.

Drea holds up her hands. "I have no idea. Her assistant in LA, Zoe, is the one who handles event planning. I imagine they're all very famous and important."

She smiles, but it's a nervous smile, and I wonder if Graffam bothered telling Dean Booker about this or if the rules just don't apply to her.

Isaac breaks away from us, in pursuit of another drink. I watch as he's swept up in the sea of bodies.

"So," I say to Drea. "What is it you do for Meredith Graffam when you're not planning parties you don't know about?"

"Whatever she needs, really. I can be a creative sounding

board, but so far I've mostly been standing in when she can't be, like, a . . ."

"Babysitter?"

"I was going to say *presence*." She laughs. "I'm also using this time to finish my Petunias because the week after Jan Term I do my first gallery show. Meredith pulled some strings to make it happen, and she just gave me the news, so . . ."

A bright peal of laughter reaches us above the bedlam, and Drea and I turn to watch Graffam across the room.

"My fairy godmother," Drea says simply.

As if she hears this, Graffam stands on tiptoes and gestures in our direction, calling Drea's name to confirm that, yes, she is needed. Drea smiles an apology and drifts away to join her.

So now it's just me. I'm still getting used to being around a lot of people all at once. Turns out grief can leave lingering side effects. In my case, a definite decrease in social stamina.

"You know who would've loved this?" Isaac has reappeared.

"Our old friend Peter."

He bumps my shoulder with his. "Who'd you vote out anyway? And you'd better not say me."

"At ease, man. You weren't my first choice." My eyes find Ramon, standing by the fireplace, mansplaining God knows what to a pair of women.

Isaac follows my gaze. "Santos?"

I nod. Drink. Attempt to swallow the guilt I feel over sacrificing one of our own.

"Yeah," says Isaac, "Tobin's annoying as shit, but he's always up for a good time. Ramon, on the other hand . . ."

"The girls must've voted out Peter, then."

As I say it, a little spark of something flames in my chest, and that's when I see her—Effy. In a black dress. Hair half up, half down. Outshining everyone else.

Maybe it's the crowded room or the blazing fire, but that little flame burns brighter. *Effy could have voted me out of this house, but she didn't.*

A clinking of glass brings me out of my reverie. The music stops and everyone turns to look at the woman in white who stands barefoot atop the balcony.

"If we could adjourn to the dining room," Graffam announces. "Dinner is served."

THREE LONG TABLES are adorned with candles and flowers and elaborate place settings. There is a flurry of movement, buzzing, and laughter as we search for our assigned seats. I find my place card at the center table, between a retired ballet dancer and Drea. Effy sits directly across from me.

Wesley appears with a brilliant blue bottle. *Whittier*, reads the label. I watch as he pours some for us lowly underage saps. "It's from a vintner friend of Graffam's," he tells me. "Nonalcoholic wine."

"Sounds delightful," I say.

Graffam stands and raises her glass, tapping it with her fork until the room falls silent.

"In this wild and precious life, we all must find community. Friends who fan our creative flame, who inspire our trust. Everyone at this table is an example of that. As the late Carrie Fisher said, 'Stay afraid, but do it anyway.' So, my remarkable six . . ."

It takes me a few seconds to realize she is addressing us—Ness, Isaac, Ramon, Leela, Effy, and me. I have to admit it feels good. As if I belong here at this table among these strange, beautiful people. As if I'm more than just Arlo the fuckup, Arlo who killed his best friend.

Graffam continues. "I have an assignment for you, both for class and for life. Build your own world. With rules and laws and a language. Give it a culture and a history. The type of world you want to inhabit. Like The Odds did before you." She holds her glass skyward and gestures to all of us, students and guests. "Slán go fóill!"

The rest of us do our best to repeat it, but it sounds more like *Slayandgofool*. I drink, and the wine is surprisingly good. Warm and sweet. Like Christmas.

The room vibrates with conversations. Graffam flits from guest to guest, introducing them as she goes. They are highly successful directors, publishers, musicians, artists. One of the women claims to be a "fixer" but doesn't elaborate.

"When I was a student here, fixers were pretty common." Graffam's voice trips across the room. "Every parent had one. That, apparently, has not changed." I follow her gaze to where Ramon sits between the piano player and the singer. He catches my eye, and his face goes pink.

"Most high-powered people do," the fixer says. "Believe me, they keep me busy."

"Places like Brighton and Hove are a lot easier when you're bulletproof." Graffam's voice is too bright. "I would have given anything for someone to have my back. Sadly, I had to bury my own skeletons."

"To having other people bury the bodies," the man with the boa toasts.

As the conversation shifts, Rosa, the dancer beside me, watches Graffam. "It's been hard for her." Her tone is thoughtful and confidential, almost as if she's talking to herself.

"I'm sorry?"

She gives me a sideways glance—confirmation that she's speaking to me—then looks at Graffam. "Everywhere she goes, no matter what projects she does, it always comes back to *The Hunt* and *The Lie*. She's had to prove herself again and again." Her eyes slide back to me. "She knows firsthand what it takes to fight for your place. Soul stamina. That's what I call it."

Across the table, Effy is watching us, watching me. I give her a wink, flash her the old dimples. She rolls her eyes and turns to the person next to her.

"Is it any wonder she prefers to surround herself with people who tell her what she wants to hear?" She nods at Drea. "It doesn't help that she's not close to anyone anymore."

"Anymore?"

"That friend who was killed, the one she wrote about in the first book?" She leans in conspiratorially, our shoulders touching. "I don't think Meredith's let herself get close to anyone since. Certainly not Paddy, not even at the height of their liaison amoureuse. Then again, the way she borrows stories and bends the truth, it's no wonder people pull away."

"What do you mean by 'borrows'?"

"Oh, you know, a family suicide here, a friend's divorce there, the death of a distant relative's child. To Meredith, everything is fodder for her craft and nothing is off-limits . . ."

Screams of laughter at the end of the table, and like that, I feel the conversation end.

The rest of dinner is lively but uneventful. Course after course is delivered until I never want to see or smell or eat food ever again. After dessert, everyone clamors for Graffam to tell them what she's working on. We fall into a comatose, carb-laden hush as she raises a hand—just a single hand—asking for our silence.

"I'm afraid I'm not ready to talk about it," she says. Groans ensue. As a consolation, she offers up the origins of The Wild Hunt, how one January night in 1922, Zachary Brighton proposed a game of hide-and-seek. A simple child's game steeped in folklore and legend.

"She does love an audience." Rosa jabs at the olive in her martini—over and over—like she's trying to spear a fish. "Still. It's good that she's working again." Her tone implies, *I guess.*

"Has she talked to you about it?" I ask her. "Because she hasn't told me anything, and you know, we're like this." I hold up crossed fingers.

"No," she says in the flat, humorless voice I've come to know and love over the past couple of hours. "But you can see it. She always looks more alive when she's in a project."

The two of us study Meredith Graffam. She glows in the candlelight, larger than life. The shimmering heat of her throwing off sparks. Catching fire and swallowing us all.

OUR GUESTS HAVE left to get a head start on the snow that's supposed to blow in before midnight. The house is quiet, and

I feel a sense of relief. As much as I love a good party—just ask my brother, my parents, the Santa Monica police—it felt weirdly intrusive having outsiders here. As if, like The Odds, this world belongs only to us.

When I can't sleep, I go where I always go. To the water. There's a layer of fog rolling in off the ocean, and I am deeply buried in my chaotic, martini-soaked brain. Which is why I don't see the figure at first, standing on the cliffs near Stray's Chasm. When Graffam appears out of the mist, I nearly piss myself.

"Jesus Christ," I say.

She doesn't respond.

I don't want the company, but I don't want to offend her either. So I just stand there feeling weird and awkward and uncomfortable. I do it for as long as I can, and then I say, "I can't sleep."

Her eyes shift from the ocean to me. Way, way out on the horizon, past the lighthouse, there are lights. A ship probably. She nods, almost imperceptibly. "Same."

"When I can't sleep, I go to the water." Something I've done since last summer.

Her expression is blank, and here on the cliffs, wrapped in a nondescript coat, lipstick faded, she looks suddenly like a regular-sized mortal person.

"That's what I call it," I tell her. "Kind of like facing your biggest fear. In this case, the thing that took away something I love. Not this particular body of water, of course, but you get the idea."

"And does it work?" She angles her head, engaged now. "Is it doing what you need it to do?"

"Not yet. But then, it's just water." I say this a little sadly. "Anyhow, you have to make sure you're doing it right. It's all in the stance. And the attitude."

I demonstrate, feet apart, legs straight but not locked, a slight bend in the knees. Hands in coat pockets. Jaw set like, *Come and get me, muthafuckas.* She imitates me perfectly because, after all, she's an Oscar-winning actor.

"Good," I say. "It's also in the— You're familiar with Peter Pan?"

"Sure." I can hear the smile rather than see it.

"It's like when Tinker Bell is dying. And all the kids have to clap their hands to prove they believe in fairies. It's a little like that. Not that you have to clap your hands, but you have to believe the water will help."

"And then it will?"

"It's not magic water. You can't expect, like, a miracle. But yeah. Then it will help."

She tilts her head to the other side, considering this, considering me. "You aren't impressed by me the way the others are."

"Uh..."

"It's okay. I respect it, actually. More than you know. The others, they're desperate for me to give them wisdom and insight. But not you. The thing I haven't figured out yet is how much that has to do with me."

"I'm not sure. But I wouldn't take it too personally. Yet."

She laughs softly. "How are you at taking compliments?"

"Oh, I'm great at it. Just try me."

It almost feels like we're flirting, Meredith Graffam and me, but she's older than my mom. It's more like there's an ease here between us. The unspoken camaraderie of a shared experience—she lost a friend and so did I.

"You're one of the best young writers I've come across in years." Her gaze is direct, no-nonsense. "I'm almost jealous."

"Of me?" I look over my shoulder, first right, then left, making sure there's no one else she could be talking to.

"Your writing seems effortless. You're not trying too hard on the page."

"Unlike, say, in person?"

I smile; she doesn't.

Graffam says, "It's a mistake too many writers make. Trying too hard. You can always tell. I work hard to appear effortless. There's a difference."

"Yeah, I'm pretty much the opposite of effortless. I mean, when I can't think of the words I want, I draw something. I think I'm discovering that I almost draw stories better than I write them."

"Which is why I invited them here—our guests. That party tonight was for you."

I know she means *you* as in *all of you*, but the way she says it makes it feel like she invited them here just for me, Arlo Ellis-Noon.

"I wanted to show you there are no limitations, only the ones you put on yourself. Everyone who was here tonight, they're all artists in their own way. They've each had to overcome something to get where they are. We all have. We still do. We're all up against something."

I stare down at my hand, at the slight tremor. *Grief is one tricky bitch*, I think, not for the first time. I should feel euphoric at the fact that I'm here, at the cold on my face that reminds me I'm alive, heart beating, blood pulsing. I've got my whole life ahead of me. That's what everyone tells you when you're seventeen. *You've got your whole life ahead of you.*

But the fact is, no one knows if that's true. I'm sure someone told you that too, Jonah Maguire, right up until you drowned.

"The important thing," Graffam is saying, "is to figure out what you're up against and then push back as hard as you can. A little like believing in fairies."

"What if that thing is you?"

"Then you push back even harder."

I imagine Meredith Graffam at my age and wonder if she was young like me, stitched together by Band-Aids and duct tape. Or if she was young like Isaac, knowing she had the world at her feet.

There's a sound from the woods, and I turn, my eyes scanning the dark. Graffam turns too. Seconds pass. Then, when nothing happens, our eyes meet and we start to laugh. She laughs so hard she doubles over, and as she does, something falls out of her pocket. I pick it up, hand it to her. Her phone.

"Habit," she says. "One I can't quite seem to break." She examines the dark, silent screen of it before tucking it back into her coat. "I'm sorry about your friend."

"I'm sorry about yours."

I hesitate because there's something I want to ask her, but I'm not sure if I should. I've read *The Hunt*. I know how she felt after her friend Lara was killed. I recognize the guilt.

Finally I just say it. "When did you stop blaming yourself?"

"Who says I've stopped?"

There's bitterness in her voice, and sadly, I get it. When I went back to school last fall, after Jonah's death, I quickly became a person to be avoided. As if my sadness might be catching.

"People can be awful," I say.

"Yes," she agrees. "Us included. Especially to ourselves."

Then, without a word, she turns toward the house and walks away, leaving me alone on the cliffs. Suddenly the night is too quiet.

"I do believe in fairies," I say aloud, filling the silence. "I do, I do." And just for the hell of it, I start to clap.

Effy

SATURDAY, JANUARY 10

(the wee hours)

I am in Ness's room, standing outside the closed bathroom door. My best friend has been in there for the past half hour. "Can I get you anything? Maybe I should find Graffam or Drea?" I want her to assign me a task, give me some direction.

A muffled *No*, and then the sound of water running. I glance around for Leela, who's off writing somewhere. Which means it's just me. I'm not good with sick people. I get awkward and weird and end up saying or doing the wrong thing. My old therapist said this was because of losing my mom so young, that I lack some fundamental nurturing skill, like a wolf that had to raise itself.

The door opens slightly, and Ness tells me she'll be out in a minute. Her hair is damp with perspiration, and there are shadows under her eyes. "Don't go anywhere," she tells me.

"How are you feeling?" I hand her the bottle of water I snagged from the kitchen.

"Empty," she says.

"Do you think it's nerves?" I think it's nerves, but I don't tell her this.

"I don't know. Either that or some sort of flesh-eating bacteria?"

I give silent thanks for the lack of Wi-Fi, which will keep Ness from self-diagnosing the rest of the night.

"Are you sure I can't get you anything?"

"Maybe more water?" She shuts the door again, and I'm suddenly energized. I have a mission.

In the kitchen I grab two water bottles from the fridge. Then go back for one more, just to be safe. As I pass the portrait of Zachary Brighton, I pause to look at the Post-it wall, our storyboard. It's sparse, a handful of questions and answers, nothing interesting or thought-provoking. I feel this overwhelming need to fill the space so that Graffam will know that some of us, at least, are taking it seriously.

I scribble down a thought that's been lingering in my mind since our first class, then add the Post-it to the wall, right in the center, smoothing it flat with a single finger.

The sudden banging of a door startles me, and I whirl around. Arlo stands there looking windswept—like a less tortured, nerdier version of Heathcliff—as if he just blew in off the moors.

"Were you outside?" I ask him.

"Yes."

"Why are you always skulking around out there?"

"Why are you always skulking around in here?"

"I don't skulk."

He shrugs. "I don't either. If you must know, I was conversing with Graffam."

The gas flame of my heart ignites, and all I can manage is "Oh." I turn my back on him, fussing with the Post-its, such as they are, rearranging them on the wall. Feigning indifference. "What did you two talk about?"

"How much we miss Peter."

Same old Arlo. Everything a joke. I continue reordering the notes. Over my shoulder, he leans in and reads what I've written: *I believe that free will exists.* I can feel his breath on the back of my neck, and suddenly I'm fifteen again, his lips exploring my throat, my shoulder, my breasts, moving down, down, down.

"You didn't write it as a question," he says.

"No. But I thought it should be up there." I look at him. "So what about you?" I try to make my voice light. "Do you believe in free will?"

"Oh. Um." He scratches his head. "Sure. I mean, someone tells me to go to hell and I'm like, *Nope.*"

"Are you ever serious?"

"What day is this?"

"Friday."

"Yeah, not on Fridays."

I glance at the clock over the sink. "Well, technically Saturday."

"Not on Saturdays either."

I stand very still, more still than Arlo has probably been in his whole life. Gran says going motionless like this is one of my greatest skills. Like a deer protecting myself from hunters, an arctic fox in the snow, a lion in the grasses of the savanna, hiding in plain sight.

He says, "See, I can't tell if you're thinking, *God, he's hot* or *What did I ever see in this asshole?* It's so hard to know."

"What you said the other day in class. Was that supposed to be an apology?"

He starts blinking rapidly. And now—*ha-ha!*—I've caught him off guard.

"No." His voice catches. He coughs. "I said it for me. I'm trying to . . . y'know, atone."

"How's that going for you?"

"Super."

"Is this a twelve-step, make-amends thing?"

"It's an Arlo-trying-to-be-a-better-person thing."

I study his face. "No one hurts me twice. I don't forgive you. But I can't hate you anymore. It takes too much energy. And I don't think it's healthy to hold on to that. If I had parents, I might not have said goodbye either. But I wouldn't have lied, especially not to get someone into bed."

"I regret that. More than you know."

I tilt my head, the anger dissipating. "You said you're never serious on Fridays. Or technically Saturdays."

"Every now and then I make an exception. Also?" He reaches out as if to brush the fringe out of my eyes but then thinks better of it, pulling his hand back before he touches me. I feel a pang of absence. "Unlike me, you, Effy Green, would never have to lie to get someone into bed."

Without thinking, I reach a hand toward him and brush that tangled hair out of *his* eyes, my fingertips leaving a trail of sparks on his skin. It's the first contact we've had in nearly three years.

I blink. He blinks. Now he's as still as I was just a moment ago.

Even as my mind is thinking of all the many, many things I hate about Arlo Ellis-Noon, the rest of me aches to lean in closer.

Since I was with him, I've made out with a half dozen boys and I've had sex with two of them. When I was fifteen, I believed sex meant something solid and permanent and that I'd feel like I belonged to Arlo and Arlo to me.

Now his eyes darken, and gradually I lose myself in them until this—what we're doing, staring at each other with no distraction—feels somehow more personal than sex could ever be.

I glance down at my arms, at the goose bumps there. And then he looks down and I see that he has them too. Around us, the Moss is silent. Just like that, whether I like it or not, the current that once drew us together is flowing again.

Arlo

SATURDAY, JANUARY 10

(the wee hours)

I stare at the ceiling for a long time, distantly listening to the sounds of the old house. The banging of the ancient pipes as someone flushes a toilet. The creak of floorboards as Isaac does push-ups in the room next door. The scratch of branches against my window.

If Moss Hove haunts this place, I haven't seen him. I wonder then if you, Jonah, still haunt the sea caves in Laguna Beach, or if you've returned to your house in Mar Vista. Or maybe you're seeing the sights—the Hollywood sign, Mulholland, the Sunset Strip, the Santa Monica Pier. Who's to say you don't haunt them all?

I remove the lens from the camera and press record.

Hey, man. It's me. Arlo. Your old best friend. So I'm supposed to do this video journal every day for Immersive Storytelling.

I blink at the camera, trying not to be distracted by my own face staring back at me.

I'm going to assume that wherever you are, you're probably all-knowing and so you're up-to-date on this whole Jan Term thing. And the Moss. And Meredith Graffam. And Effy.

I press stop.

Of all the things we've done since we got here, recording this video journal is the one thing I truly hate. Self-reflection is my least favorite activity, right up there with solving equations and doing triathlons. I would much rather draw. Or write. Or read about cryptozoology in all its hopefulness.

I lay my Lakers cap on my chest. It rises up, down, up, down with my breath.

I know better, even if my heart doesn't, than to hope Effy and I will ever be more than that moment in the kitchen. But it's something. Maybe this is what they call growth.

I press record.

And now, suddenly, I'm talking to her.

I figured if you knew I was going away, you'd wake up and realize we never should have been together. This isn't just about sex. It never was. Okay, not completely. It was about getting close to someone, which I'd never been able to do because I was never there long enough. It was about wanting to. Because you're you. Effy Green. And I'm me. And this is before Jonah died. Me right now is even less worthy of you.

Jonah should have been the one to survive. He was the brave one. The one who could swim for miles without swallowing half the ocean or getting a cramp in his entire body. The one who could surf without wiping out or giving himself a concussion with his board. The one who drove miles across town to buy his sister the gluten-free doughnuts she loved. The one who brought food and clothes to the homeless woman who lives outside the CVS on Wilshire. The one who sat and talked with her and listened to her stories. You would have loved him. Everyone did. But the thing is, if I hadn't known you, I never would've let myself get to know him. The second friend I ever had.

After you.

Effy

SATURDAY, JANUARY 10

I'm awake and getting dressed for the day when I hear the slam of a door. In the driveway below, a car idles, steam blowing from the tailpipe. I lean into the window until my breath fogs the glass. Not Dean Booker's SUV, not Wesley's truck or Drea's rental van. The car is black and nondescript.

The driver's side door opens, and a man in a suit gets out. The Moss is surrounded by acres of forest and fifteen-foot perimeter walls. I wonder who he is and how he got past the gates.

Downstairs, I hear clattering, voices, doors opening and closing. And then the man reappears, lugging suitcases, followed by several figures bundled in coats and scarves. I try to make out who they are, but it's impossible to tell as they climb into the vehicle. Then Graffam walks out, hair fluttering in the breeze. She doesn't wave or say goodbye, merely stands there watching as they drive away.

* * *

SNOW TURNS TO rain, and by afternoon we're trapped inside, left to our own devices. Graffam is occupied, and we are supposed to spend the day writing. For all her talk of The Odds creating their own society, most of our time here is spent in solitude. Everyone works alone, as if our projects need guarding. There is no sharing of ideas or inspiration, only each of us cloistered off in the rooms we've claimed as our own. Ness and I seek each other out now and then to share something we've written or ask the other's opinion, but that seems to be happening less and less the longer we're here.

Around seven p.m., the six of us wander down for dinner one by one. As usual, we've dressed for the occasion, only to discover the table set but the kitchen empty. No chef, no Wesley, no Drea, no Graffam.

We're like the Lost Boys from *Peter Pan*, pillaging through the cabinets and pantry in this New England Neverland. No adults, no supervision. The day has left us feeling pent up and sluggish, like children during summer vacation. The boys whip off their ties and jackets. Ness removes her earrings. I remove my heels.

"There's a note," Ness says, taking a slip of paper from the refrigerator door.

> *Chef and her crew had to return to California, but good news—I'm a bit of a cook in my spare time. I've left you something (with heating instructions) in the fridge.*
>
> *xx MG*

She doesn't say where she is or when we'll see her again. But we are ravenous, so we eat the spaghetti cold right out of the containers. We make small talk, like strangers, avoiding the subject of our own work but trying to suss out how the others are coming along.

"We should do something," Isaac says afterward.

"Like a team-building exercise?" asks Arlo.

"I'm planning to keep working," Ramon says, but no one seems to hear him. Instead we throw out ideas. *Explore the house. Play cards. Play pool. Play truth or dare. Find the liquor cabinet. Raid the liquor cabinet. Charades.*

Leela suggests a scavenger hunt. The rules are simple—run from one end of the Moss to the other, collecting an item significant to The Odds along the way. Then we'll regroup in the library to compare our spoils.

As the race begins—everyone sprinting ahead—I pass through the theater and pause at the foot of the staircase that leads up to Graffam's wing. Something compels me upward onto the balcony, where I find two doors, one closed, the other open.

I move toward the open one, inhaling the scent of fresh flowers. Inhaling—somehow—Graffam herself. The room is painted a cheerful coral, with bronze-colored curtains framing the windows. A suitcase lies open on the four-poster bed, and a broad desk is covered in papers, notebooks, magazines. Graffam's white kimono dress from the party is flung over the back of the chair.

I want to step inside and shut the door and snoop through her things. Maybe I'll discover something we have in common, a connection that will give me an edge over the others.

Instead I stand in the doorway, feet rooted to the floor. If she catches me, I'll probably be thrown out like Joey and Peter. There won't be any more second chances after that.

I force myself to back away, then turn to the closed door at the other end of the balcony. I press my ear to it but don't hear anything. I reach for the doorknob, and realize there isn't one. Only a flat panel covering the place where the hole should be.

Gran says I'm like a cat: I hate closed doors and don't like to be told no. I run my hand across the soft blue paint and gilt edges of the wood, giving a push every few inches in case there's a hidden spring. But the door remains closed.

The shout of happy voices below. I force myself to go downstairs and rejoin the others. Eventually, I find a small, framed map on the wall of a study. At the top someone has written *Realm of The Odds*. There is Murton Wood, the Moss, Brighton's Woe, the lighthouse, and a few other landmarks I don't recognize.

Back in the library, we pool our treasures—photos, mostly, and a book on magic by Odds member Laszlo Csaba. The map is probably the most interesting item, but Isaac wins because he was fastest. With some prodding, he shows us the secret passage he used as a shortcut, the one running parallel to the theater. We duck inside and feel our way to the end of it and then back, moving through the Moss like shadows.

Once we tire of this, we discover a mudroom, where, in the back of a closet, we unearth a bunch of old badminton rackets and something else: a trunk full of black cloaks and elaborate masks—grotesque animal masks with feathers and fur. At the bottom of the pile, we uncover a book titled *The Wild Hunt*, with the name *Moss Hove* scrawled inside the front cover. I run my fingers across the letters, as if by doing so I might conjure him. The pages are filled with notations—dates mostly, keeping track of when they played.

The book contains an introduction by the author, Yvette Manks, another of The Odds. *This game is meant for entertainment. But it should also be taken seriously. As in life, your belief influences the outcome.* It also includes a brief history of Perchta, the German goddess and leader of the Hunt, whose feast day was in January. And a set of rules:

> Those who are not hunting are the Living . . .
>
> The goal of the Hunter is to collect as many souls as possible . . .
>
> Ruler of the Forest is awarded to the Hunter who collects the most souls . . .

The cloaks are a rich, heavy velvet, but we handle them as if they're made of glass. Judging by the smell of mothballs, and the frayed hems, these are the same cloaks worn by Moss Hove and his friends, passed down throughout the decades each January. I drape the cape around my shoulders, letting it enfold me, thinking of those who came before and those who will come after we've gone.

I choose the tiger mask, its fur a vivid orange with black stripes that shimmer. It looks alive, ready to pounce, but behind it I feel closed off and confined, my warm breath blowing back on my face. I push the mask onto the top of my head and see that the others have done the same.

Leela, the grizzly bear, says, "We should play the game."

"No," says Ramon, shaking his head so hard his raven mask falls off. It lies on the floor, beak open and pointing to the sky. "The Wild Hunt is played on the last night of Jan Term. We can't break tradition. It's against the rules—"

"Do you think Perchta is going to rise from the dead and collect your soul? Give me a fucking break." Unsurprisingly, Issac picked the lion. "There's no such thing as Perchta and no such thing as the boogeyman."

"Go ahead." Ramon is still shaking his head. "You can leave me out of it. But don't blame yourselves when you get sent home and I win Jan Term."

"The day you win is the day hell freezes over. 'Cause Isaac Thelonious Williams III does not lose." Isaac cups a hand to his ear like he's listening to applause.

Arlo drops his mask—a wolf—back into the trunk and swoops up a corner of the cape, peering over it like a movie vampire. "What about badminton? Are there rules about that too?"

"We really shouldn't play it inside . . ."

Arlo holds up a hand in Ramon's direction. "All work and no play, Ramon. I mean, really. Don't spoil the fun."

Gingerly, we return the cloaks and masks to the trunk, and I feel both lighter and heavier without them. Arlo distributes the rackets. Music starts to blare through the in-house speakers, and Isaac appears with another bottle. Its blue glow like something from *Alice in Wonderland*.

Leela groans. "Couldn't you find anything alcoholic?"

"Check the label," Isaac tells her. "Same vintner, but this one has booze. There's an entire cabinet of bottles. Nonalcoholic.

Alcoholic. Percentages listed on the labels. This one's twenty-five proof."

Juggling rackets with wineglasses, we stumble into the solarium and launch into a wild game that bears only the faintest resemblance to badminton. The evening feels psychedelic and loud, the house breathing and expanding around us like some sort of beautiful, consumptive accordion. I'm not sure where Graffam and Drea are—downstairs or in their rooms or someplace far, far away—and I feel this sudden sense of freedom, as if we've escaped our parents, our teachers, and all other adult authority figures.

The game grows wilder and wilder, until Leela scales one vine-covered wall to hit the birdie and there's a terrible crashing sound.

"I'm okay," she calls from the floor.

And then Arlo goes, "Fuck. Me."

All around us, like glittering confetti, lies what's left of an enormous, ancient-looking gold mirror.

AFTER WE TIDY up the crime scene and dispose of the evidence, we retire to the theater, tails between our legs. We choose the safest, most wholesome activity we can think of—roasting marshmallows over the fire.

"Well." Arlo breaks the silence. "It was nice knowing you all. Some more than others."

We pass the marshmallows penitently. The fire lulls me into an introspective state.

"If you actually died tomorrow," I say, "what's something

you'd want people to know about you? Or what's something you'd want to do?"

No one answers right away. Finally Ness goes, "I don't want to make myself so goddamn small anymore." She rotates her stick, round and round, watching as the marshmallow catches fire. "I'd like to make myself as large as possible. And I'd like to feel like I belong."

"You do belong," I start to say, but she levels me with a look. Because this is what I do—rush to her defense, whether it's other people picking on her or Ness picking on herself.

And then she accidentally drops the stick at the edge of the fireplace, dangerously near the rug. I have a vision of the whole house going up in flames and Graffam returning from wherever she is to the smoldering ruins of the Moss.

Isaac stamps out the fire with his shoe, then sits back on his heels. "It's strange," he says, rubbing a hand across his skull, "to feel small and insignificant, but also like you're all that matters."

Then he tells us how his parents disowned his sister for becoming a teacher and marrying her girlfriend. That they changed the code to the gate and the locks on all the doors, even to the shed where the gardener kept his tools. They told her to think of them as dead.

"That's what they said." He glances up at us. "'Think of us as dead.' Of all the rotten things they've done, of all the people they've wronged, that was the worst."

"I don't have many memories of my parents." I lay down my stick. "But if my mom had lived, if my dad hadn't gone away—I wonder sometimes how they would've disappointed me. Because at some point even the best parents are going to let you down."

I think about Mary Shelley, who was my age when she wrote *Frankenstein*. Her mother died eleven days after Mary was born, which—even more than my mother's notes in the margins—is why I love that book. It was written by a teenage girl who knew what it was to be motherless.

Leela says, "I've got good parents, still alive. Siblings I actually like. But sometimes I feel guilty over it. Like, why me? Why not Effy? Why not Isaac?"

We go around, talking about the people we love, the ones who are here and not here. Everyone except Ramon.

"Not to rain on this super-fun parade." Arlo rearranges himself, leaning back on his hands, legs out in front of him stretching on forever. "But does Graffam ever seem off to you?" His eyes spark like the fire, as if he knows all.

"Off how?" Leela asks, mid-chew. She sets down the bag of marshmallows.

"Like, *intense*. Not just jumping in the ocean and, oh, jumping off the roof, but . . ."

He looks at Isaac like, *Help me out here.*

"She told us her methods would be unconventional." I sound huffy, almost indignant. Arlo raises his hands in mock surrender.

"I think she's awesome." Leela wipes her mouth. "She took all this shit for lying about something that wasn't actually her fault, and when everyone called for blood, what did she do? She came back stronger than ever."

"Exactly," I say, sitting up, leaning in, suddenly reanimated.

"We wouldn't be talking about this if she were a man. People are so suspicious of a successful woman, or any woman who doesn't conform to societal expectations . . ."

Isaac mutters something like *Especially a crazy one*, and Leela goes off on him about how dehumanizing the word is, how it perpetuates gender-based stereotypes and stigma around mental illness.

"Well, I don't like her," Ramon says. "The fact that she doesn't have a penis has nothing to do with it." He looks at each of us, lips pursed so they're barely visible. "I think her methods are weird. I think she's lucky to have gotten as far as she's gotten in her career."

"I think she's fierce. And brave." Ness gazes up at the ceiling, a little smile on her face. "She did tell me this story though." The smile fades. "I'm not sure if it was real or maybe . . . exaggerated a little. Anyway, when she sold *The Lie* to her publisher, she was in the middle of a divorce . . ."

As she talks, I'm feeling a myriad of emotions, none of them good. The biggest and most disturbing of them—a white-hot jealousy of my best friend. *I am not the only one Graffam has been confiding in.*

"Her ex-husband accused her of plagiarism," Ness continues. "He said she'd stolen *The Lie* from him, even though it's a story about her friend's murder. Like, the whole point of that book was Graffam apologizing. And then he accused her of writing about his parents, his childhood, private things he'd told her that weren't meant for anyone else. He claimed she started fights in their marriage so that she'd have something to write about, like she was orchestrating everything."

Ness shakes her head, her curls going *swish swish*. "So Graffam added something—mushrooms maybe?—to his food one night. And he got sick. I mean, he was fine, but it was, I don't know, the way she told it. It was just so . . ."

Casual, I think.

"Fuck the patriarchy!" Leela cheers, and throws a handful of marshmallows into the air.

They rain down like confetti, and then Ness starts tugging at my sleeve.

"Oh," she breathes, her voice suddenly filled with wonder. She sits up straight and points at the window behind the piano. "Snow."

OUTSIDE IT'S A winter wonderland once again. We make angels, arms moving in white powder, faster and faster until we're flying. I picture myself leaving the ground and taking off into the sky.

"I don't want to go home yet," Ness says next to me.

A terrible thought flits into my mind—if Ness went home, Graffam would confide in me. Only me. "Who says we're going home?"

But she doesn't seem to hear me. "I want to see what happens next. I feel like I can, I don't know"—Ness spreads her arms wide—"do something valuable."

Another rush of jealousy. I search my memory for a time I've ever felt this way. As far back as we go, we've only been good and harmonious and noncompeting. With Ness, I can be the Effy Green who withers people with a look and shines academically and is basically fearless and loyal.

I try to push away the feeling of something coming, like the feeling you get before a big storm. Maybe it's grief or maybe it's because I've realized just how much I need to be here. How much I want to be the last one standing.

For the next hour, we roll and jump and play like kids. We throw snowballs and catch snowflakes and I forget about Graffam. As my eyes meet Arlo's, I think, *He may be the most awake of us all.*

In that moment, I decide it's not all bad being cut off from the world. There is magic here. And understanding. There is something to be said for sharing a place and a time that no one else could ever understand.

Arlo

Sunday, January 11

It's not until the next evening at dinner that the shit hits the fan. The six of us are seated at the table, in our best athleisure—no more formal attire for these kids—when Graffam blows in like a Category 5 hurricane. We go deathly still. It's as if we're playing that old childhood freeze game, forks hovering in midair, mouths open mid-chew, glasses raised to lips, bracing for impact.

"I don't need to tell you how priceless the mirror was." The temperature of Graffam's voice is subzero, a frigid Nordic lake. "How irreplaceable."

"To be fair," I hear myself say, "why would you let a bunch of teenagers stay in a house packed with priceless treasures? Not *you* as in you, Meredith Graffam, but *you* as in the establishment that is Bullshit Prep."

She shoots me a withering look.

"This wasn't any ordinary mirror. This was an early

nineteenth-century chinoiserie English Chippendale giltwood overmantel mirror bordered by a pair of ho-ho birds—"

"Sorry." I can't help myself. "Ho-ho birds?" My mother says this tendency of mine is compulsive, that I came out of the womb running my mouth and cracking jokes at inopportune moments.

Graffam is not amused. "They are a mythical version of the phoenix. Any other questions, Arlo, or may I continue?"

"Sorry."

"Were you drinking?" She scans our faces.

"A little," admits Ness when no one else speaks up. "We may have gotten into the wine."

"None of this was my idea," Ramon pipes up.

Graffam wheels on him. "Did you participate?"

When he doesn't answer right away, Leela volunteers, "He did."

"Fine," he snaps, "but you were the one who broke the mirror." He turns to Graffam. "Leela broke the mirror. I didn't have anything to do with that."

"Wow," I say. "You really aren't here to make friends, are you, Bachelorette?"

"Arlo?"

"Yes?"

"Be quiet."

Graffam's eyes take in the whole depraved lot of us.

"I promised Dean Booker that I would take full responsibility for your time here. I chose you—all of you. And frankly, I expected better."

I expected better. I feel the sting of those three words. *Once again, Arlo, you have let someone down.*

"Dean Booker may want to send you home. He may want to send Drea and me home. I know you're young, but you're also smart and you've been through enough in your lives to know how to behave. You cannot expect to be given second chances. You have to earn forgiveness. You have to earn the chance to start over."

She looks taller and more formidable than the woman I first met on the cliffs. I have to check to make sure I'm still here—feet on floor, body in seat—and that I haven't shrunk down to nothing.

"Right now, I can't imagine a scenario where Dean Booker lets us stay. But if for some reason he's feeling charitable enough to give us an opportunity to prove ourselves, we have to trust each other. I have to trust you. I just hope it's enough."

And that's when the shit, as they say, suddenly gets real. She is looking at us like we've run over her dog.

"Isaac." She swings around to face him. "You lead with false bravado instead of truly investing yourself emotionally. You look down on others who don't share your pedigree, yet you fear you come up short when you compare yourself to your parents' legacy. Do you *really* want to be them? How about living up to yourself instead?"

For once in his life, Isaac doesn't have a rebuttal. He catches me watching and flips me off.

"Ramon, everything in your life is governed by a rigid system of rules you've created—from your art to your relationships. Try forgiving others for disappointing you. Try tolerance. Try patience. Try not being so disapproving of anyone other than yourself."

Ramon sits, arms crossed, unblinking. She's clearly running down the list of us, and my mind starts racing as I try to imagine what she'll have to say about me.

"Leela, you know who you are, which can be a good thing, but you get carried away. You're an instigator for instigating's sake. You have a chip on your shoulder. And you dig your heels in—"

"Since when is knowing who you are a bad thing?" Leela interrupts, chin out.

"Since now. If you only ever stand your ground, you end up standing still and alone."

Then, dear God, she turns to me. And there is a beat—two beats, maybe three—before she speaks.

"Arlo, you're a funny guy. But it's not a joke if you're the only one laughing. You need to put aside the flipness now and then and let the feelings in, no matter how uncomfortable they make you."

Like that, her gaze moves away.

"Effy."

Effy's eyes glint at her. A challenge or maybe a flash of fear. "You are too guarded and too suspicious, and yet you're obsessed with building your walls even higher. You can't see how your defenses have become a cage. And both of you," she says to Effy and me, "need to let go of the grief that's defining you, or at least find a way to live with it. Don't let your story start and end there."

"Don't lump me in with him," Effy starts, but Graffam holds up a hand that says, *Stop*. Effy's eyes flutter to her lap.

"And you, Ness," Graffam says, "are too self-conscious. Stop trying to make everyone happy. Stop doubting yourself. Stop trying to make up for the world's ills. And if that doesn't work, lie to yourself about being brave. That's all any of us do. We lie to ourselves. You need to learn how. Or maybe you already do." A smile shimmers across Graffam's face. "And after a while, those lies will turn into something real. And you'll be able to rely on you. No one else. You."

Graffam rubs at the V between her eyebrows as if she suddenly has a headache. For the past few days, I've been feeling like we are her chosen ones. In one night, we've ruined all of that.

No one speaks. There is nothing we can say.

Finally, Graffam lets out a deep sigh, as if to expel her anger. "I remember what it's like to be a teenager. I have a lot more in common with all of you than you can imagine. My own ego has been known to get in the way. I struggle with patience and forgiveness and digging my heels in just for digging's sake. It can be hard for me to let the feelings in, to meet others halfway. And I wish I could always believe in myself."

In my short life, I've never had an adult speak to me like this, like they get it. Most of the adults I know are too busy, too distracted, to stop and pay attention.

"Wesley has already disposed of the mirror, so you can apologize to him the next time you see him. I need your completed world-building assignment tomorrow. Work on it. Go to bed. Don't let me see your faces till morning."

* * *

AS A GROUP, we make our way to the Hall of Oddities to finish the assignment. None of us want to let Graffam down again, so there's a renewed sense of determination as we arrange ourselves on sofas and chairs beneath the unblinking eyes of Moss Hove's extensive taxidermy collection.

All around us, glass-fronted cabinets display butterflies and insects with their wings pinned back. Every spare inch filled with stuffed rodents and bats and birds. Again with the birds. Glassy eyes staring, wings outspread, like any moment they might launch themselves at us.

We hash out the world Graffam wants us to create, arguing more quietly than usual, as if the air and the fight have gone out of us. Effy has the neatest handwriting, so she copies down our bylaws.

I glance around at the room as she writes, head throbbing as if I'm still hungover. When one of the birds seems to stare directly at me, I stare back. Isaac makes a crack about how the crow and I are having a real meeting of the minds. Its right eye catches the light, but the other is dull and dead.

"Arlo," Effy snaps. She shakes the paper. "You need to sign your name."

AS THE OTHERS wander off to bed, I roam the halls until I find Wesley in the laundry room, reading from a textbook propped atop the dryer. I clear my throat, and when he looks up, I say, "I just wanted to apologize for our shitbag behavior." He blinks at me, so I clarify. "Breaking the mirror. The priceless ho-ho mirror, or whatever you call it."

"Oh. Right. You don't have to apologize to me."

I watch as he starts moving a load from the washer to the dryer. When the machine begins to whir, its familiar thumping fills me with homesickness.

"Just out of curiosity," I say, "how much do you think it's worth? The mirror. You know, in case it ends up coming out of our pockets."

"Oh jeez." He busies himself putting things away—dryer sheets, detergent, the remnants of his chores. "It's really hard to know off the top of my head. There's a lot of priceless stuff here."

He glances past me at the door. I turn to see what he's looking at, but there's no one there.

"Sorry," he says. "I've got to get back to it."

"Yeah, man. Of course."

He gives me a quick smile and tucks the book under his arm, then he's gone, feet heavy on the stairs.

I stand there another minute, lulled by the *thump thump thump* of the machine, reliving some long-ago day at the beach, clothes damp from the ocean. Mom always wanted us to wash them right away when we got home, but I liked the smell of the salt and the waves. Sometimes, when she wasn't looking, I'd strip naked and throw my shirt and shorts straight into the dryer. Then they'd be warm and ocean-scented when I put them back on, and I'd carry the day around with me.

Effy

MONDAY, JANUARY 12

(the wee hours)

My room is dark except for the glow of my laptop. In here, it's just Clay Reynolds and me.

Over the years, writing to my father has become instinct—something to do when I can't sleep or feel blocked. Before he was released from prison, I imagined him in his cell, reading my letters—the ones I never mailed—and dreaming of life outside those walls. Now that he's free, I don't know where to picture him. In a house or apartment somewhere in Boston, with a new wife or a new truck. *Free.*

I try to write to him now like I've done so many times before. But without prison bars, barbed wire, guards, there's nothing to separate us. If I send him a letter, he might actually answer or, worse, show up in person.

And so I sit, frozen, staring at the blinking cursor on my screen. When I hear knocking, my first thought is, *I am being sent home.*

If I don't answer, maybe they'll go away and take someone

else. I hold my breath. We weren't told to leave our suitcases outside the door tonight, but that doesn't mean Graffam won't pick a sacrificial lamb in exchange for the mirror.

After a few moments of silence, I resume typing. I hear my door open, footsteps on the stairs that lead up to this belfry. I close the laptop and draw back against the headboard, making myself invisible.

A head appears, followed by a body, and then Arlo is standing at the top of the stairs. "Hello?" He flips on the light switch, and the room is suddenly too bright. I hold up my hand to shield my eyes.

"I thought you might be up."

I emerge from the shadows, squinting like a mole. "Can I help you?"

He leans against the doorframe. "I don't know about you, but this was a strange, unsettling day and I'm feeling pretty shitty." The usual smirk is gone. He looks almost sad.

"Same," I say.

"So I figured, since this all may end tomorrow . . ." He drifts off.

He has more to say, I can see it on his face. But whatever it is, he keeps it in. In this moment, it feels as if we're the only two inside this house. I'm used to all the world asleep while I'm awake, but I'm not used to having someone else with me.

"I never sleep," I tell him.

"Me either."

"I try," I say, "but my mind gets going and it's like I've got this assembly line of feelings coming faster and faster, like the machine isn't working. All the wires are fried and I just give up."

He says, "I feel like I've got eighteen cats running around in my brain. Like I'm a human cat café and it's kitten season and they're in there just having a ball. Rolling around and scratching everything and running and jumping and doing their cat things."

He smiles at me and I smile back. His smile makes me feel like the world is righting itself, if only a little. He circles the room, taking it all in, pausing here and there to examine a portrait or pick up a vase. He pretends to admire himself in the mirror and then browses the books on the mantel.

"I see you have the orphan collection."

"What?"

"*Anne of Green Gables, Great Expectations, Heidi, The Secret Garden* . . . Orphans."

It hadn't occurred to me, but he's right.

"What about the books in Ness's room?" he asks.

"They're a mix. *Jane Eyre. The House of Mirth. Rebecca* maybe? Then there's Emily Post. Other old etiquette books."

Arlo nods, wise and knowing. "So she got wallflower spinsters and *Let's teach you to be more confident*—you know, in a nutshell. But those don't exactly scream Leela."

"What do you mean?"

"They share a room. There must be books in there for her too."

I have to think about it. "*East of Eden. Twelfth Night. The Bobbsey—*"

"*Twins,*" we say at the same time.

Arlo considers. "Isaac's shelf was all Grimms' fairy tales. Which I guess could mean cautionary stories about egotistical or wicked people getting what they deserve? I need time to think on that one more. It appears that whoever assigned our rooms chose them for us based on theme. Or maybe it's the other way around?"

"You mean someone curated our bookshelves based on who's staying in which room?" Even though I'm not convinced, I'm irked that Arlo saw it first.

"The books in mine feature drownings. So. Yeah." Then he looks at me, his smile fading. "Do you hear that?"

"What?" I freeze, listening.

"The sound of the whole world sleeping. Everyone but us. It's usually just me, but it's nice to share it."

It takes me a second to realize I haven't uttered my thoughts aloud and that, somehow, he's read my mind. I'm left with this strange, private moment that feels intimate, and there's that feeling again of being the only two people in the house.

Without thinking, I walk over to him until we're just inches apart. Then. *Then.* I reach up to brush the hair out of his eyes. Which catch mine and hold them.

Like that, everything else fades away—the sealed room, the Moss, Graffam, the broken mirror.

We are close now, our bodies taking up the same small space in a great big world, the only two people awake. I'm suddenly aware of my breath and his. I can almost feel his lips on mine. A bird cries outside. The tide thunders in, and my heart pounds along with it.

And then I take his face in my hands and I kiss him.

Moments like this I cease to be everyday Effy, freed from the anger and self-doubt that have followed me since the day my mom was killed and my dad went away for killing her. The day I learned that anyone could be taken from me at any moment.

Right now, I'm barely thinking, only doing what feels right. Call it free will. Call it the effects of this house or this whole Immersive Storytelling experience. Whatever it is, it feels like the purest form of emotion I've ever known. A losing myself and finding myself at the same time.

And then we're up against a wall, my hands on his chest, his hands on my face, just kissing, nothing more, although I can feel him through his boxers, as hard as the wall at my back.

I shouldn't be kissing him because this is Arlo and he once hurt me more than anyone has ever hurt me, next to my dad. But again, what do I have to lose?

His lips are new but also familiar. The lips I remember, but also somehow *more* than I remember.

We kiss until I feel myself falling down the rabbit hole. And this, I think, is unknown, unmapped territory. This is a whole new world. But there's a part of me that resists. *No*, it says. *No. No. No. Not again.* Not with Arlo. I promised myself no more mistakes.

I push him away. "This can't happen."

He looks a little dazed, a lot happy. He smiles. "Oh, but it did."

"It can't happen again. You need to go. Now."

He laughs. "That's one of the things I've always liked about you, Effylou. Your subtlety."

"Good night, Arlo."

I LIE DOWN. I get up. I lie down. I get up. My head spins. My lips throb where Arlo kissed me. Where I kissed him. *Jesus, Effy.*

When Gran's back went out last year, her doctor prescribed a TENS unit for the pain—transcutaneous electrical nerve stimulation delivers mild shocks through electrodes. It floods the nervous system, blocking pain signals and triggering an endorphin rush. This is what it feels like to kiss Arlo—little electrical impulses flooding my nervous system.

Looking for a distraction, I grab *The Hunt* from my bedside table. Graffam was only two years older than I am when she wrote it. It's impossible to picture her as a person my age, fallible and scared, dealing with her own grief. I skim a few pages, and then I turn to my favorite passage, which has been underlined and highlighted and flagged.

```
I look for her in Parkerton and in every
person I pass on campus. I will probably
always be looking for her. Even when I
leave here to go to a place where nobody
knows me. Where I can be all the me's I've
ever wanted to be.
```

Every time I read them, the words have this way of digging in a little deeper than the time before, as if they're making a nest in my heart. I don't know what it is about them; I only know they make me feel less alone.

Then I pull my father's letter out from under my pillow. It weighs almost nothing, which is fitting because the words it contains can never be enough. With the envelope still in my hand, I slip out of bed and pick up the camera. I turn it on myself and press record.

A tiny part of me holds out hope that maybe, just maybe, there's a clue in here as to why. *Like if I just keep rereading it, I'll see something in a new light, something that explains what happened that night and lets me know if I should give you another chance to be my dad.*

In the viewfinder, in the shadowy light, I look like a younger version of my grandmother. As if the likeness skipped an entire generation and my mom never existed at all.

My biggest fear is being surprised by sudden, horrific change. That's your fault. I don't remember feeling that way before you killed her.

For some reason it's easier to talk to him than it is to write the words down. *Do I have it in me?* I think. *To write about the painful things?*

Arlo

MONDAY, JANUARY 12

(the wee hours)

I am standing on the cliffs, lost in thoughts as warm as clothes from the dryer. *Effy Effy Effy* . . . I rub my bottom lip, so recently connected to hers. I could be braving the East Antarctic Plateau, the coldest place on earth, and I wouldn't feel the chill.

When Graffam appears beside me, it takes me a minute to register. But then my mind boomerangs back to the shattered mirror, the things she said to us at dinner, the position we put her in.

"I'm sorry," I tell her.

At first I don't think she's heard me. Then she says, "I sent Leela home."

"Did you just say—"

"Story is everything, Arlo. It's all we have. Without stories, what do we leave behind when we leave the world? Our stories *define* us. That's why they're so important. Without them, it's as if we never existed." Her tone is suddenly feverish, her words rushed. "The thing about Perchta, the ruler of The Wild Hunt, is that she had two sides, one true, one false. She could appear as this beautiful young woman. But she was also someone who—once she drew people in—entered their homes while they slept and gutted them, stuffing their bodies with rocks."

"So what you're saying is do it for the plot." I mean to sound lighthearted, to lead her out of this strange, serious place we've suddenly found ourselves in, but my voice cracks. I know Meredith Graffam is, as Drea says, human. But for the first time since I got here, there's a gap in the old curtains, and through it I'm able to glimpse daylight and shadow and someone moving around. I'm just not sure whether that's a good thing.

"Yes. Do it for the story. Always. Get along with them, Arlo, but don't trust them. Guard yourself and your talent. You're good, but you could be extraordinary. Don't let anyone—not even me—get in your way."

And then Meredith Graffam walks off, dark hair blowing like a kite, leaving me alone in the night.

week two

Immersive Storytelling

Monday, January 12 – Sunday, January 18

> **SESSION TWO**
>
> - Know when and what to reveal.
> - Build your vision.
> - Keep your enemies close.
> - Don't be afraid to stir the pot.
> - Remember that timing is everything.
> - Find the fatal flaw in your competition, and use it to destroy them.
> - Distract. Defy. Discombobulate.

One should not be too straightforward. Go and see the forest. The straight trees are cut down, the crooked ones are left standing.

—**Kautilya, third century BC**

Arlo

MONDAY, JANUARY 12

It's the nicest day we've had so far, a clear, bright blue, the air crisp as a full red apple. We are loaded into Drea's rental van. Graffam sits in the passenger seat. She looks up and says hello, her tone—in that single word—indecipherable.

Drea drives us north through the woods in the opposite direction of campus on an old, rutted service road, choked with snow and mud and vegetation. According to Graffam, the weather report says we're expecting a snowstorm, which means soon this road might be lost entirely under a blanket of white.

No one speaks, and I'm aware of an invisible fracture in our group, as if Leela's departure has broken us in some way we aren't yet aware of. There's more going on though—a collective holding of breath as we wait for Graffam to tell us she's spoken to Dean Booker and we're all being sent home, never to return to Bullshit Prep.

"I've decided," she begins, "not to let your dean know about what happened. It was my fault for believing that you could behave yourselves without adult supervision while Drea and I were working, because in my eyes I see you as adults. We all deserve second chances. Years ago, I was given one. You should be too."

Even though I haven't known her long, this is a person I don't want to disappoint, and I feel the sting of her words somewhere deep in my chest.

"Replacing the mirror is impossible. It's a rare piece, valued at nearly thirty thousand dollars. The frame itself is still intact. I've managed to find someone who restores antique glass. She rarely takes commissions because it's a painstaking and expensive process. But I've called in a favor and will pay to have the mirror restored."

Finally, she turns to look at us.

"Dean Booker doesn't need to know. We will keep this between us. But *I* need to know that I can count on you going forward. I need to know you are all in."

It hits me at once—relief. Graffam could have sent us home, but furious as she is, she has our backs. And now, through some unspoken pact, we've got hers.

I try to catch Effy's eye, but she won't look at me, even though I can still feel the imprint of her lips on mine. So I settle for a fist bump with Isaac.

At some point, we run parallel to the walls that encircle Murton Wood, the old stone disappearing and reappearing behind shadow and vegetation. The property is so enormous, it's easy to forget we're corralled in here like farm animals. I wonder if the walls did what Moss Hove wanted them to do—if he ever missed the world outside them.

And then we come to what Drea tells us is the former service gate. It looks neglected, vines growing up and around it. Graffam pulls out one of those ancient-looking skeleton keys and climbs out of the van. We watch as she unlocks the gate and pushes it open. If they cryogenically freeze my body and bring me back to life centuries from now, I'll never forget the sound it makes—a low, suffering groan.

Ten minutes later, we reach the northern entrance of Murton Wood. Unlike the southern entrance, which spills gently into the bucolic campus of Brighton and Hove, this entrance spits you onto Highway 127.

The van rolls to a stop on the shoulder, and without a word Graffam opens her door and gets out. While Drea sits inside in the warmth, engine idling, the five of us assemble on the roadside, our backs to the forest. I can feel the energy of the others as if I'm plugged into them—it's a new energy, the kind of second wind that comes from seeing the other runners in the race drop away, knowing you have a shot at the finish.

Traffic rushes by as Graffam, white coat matching the snowy ground, hair the color of a burnt match tip, crosses two lanes of highway to reach the center yellow line.

"What's happening?" Effy says to me, to all of us.

We watch from the shoulder, scarves fluttering from the whoosh of passing cars, hearts fluttering from the sight of Meredith Graffam standing in the road. It's not the busiest stretch of highway, but it's the only artery that links the town of Parkerton to the outside world, so there's a constant flow of traffic. Right now that traffic keeps rushing past as if there isn't a woman—an extremely famous woman—standing in the middle of the highway. Nothing to keep her from ending up as roadkill except the reflexes of the drivers.

And then she closes her eyes. Opens her mouth. And screams.

Effy starts toward her, and I pull her back before she gets flattened by a semi.

In a panicked voice, Ness says, "What is this? What's she doing?"

Isaac murmurs something about a psychotic break, and Ramon starts ranting about how he *almost* didn't apply for Jan Term but at the last minute allowed himself to be persuaded and now he doesn't even know if writing is what he wants to do anymore. On and on in my ear.

Meanwhile, Graffam's scream has turned into a deep, guttural roar that seems to emanate from the catacombs of her soul. Every hair on my body spikes into quills, and my hand starts to shake. Whatever is making her scream like this, it's not something we should be witnessing.

And then I see the car—a Dodge Challenger—rocketing around the bend because drivers always drive too fast on roads like this, especially in cars like that. A blast of the horn, and the Challenger does its best to slow, but there's no time. The horn blaring, the five of us shouting from the grass. The car veers off the road to avoid hitting Graffam, and now the man is screaming out the window at her as he steers back onto the asphalt and away, disappearing around the next curve.

As I stand there, a horrible thought enters my head: *What if Graffam is truly unstable?* I mean, how well do we even know her? We *think* we know her because she's famous, but all we really know is that she's gone out on a limb to protect us from expulsion. For the first time, it occurs to me to ask why. Why would she do that? What's in it for her?

If you were here, Jonah Maguire, you would say this is just me overthinking things with my sleep-deprived brain, and you'd probably be right. You almost always were.

Graffam turns to us now, eyes open and wild, face lit with exhilaration. Another car passes, horn blaring. And another. Another. They come, fast and furious, from both directions. My lungs feel blistered, my breath shallow. I'm trying to remember how to breathe.

Over the sounds of the highway, Graffam shouts, "If you don't feel like you are standing in the middle of a busy street with a car speeding toward you at sixty miles an hour, then you aren't writing the way you need to be writing to stand out above all the noise. There are times I hate what I do. Hate the industry. Hate the actual work. But I wouldn't trade it because it's who I am and it's the only way to take all the messy, raw, reckless energy inside of me and turn it into art. Do you trust me?"

"Yes!" I hear myself cry along with the others, and in that moment—in spite of my doubts—I decide that sometimes you have to take a leap of faith, even if it's just to get your teacher off the road and out of harm's way.

Graffam closes her eyes again and opens her arms wide.

"Then I trust you. Now guide me back." Her eyes remain shut, and I get it—it's up to us to guide her across the road.

For several minutes, the stream of cars is too steady. I imagine the call to Dean Booker—*We've had to leave Graf-fam in the middle of Highway 127.* And then the call to my brother. *Hey, so, my teacher thought it would be fun to play in traffic, and I'm going to need a place to crash till regular semester starts.*

Suddenly there is a break, the oncoming traffic just visible on the horizon.

"Now," we shout. "Run!"

Instead she strides casually toward us, eyes still closed. My gaze jumps between her, the coming traffic, her, the traffic, back and forth, until finally—with seconds to spare—she steps onto the shoulder, cool, composed, her breathing steady, unlike ours.

She opens her eyes again. "Now it's your turn."

"Our turn," Isaac repeats.

"Your turn," she says again.

"To stand in the middle of the road?" asks Ness.

"Yes. Scream, shout, cry, purge any pain that's taking up too much space. Get it out of you. Anything that's holding you back. Anything you need to say."

I can't explain it, but there's this thrill that shoots through me. A kind of sickening excitement. I want to hurl. I want to run for that yellow line. I want to climb in Drea's van and hide under one of the seats. I want to feel the flow of cars speed by me as I scream out everything I'm carrying, just unload it right there in the middle of the asphalt.

Unsurprisingly, Isaac is the first one to plant himself on the center line. I can see him thinking, processing, trying to figure out what to say, maybe even how much to say.

"No editing," Graffam shouts. "This is whatever is right there." And I know what she means—the thing or things that hover just below the surface of all of us, the things we're desperate to hide from everyone else.

Isaac must know what she means too because he closes his eyes and all of a sudden the words pour out of him. "*Don't do that, don't go here, don't go there, don't want this, don't want that. Think of the family name. Think of our reputation.* That's *your* reputation. Not mine. And the things you've done to protect that reputation. Making employees take the fall. Making my sister take the fall. I listen. I hear things. I know where the bodies are buried. So many fucking bodies."

The whole time, cars are whizzing past. Faces staring out of windows. Mouths moving. Horns blaring. Drivers swerving. The motion of it causes Isaac to sway, to swerve too, and we shout at him to stand still, to freeze right where he is.

"All this time I've been feeling like I'm not enough. I can't keep up. But guess what, you're not enough for me."

He does this wild fist pump in the air like he's scored a touchdown, and he starts walking toward us, eyes still closed. A truck is heading directly for him, and we shout at him to run, goddammit, run. He opens his eyes then and dives onto the shoulder, and for a second he looks surprised, as if he forgot where he was. I can feel the roar of the truck, which doesn't slow down. And why should it? Isn't that the whole point of this little exercise? *Don't slow down for anyone.*

Ramon leans toward me. "You're not actually going to do this, are you?" I look at him, and in that moment I'm like, *I can be a Ramon, or I can be an Isaac. And I'd rather be an Isaac.*

I glance to the right, to the left, to the right again, and then jog on over to that middle line. It feels like crossing the desert, like the line is miles from the shoulder. Ahead of me and behind me, just traffic and more traffic. I close my eyes and have this sensation of gravity shifting. The noise, the darkness, the motion of the cars hurtling past—everything feels far away and close up at the same time.

My dad has always loved challenging Aaron and me with moral paradoxes: *The train's brakes have failed. If you do nothing, you will kill five workers who stand on the tracks, but if you change the train's path, you will hit only one person. How do you know which life to save? What makes one person more savable than another?* Dad doesn't ask these questions anymore. Not since a lifeguard had to choose between saving his son and saving his son's best friend. But I think about it all the time. The train with no brakes. The tide coming in. Two teenagers in a sea cave.

The novel I originally proposed for Jan Term was about Tyler the lifeguard, the day he was forced to choose which person to save, and the weight he carries. But you can't always carry it around, can you? If you do, you'll snap in half from the weight of it.

"I'm sorry," I say now.

My voice gets lost under the noise of the traffic, and Graffam yells, "We can't hear you." On the heels of this, Isaac hollers, "Set yourself free, little man."

Usually I'd be like, *Fuck you, Isaac. We're the same fucking height.* But that's just Isaac. That's just what he does.

"I'm sorry."

Louder, I can hear you say.

"I'm sorry. You were right. We should've gone to Zuma. You knew it was a bad idea, but you were always coming up with where to go and what to do, and this was me trying to make my own small contribution so that you didn't figure out what everyone else had—that you should never have been hanging out with me."

The noise of the cars dies away. And now it's just Jonah and me out here.

"Fuck you for dying and fuck me for living, and I'm sorry that it's all my fault."

I feel a burning behind my eyes and in my throat and in my chest, and I can't tell if I'm about to burst into tears or spontaneously go up in flames. I throw my arms out wide because I've forgotten where I am, and Effy, Isaac, Ness, they all shout, telling me I just missed an oncoming car.

I'm done then. I don't have to tell them because they can see it. They guide me back to the shoulder and I'm safe and alive. I open my eyes and the sky seems brighter and we look brighter beneath it.

Ness is on that yellow line now, but I barely hear her because I'm lost in my own world. Then she is back in one piece and jumping up and down and hugging Effy, who tells her, "You're such a good person. The best person."

"I'm not, I'm not, I'm not," says Ness.

And as I watch them, it makes me think of you, Jonah Maguire. But with maybe a little less guilt and a little less pain than I had this morning.

Effy

Monday, January 12

My mind flashes back to that twisty and narrow section of I-95. The screech of brakes, the crush of metal, the wail of sirens. I wasn't there that day—I was at home with Gran—but I didn't need to be there to see it. Of all the nightmares I have, this is the one that feels the most real. I can smell the burning of rubber. I can feel the damp of the sea in the air. The tremor of the earth—a great, horrifying shudder—as my mom was killed.

Then I march out into the middle of the street, feet straddling the yellow line. I shut my eyes, throw my head back, and yell at the sky, "You cannot predict the future. You can't guard your life like a watchdog. You can be angry. You can even be angry at your mother for letting him drive in the first place. But you can't change what happened. You don't have that power. No one does."

Not even my father.

I feel my legs go out from under me. I will not collapse here in the middle of this road. I turn back toward the others before I can think. I hear the car before I see it. Maybe just one, maybe a line of them. I open my eyes, and for some reason I can't seem to move my legs at all now. It's like a dream where you're being chased and you know you have to run for your life but your body is paralyzed. A dream where a car is racing toward you at sixty miles per hour, the driver staring down at his phone, and you cannot move.

Everyone is screaming my name, but it sounds as if they are far away. And suddenly I'm hit by something hard and swift that sends me rolling into the soft grass of the shoulder. I bounce against the ground, the wind knocked out of me. I feel a sharp stab in my ribs.

My eyes are still closed because I might be dead or trapped beneath the wheels of the car and I don't want to see.

"Look at me," a voice says. "Effy. Look at me."

So I look.

Arlo's arms are wrapped around me, and his eyes are on mine. His mouth is moving, but I can't hear him over the sound of the vehicles racing by. "Not a car," I say. "That was you."

I count four faces above me—Arlo, Isaac, Ness, Ramon. One, two, three, four. I turn my head and stare at Graffam. From down here, she seems stretched somehow, an exaggerated version of herself.

Arlo helps me to my feet and brushes off my jeans, coat, hair. He starts patting me like a child, feeling for broken bones.

"I think you broke one of my ribs," I tell him.

"You mean just now, when I saved your life?"

A few yards away, Graffam speaks through an open window

to one of the drivers who has pulled over. Ness and Isaac are chattering at once, voices high and excited.

I think of the feeling I had in the middle of that road. One of fear but something else—invincibility. All around me the drab winter palette is suddenly vivid and beautiful, not dead but alive.

"Are you okay?"

I have created these worry lines in Ness's forehead. Just minutes ago she was on top of the world.

"Yes," I breathe. *I am miraculous.*

We watch while Graffam signs something for the driver, an autograph probably, and then the car continues on its way.

"Everyone all right?" she calls.

For some reason I think of that line from *Alice in Wonderland—We're all mad here.*

"Yes," we answer. *Everyone is good*, I think. *Everyone is invincible.*

Graffam only smiles and nods and goes, "Ramon?" She tilts her head at him.

"There's nothing anywhere that says in order to write you need to stand in the middle of a road and risk getting run over. It's reckless. And it has nothing to do with storytelling, nothing to do with trust." I can feel his eyes bore into me. "You, Effy, out of everyone. I don't see how you can be okay with this."

"Jesus."

"No," I tell Arlo. "He's right."

The thing I can't explain to Ramon or Arlo or anyone else is that in some bizarre way, I needed this. It was like a plunge into the void. And I survived.

"You all are the biggest bunch of hypocrites," Ramon

continues to Graffam, to the rest of us. "I don't trust you. I don't trust any of you. Like you all wouldn't throw me under the bus at the first possible moment. Figuratively and literally. The way you did with Peter Tobin." He waves at the road. "'Stir up the waters,' right? Because it's a competition. Why are we pretending it isn't?"

Ramon stomps off toward Drea and the van, and she must see him because she pops out and opens the door for him. He's halfway in the vehicle when Graffam says, "Drea, shut the door. Do not let him in there."

"But," Drea says, "it's freezing out here—"

"He can take the trail back to the Moss."

"Sorry?" Drea's forehead is creased with confusion. "But, Meredith . . ." She glances at us, at Graffam. "We're responsible for—"

"No." Graffam gazes at Ramon. "The time will be good for you to think about why you're here and what you really want out of the next two weeks. I think we can both agree you've been having some trouble adjusting—"

"Hey," Arlo interrupts, Mr. Congeniality. "We can't really let him walk all that way, even if he is a bit of an ass . . ."

"It's, like, miles back to the house," seconds Ness. "And it might snow . . ."

Graffam turns to the rest of us. "You're either in or you're out. Honoring your principles, marching to your own drumbeat, these are important. But so is flexibility. So is a willingness to join in and be here wholeheartedly."

"Yeah, but there's also personal safety." The afterglow has disappeared from Arlo's face. "Books told us to stay out of the woods. It was pretty much a direct order. In case you forgot, a girl was murdered there. We don't call it Murder Wood for nothing . . ."

Graffam flinches at this, her face closing up, even as Ramon wheels on the four of us. "Like you've got any allegiance to me? Now, what, we're suddenly best friends? A team?" He looks at each of us and laughs. "Give me a break. Like Isaac Williams has ever been interested in anyone other than himself. Like any of you—let's be honest—give an actual shit about me."

"Ramon . . ." Ness steps toward him.

"Screw you, Ness. Screw all of you."

He spins away and—just like that—disappears into the trees.

THE MOSS RISES up, a dark silhouette against the blue of the sky, as if it's anticipating our return. Inside the van, I am alternately thinking about Ramon and Highway 127.

As we make our way inside, Graffam says, "I want you to spend the rest of the day on your projects. Don't worry about Ramon. Worry about yourselves and your work. We'll reconvene at dinner." And then she's gone.

Everyone but Drea hangs their coats on the hooks in the mudroom. She says, "I'm actually going to take a walk. I'll keep an eye out for him."

As she ducks outside again, the four of us move toward the stairs.

"We should check his room," says Ness. "See if he's here." It's too soon. He won't have beaten us back. But the exercise in the road has left her emboldened, and one by one we follow her up the main staircase to our floor.

The door to Ramon's room is open. The bed is made, his bookbag at the foot of it, and inside the wardrobe, his clothes hang neatly. Everything just as he left it.

"So he hasn't gone," Ness says, letting out a breath, a kind of *Phew*. "I mean for good." Then her forehead crinkles up again and she goes, "But where do you think he is?"

"I wouldn't worry about Ramon," Arlo tells her, his voice purposely light, his eyes dark as a bruise. "He's a tough old bird. He's probably getting a much-needed break from the rest of us. I'm sure he'll be back soon."

Arlo

Monday, January 12

By sundown, Ramon still isn't back. Night comes quickly, the moon and stars engulfed by dusky gray clouds. Outside, I circle the Moss, tracing its chaotic, drunken footprint. From this angle, up close like this, the house looms as if it has doubled in height, and I move inside its shadow. Its illuminated windows are a hundred staring eyes. Seeing. Watching. Welcoming. Beckoning. *Come in*, they say. *Come back. Get warm. Be safe. Stay.* Instead I head for the forest.

I've never been in Murton Wood at night. As I step onto the trail and into the trees, instantly the world goes quiet. It's as if I've entered a tomb, the wind and the moon walled out, everything vast and shuttered.

I begin to call his name.

"Ramon..."

A slight echo, as if my voice has nowhere to go.

"Ramon..."

The deeper in, the darker it gets, all light walled out along with the wind and the moon. And then, in the not-so-distant distance, something moves. *It's just a deer*, I tell myself. *A harmless wood-dwelling animal.*

"Ramon," I call. "Ramon!"

"Arlo?"

A woman's voice, followed by the crunching of snow and the shaking of tree limbs. Drea emerges from the darkness, flashlight bobbing.

"What are you doing out here?" she says. Her breath makes little clouds.

"Looking for Ramon."

"Me too. I don't like the thought of him out there alone."

The way she says it—*out there*—makes it sound as if Ramon is wandering some distant planet.

"On the bright side, the woods have been murder-free for the past thirty years." *As far as we know.* As pep talks go, it's not one of my better efforts, and I don't need Reddit to tell me I'm the asshole here. "Sorry. Humor is my coping mechanism."

She gives me a thin smile, but her heart's not in it. I'm grateful for the attempt though. She says, "Lara wasn't killed in the woods."

"Isn't that the whole point of keeping us out of them?"

"They—she and Meredith—were attacked in the woods. But her murderer chased them to the cliffs and pushed Lara into the chasm. Meredith got away from him, although she was pretty battered and bruised."

"That wasn't in her book."

"No."

Drea doesn't explain how she knows this detail, and I don't ask. They never found the man who actually killed Lara

Leonard. An unsettling thought when someone you know is out there wandering in the dark. I find myself wondering where Timothy Hugh Martin is now and if they know absolutely, conclusively, without a shadow of a doubt that he was innocent.

There's a sudden rustling noise, and I nearly jump out of my skin. Drea lays a hand on my shoulder—a kind, maternal gesture—and trains the beam of her flashlight on the undergrowth.

"Ramon," we call in unison. "Ramon!"

The breeze picks up, cutting through the walls of the forest. Drea shivers. After a few more minutes, she clicks off the light and we turn toward the house.

She says, "I can't imagine coming back here after all that happened. If it were me and I'd been through what she went through . . ." She shakes her head. "This will sound selfish. I don't mean it that way. It's just—I want to finish the next couple of weeks with her and then do the art opening in New York. And then I plan to leave and branch out on my own."

We're blinded by a sudden burst of light. The two of us jump. I let out a little scream. A voice reaches for us in the dark. "Any sign of him?"

"Dude," I tell Isaac, shielding my eyes. "Cannot see."

"Sorry." The night goes dark again.

"No sign," Drea tells him. From somewhere, I hear a buzzing sound. She pats her pocket and excuses herself, red hair swinging as she runs toward the house.

Isaac says to me, "I don't love the guy, but that was pretty fucked up making him walk back."

We look at each other, and I can see he feels it too—

something is rotten in the state of Denmark. But it's not a something I'm ready or able to name.

Without a word, we walk back to the Moss.

"RAMON IS FINE," Graffam tells us when she arrives for dinner that night. She has just spoken with Dean Booker, who let her know that Ramon arrived on campus cold and tired, but unharmed, and is back in the dorm even as we speak. Someone will be stopping by tomorrow to collect his things.

It takes time for this to sink in. For the past few hours, I've been picturing Ramon lost and wandering, maybe even dead, knowing it's not my fault but still feeling like somehow it's my fault because I was there. I could have stopped him from walking into the woods alone.

"He's okay," Graffam says. "Ramon is fine." And I realize I'm not the only one feeling like this. I see it on the faces of the others. She repeats it. "He's okay. He is fine." Like a parent soothing an anxious child. The tension in the room begins to ease.

Without thinking, I say, "I didn't hear the phone ring."

"What?" Graffam turns to me.

"The landline. It didn't ring."

"Because I called Dean Booker," she says. "Not the other way around. I've been calling him ever since we got back." The two of us stare at each other as everyone else stares at us. "You of all people, Arlo, should understand what it feels like to hold yourself responsible for someone else."

The others lose interest in our exchange, digging into their plates as if they haven't eaten in months. Only Drea pokes at her food while Graffam leans forward, chin in hands.

"I'm proud of you," she says to Isaac, Ness, Effy, me. "I know it isn't easy, but you are opening yourselves up and letting yourselves be vulnerable. What you did today, not everyone could do that." She raises her glass. "'May your glass be ever full. May the roof over your head be always strong. And may you be in heaven half an hour before the devil knows you're dead.' Sláinte!"

We all drink, and then Isaac flashes her an expectant grin. "So who won?"

Graffam seems to consider this. Given the moment and the mood, I almost expect her to tell us no one has won, that it wasn't actually a competition. Her eyes alight on each of our faces.

"Ness."

"Ness?" A note of incredulity in Effy's voice.

"Yes," says Graffam. "Who do you think should have won, Effy?"

Effy doesn't answer.

As Ness frowns at Effy and Effy frowns at the table, I think, *And now we are four,* and feel this rush of togetherness and camaraderie that comes from sharing an experience no one else can possibly understand. And I feel something else—an undercurrent of electricity. In that moment, it's as if Jan Term truly begins.

The conversation turns to The Wild Hunt, which Graffam promises we will play the night before we leave. "Jan Term," she tells us, eyes shining in the candlelight, "was what I'd wanted

Brighton and Hove to be from the moment I set foot on campus my first year. During The Wild Hunt, we moved like wild things in the forest. I won the crown, and afterward I didn't just feel like I ruled the wood. I felt like I ruled the world."

Lulled by the food and the sound of her voice, I sit thinking that I wouldn't mind feeling even for a minute like I ruled the world.

Eventually the meal winds down. We're pushing in our chairs and clearing our plates when Graffam calls my name. Everyone turns as she presses a book into my hand. A hardcover with a faded dust jacket. *On Writing* by Stephen King. I open it to the front page and see the signature.

"A signed copy?"

"A signed first edition. It's one of my favorite books on story. Years ago he was nearly killed in an accident, and he talks a lot in here about writing and living."

The others are still standing there, as if waiting for their own copies. But then Graffam bids us good night.

I TRAVEL THROUGH the house with only my book for company because Effy, Ness, and Isaac have abandoned me. Funny how as soon as we were four, I am now one. The book is warm in my hand, the promise of all those words neatly locked inside.

She has to know, with all her talk of competition, that gifting me a signed first edition of a book—not just any book but a book on writing—in front of my peers will be seen as playing favorites. And I don't even think I am her favorite. If I had to guess which one of us she likes best, I'd guess Ness or Effy or maybe no one at all. So why do it tonight in front of everybody else?

In the game room, I pull open the window seat and descend the stairs into the secret hollow below. Inside, everything is just as I left it, the dusty air undisturbed.

"What's your angle, lady?" I say to the ceiling, which—I notice for the first time—is painted with stars. I search for Ophiuchus, but these are just stars, not constellations. I sink into the daybed and begin reading.

When I get to page 37, there is a Post-it note marking a passage. The passage says:

```
Good story ideas seem to come quite
literally from nowhere, sailing at you
right out of the empty sky: two previously
unrelated ideas come together and make
something new under the sun. Your
job isn't to find these ideas but to
recognize them when they show up.
```

The note says:

What about a graphic novel? But not in the traditional sense. What if you alternate chapters between prose and art?

MG

The idea hits me like a lightning strike. I lie there imagining how it would look, how it would work, and then decide I don't need to figure that out yet.

I read a little more before stopping. Of all the wisdom King imparts on these pages, this is what sticks: You've got to show up.

There were times in August and September of senior year when I wasn't able to show up at all. That was when I missed all those weeks of school. It wasn't until my brother flew out from New York and forced me to leave the house and go with him to the beach that I started thinking I might be able to show up again.

I've been trying to show up ever since.

Now I close the book and get to my feet. I'm on the bottom step when I notice the Scrabble board. It's in the exact same place and exact same position it was the last time I was in here. Only now there is a word in the center of it:

Effy

Tuesday, January 13

(the wee hours)

When he opens the door to his room, Arlo looks rumpled, preoccupied. I brush past him and drop into the desk chair, glancing at the open laptop, at the black Moleskine notebook and drawing pencils, at the signed first-edition Stephen King book Graffam gave him. Too late, he notices and flips it over so that it's face down.

I cut to the chase. "Who you were talking about today? In the road? You don't have to tell me."

"Okay." He doesn't sit. Instead he stands at the foot of his bed, looking as if he's on his way somewhere.

"But you can," I say. "If you need to."

And then I wait. I settle back in my chair and stare at him, making it clear that I'm in no hurry to leave. To be truthful, I don't fully understand why I'm here except that he's lost someone and so have I and he knows what that hole feels like.

"You're not leaving until I tell you?"

"No."

"Okay," he says again.

And then he sinks onto the bed.

"My friend Jonah. He was the one who died." His voice sounds quiet and un-Arlo-like. "It was last summer. He liked to surf. And he was good at it. Good enough to have gone pro. We always went to Zuma Beach, even though we didn't live in Malibu. But it's got this wide, soft sand, and the surfing is famously good. I'm not the surfer Jonah was. I can basically stand up for about ten seconds before wiping out. But it was something we did together. Anyway. There's these sea caves down in Laguna—you can go there at low tide and see all sorts of sea urchins and fish in the tide pools and walk all the way through to another cave just beyond. So, I convinced him to come with me, only I misread the tide. It flipped while we were in there—in the caves—and he told me it was coming in, but I said *No, we're good,* and we argued about it. And then . . . we got trapped." There's a tremor to his hand now.

I don't say anything. I wait in case there's more.

He makes a fist with the shaking hand. Opens it flat. Clenches it tight. Over and over. And then he says, "There was one lifeguard at the beach that day. He couldn't save us both. He had to choose. It was my idea to go there, but Jonah was up ahead, farther in, and he was the stronger swimmer. The stronger everything. So the lifeguard—his name is Tyler—he saved me." He looks up at the ceiling. Looks at me. "Jonah's whole family—they took me in like I was one of their own. This was before, of course. I was going to live with them this year after my parents went back overseas. I haven't talked to them since the funeral."

"By your choice or theirs?"

"Mine. But I can't imagine they want to see me. I'm the one who dragged him down to Laguna. I was the friend who never could keep up. Who always needed saving. Which was why the lifeguard chose me. I didn't know Jonah long, but I knew him well. If that makes sense."

"It does."

"His parents gave me the hat." He plucks it from where it hangs on the bedpost. "He never missed a game. His granddad went to the championship. He got Magic Johnson to sign it. So." He places the hat on his head. "I wear it."

"Like a talisman."

"Kind of." A beat. "I'm sorry about your mom."

Around us, beneath us, above us, the house settles and sighs.

"I miss her," I say simply. "But I was only six, so I miss the version of her that I knew as a six-year-old. I'd be a stranger to her now. I don't even know if she would like this me."

"I'm sure she'd love you even more."

"I didn't say it so you'd reassure me. But. Thanks. When my dad got out a few months ago, he wrote me a letter." I reach for it and then remember that I'm not carrying it with me. I haven't carried it with me in a day or two. "So. Yeah. Basically he just wants to get to know me again."

"Whoa."

"Yeah."

The two of us sit across from each other more naked than we were when we were literally naked at the end of sophomore year.

"Effy?"

"Yes?"

"I'm really sorry I ghosted you."

I can tell he means it, but suddenly I don't want to talk about us or what happened. I don't want to talk at all. The sound of my heartbeat fills the room. And then it's like I can hear the sound of his heartbeat too.

At the same time, we stand and move toward each other.

He takes my face in his hands. And then—he kisses me. Barely brushing my lips with his own. His nearness sends me whirling. The almostness of the kiss.

Once again, he feels the same as he did before, but different. His hands on me feel broader, stronger, surer. His lips are softer somehow. Everything else just melts away and I fill with a delicious ache, like I can't get close enough to this boy.

We take our time, touching and almost touching, our breath hot, our hearts quickening. I think of this instrument Gran told me about once—one you play without actually putting your hands on it. The theremin.

That's what we are right now. We are the instrument, making our own weird music from the electricity of us.

"Have you ever heard of a theremin?" I look up at him.

"Of course," he says. "It's like the unofficial sound of every 1950s sci-fi movie." He points to his shirt. *Welcome to the Twilight Zone.* "You know why there're so few theremin players in the world?" His voice is warm. A late-night, closed-door voice. "The sound it makes is different for each person, so there's no single way to play it. We conduct the air. We become part of it."

I kiss him then, feeling the warm skin of his back under his shirt. His hands twine through my hair. His tongue finds mine. Then his lips find my neck. It's a kind of hunger. I kiss him till I feel like an explosion ready to go off, and then he picks me up, my legs wrapping around him, and carries me to the bed.

He sets me down, and I pull him closer. His lips are on my throat, my ear, my mouth. My legs are still wrapped around him as I pull off his shirt and toss it. It lands on his head and we laugh, but only for a second, and then I start to unbutton the flannel nightshirt. He tries to help me, but one of the buttons pops off, shooting across the room, ricocheting off the wall.

I bolt up, and he goes flying off the bed, landing on the floor.

"No," I say. "No, no, no." I stare down at the nightshirt where the button used to be. "Did you see where it went?" I frantically walk the room, examining the floor, the desk, under the bed. "Don't just sit there."

He scrambles to his feet. "We're looking for the button?"

"Yes, we're looking for the button."

There are little spaces between the floorboards, and I am on my hands and knees checking these with my eyes, with my fingers.

"You know," he says, "they have this thing called the internet where you can order nifty items like—"

"Don't be a smart-ass. Not right now." I feel feverish and

frenzied and angry that I've got an audience, even if it's just Arlo. I tug hard at the nightshirt. "This was my mom's."

It's just a button, I tell myself. *It's not your mom.*

He drops down and begins to crawl along the floor. In silence, we cover every inch of space. He moves the bed away from the wall. Then the chair. Then the desk.

When the clocks chime, I sit back on my heels. Feverish and frantic have given way to weary and defeated. "I think I'm going to go to bed. Thanks for helping me look." I rub at my eyes, which burn from tears I refuse to let out.

He follows me into the hallway.

"We'll find it if I have to pry up every floorboard." He brushes the hair out of his eyes.

"I do realize it's just a button." It sounds defiant. "But it's all I really have of hers, and that copy of *Frankenstein*. After she died . . . My grandmother isn't a sentimental person. She's loving. But she doesn't need things to remember people, so she gave most of my mom's belongings away."

"When you lose someone, objects change their meaning," he says softly. "They start being a lot more than what they originally were. And that's okay."

I hesitate and then lean into him. I want to thank him for getting it, for getting me. But instead I kiss him, just once, and his lips are warm against mine.

IN THE HALL, the door to Ramon's room stands open. The wardrobe empty. The books have been cleared off the dresser. All his things are gone, as if he was never here.

I stop outside Ness's room, the warmth of Arlo enfolding me, making me feel generous and calm. I will tell her I'm sorry for having a single negative thought about our friendship. She won today's challenge fair and square. *Sisters*. Like Graffam said—we're more like sisters than friends.

I almost walk right in, but then I hear laughter and voices, and I freeze. I hear Ness say, "But the way you broke out."

"I wish you'd seen me then. She changed me forever."

"Do you wonder what would've happened if she were still here?"

"Yes. But we can't look back. As much as it's the human instinct. Regret. Guilt. Grief. The only thing we can do—we owe it to ourselves—is to look forward."

Graffam.

Without thinking, I turn away from all of it—Ness, Arlo, my own room. On the landing with the birds of prey, there is an old black rotary phone sitting on one of the shelves. It's almost midnight, but I suddenly need to hear Gran's voice. She's a night owl like me, so chances are she's awake, and if she's not, she'll still talk to me because Gran is always there. Gran has always been there. She's the only person I've ever been able to count on.

I pick up the receiver, put it to my ear.

There's nothing but air.

I hang up, try again.

Nothing.

I do that thing I've seen people do in old movies—jiggle the prongs in the cradle over and over. If tears weren't burning the backs of my eyes, it would be kind of cool—the big old house, the old-fashioned phone, a mystery to solve.

I think of the storm that's on its way, that may already be here. The woods separating us from Parkerton, from Brighton and Hove, from Highway 127, from everything and everyone. And it hits me, for the first time, just how cut off we are from the rest of the world.

Arlo

Tuesday, January 13

Brighton's Woe sits about 1,500 feet offshore. Graffam says the water today is smooth enough to get there, as long as we leave now, never mind the several inches of snow forecast this very evening and the darkening horizon.

The boat has an outboard motor and seats six. We're over the required age for wearing life jackets, but we don them anyway because the ocean is rougher than it looked from the dock. Effy's hair swirls around her, as if casting a magic spell, but the rest of us look as miserable as we feel. Graffam navigates over whitecaps and waves, and by the time we reach the island, we are wet and shivering.

Isaac crouches in the bow, holding this orange stake tied to a rope. As soon as we scrape rocky bottom, he jumps out, into the shallows, and plants the anchor in the sand. I notice that he alone is wearing waders. I can't help wondering what Graffam told him about this little outing and what else they might have talked about.

My own feet get soaked as I climb out of the boat. Without stopping, I head straight up onto the cliff above.

Graffam appears beside me, followed by the others. "Your setting and your narrative are intimately involved," she says over the wind and the waves. "Tone is your emotional landscape. Atmosphere is what controls an audience's reaction, their ability to immerse in your story." She gazes around us. "I want you to absorb this place and focus on how it makes you feel."

The sky right now is low and heavy. The island is small—really just a slab of rock with a lighthouse at one end and the ruins of a cottage on the other. A few trees grow along the wind-battered eastern coast.

Graffam tells us to be careful exploring, and we scatter like leaves. As Effy starts to flutter away, I call her name.

She turns, squinting at me in the bright light. When she turns, I hold out a hand, and she hesitates before taking it. Together we climb the front steps of what was once a house. From here there's a clear view of the Moss.

"Look," I say.

She follows my gaze across the water. And for a moment, we see it—the Moss as it was, the bright sky, the meadow, the gardens running right up to the shore. I have this sudden urge to draw it the way it used to be.

"Do you think Moss Hove was trying to swim here when he drowned?" she says, her voice hazy and far away.

"Yes."

"Do you think he and Zachary Brighton haunt this place?"

"I think they've moved on together to whatever's next.

When I die, I'm going to haunt the Cascade Mountains of Washington state. Where the most Bigfoot sightings are—8.9 sightings for every hundred thousand people. I figure my odds of seeing this magnificent creature, especially if I'm there for eternity, are pretty good."

"So we're assuming Bigfoot exists?"

"Oh yeah. As *The United States of Cryptids* says, your backyard is full of monsters. Even if you don't see them."

Someone calls her name, and in unison we turn. Ness waves from the base of the lighthouse and hollers something I can't make out.

Effy frowns, not waving back. "I think I'm supposed to join her." But she continues to stand there, and I tell myself it's because she doesn't want to leave me. My hand is on the sketchbook in my coat pocket. I have a sudden instinct to show Effy the Effy I've drawn, still incomplete but also pretty good, if I say so myself. But then Ness shouts her name again.

"Do you need to get that?" I ask.

"Probably." She starts walking away, then stops. "Hey, Arlo? I'm sorry about last night."

"Love means never having to say you're sorry."

"What?" She frowns, crinkling up her face.

"It's from an old, very sad, incredibly sappy movie about two sweet, mixed-up kids from opposite sides of the tracks. He's studying law. She's studying music. And then she dies of leukemia. But before that, early on, he fucks up. And she tells him, 'Love means never having to say you're sorry.' And then later, after she's gone, he repeats those words to his estranged dad."

"So you're telling me you don't believe in apologies?" She cocks her head, eyebrows arched. A most unnerving expression.

"I'm saying you, Effy, do not need to apologize for anything. I'm a different story. In my limited experience, love is *always* having to say you're sorry."

"Mm" is her only response before she walks off, for good this time.

I sit on the steps and begin to sketch, at first the house across the water, a serpentine hump representing the Gloucester Sea Serpent in the foreground. And then I flip to the drawing of a girl with dark fringe and green eyes.

When I look up again, Graffam is there, camera in hand, scrolling through the viewfinder. Without meeting my eye, she says, "So what do you think of the water from this angle? Does it still work?"

"That depends on the view. Ideally, when going to the water, you just see water—otherwise you're looking at land, and that defeats the purpose."

She trains her camera on the opposite shore, and for a second I think she's not listening. Then she says, "I've been thinking about your friend. I lost a friend once and I know how hard it is."

For some reason my pulse quickens. She's talking about Lara Leonard, the girl who was murdered. As far as I know, Graffam rarely talks about that night.

"Everyone tells you it gets better," I say. "And I guess it does. But it also doesn't."

"It just gets . . ." She points the camera at the sky, as if searching for the words there. "Different. It just gets different." She holds the camera at her side now and meets my eyes.

"An old professor of mine said a story is a series of events that build toward unalterable change."

In the distance, there's the sound of Effy and Ness, a conversation shouted over the wind. I turn and watch them—on opposite sides of the lighthouse. When I turn back to Graffam, I say, "Hey, thanks, by the way. For the book and the advice."

Her eyes darken, matching the sky. "I'm going to tell you something, Arlo, and I want you to really hear it. You can write about your friend and let that decide you. You'll be that guy who writes about his dead best friend, who explores grief in every project he does, who looks at it backward and forward and inside and out, over and over and over. Or you can use it once and then move past it, just keep going. Don't look back. You don't need to. Because you're more than what happened and you're more than your friend. If you never went through that experience of losing him, you'd still have things to say. Don't let anyone tell you otherwise."

My mom and dad spend their lives in war zones. They don't have time for grief. When they lose friends or colleagues, they keep going. But after Jonah died, I stopped everything. Graffam though—she lost her best friend when she was my age. I figure if anyone knows how I feel—as she herself has pointed out—it's her.

"Don't push it away," she's saying. "The guilt. The grief. Don't try to make it fit anyone else's timeline or anyone else's preconceived ideas. I'm not saying wallow in it. But you can use it. Let it fuel your writing, but don't let it consume it. Don't let it consume you. Then move on."

"Just like that?"

"Just like that."

I catch sight of Isaac in the distance, watching us. I have this instinct to throw my head back and laugh uproariously, to snap a selfie of Graffam and me, something that will burn him up. But the moment is peaceful, and—for now—so am I.

Effy

Tuesday, January 13

When the sun starts to set, the temperature drops, and the wind picks up. I head to the beach, suddenly worried about being left behind. But the boat isn't there. I look toward the cliffs where we climbed up. Then back out to sea. I'm sure this is where we anchored, but just in case I go up the hill and walk it a ways before coming down to the beach again in the exact same place.

Nothing.

I roam the beach and then scale the path up to the cliff once more. In the distance, I spot Arlo and Ness, and Isaac up in the tower of the lighthouse like he's surveying his kingdom. I wave, but no one seems to notice. My heart is racing, even though I tell myself, *Be calm. There's a good explanation. You don't have all the information yet.*

I start to follow the current, which seems to be pushing east. This time I walk along the waterline, eyes on the fading sun, which has dropped to the horizon. Because of the tide, most of the sand has disappeared under the waves. I pick my way across the shallows and the rocks that grow up there, sometimes scooting along on my hands and knees when it's too slippery to be upright.

I cannot think about the snow that's on its way or the distance between us and the Moss. Or the fact that we have no way of calling for help or letting anyone know where we are.

I round the eastern side of the island, where the wind has a cold bite to it, slamming the waves against the rocky shore. And that's when I see Graffam standing on the rocks, gaze fixed on the horizon.

Where the boat is floating away.

It must be at least twenty feet offshore. I start to run. "What happened?" I cry, my voice carried off by the wind. I shout it again, and this time she turns.

She looks wild and scared. "It was gone. I came down to the beach, and it was just gone." She rakes at her hair, long, billowing. "I don't know what . . . I don't know . . ." She darts forward into the surf, then back, forward and back, like a bird trying to outrun the waves. "And the storm . . ." The ends of her sentences drop off, swept away into the current.

I'm trying to think, but there's no time to think because the boat is drifting farther away. For the past week, Graffam's been telling us to jump, not overthink, not stay safe, so this time I don't think at all. I wade straight into the water, Graffam screaming my name. As soon as I'm past the rocks, I dive below the surface.

Immediately the current and the cold knock me senseless. It's how I imagine it would feel to be struck by a car—the impact, sharp and paralyzing. Water fills my nose and ears and eyes and mouth, freezing me from the inside until I'm hard and brittle, like diamonds. I cut through water like I'm cutting through glass.

I come up for air when I need to and then go back under. Up. Under. Up. Under. It takes everything I have to keep moving. Because I have to keep moving. If I don't, I'll freeze to death.

I may or may not hear my name from the island, may or may not see figures gathered around Graffam. The only thing I'm focused on in my dull, distant mind is the boat. *I have to keep moving.*

I push harder than I've ever pushed for anything, no longer able to feel my limbs or my heart, which throbs like a dull, distant drum. The only reason I know it's still beating is that I hear it from far, far away. Time has slowed down. I have slowed down. My breathing. My pulse. The air. The sky. It's as if they all live inside me now.

And then. I lift my arm, and it smacks hard against wood. I uncurl my fingers, expecting them to break in half as I do, and force myself to grip the side of the boat.

Next is the rope, which glides in the water like a snake. I watch it coil and uncoil, and then I reach for it with the other hand, which is locked in a fist, but I don't want to let go of the boat, not even for a second. As my fist brushes the rope, it somehow uncurls, and I realize I am doing this—I am opening that fist. And then I am fitting the rope into my cold, dead hand. And I am starting to pull the boat toward shore.

My eyes are blurred with salt water and wind and the cold, cold, cold. I'm starting to close them when I feel an arm loop beneath my shoulders and the rope break free. I reach for it, and suddenly there is Isaac, taking the rope, guiding the boat back to the beach. And there is Ness, swimming alongside me, and Arlo with his arm around my chest.

I want to tell him I'm sorry he had to get into the water. But love means never having to say you're sorry, so instead I hold on to him, my hand on his, hoping that the things I want to say are somehow flowing from me into him through this contact of skin and tissue and bone.

IN SPITE OF the lights burning and the fires in the fireplaces, the Moss is too dark, every window blacked out from the storm shutters, which have closed us in. Even in the Sky Room, it feels as if we're locked inside an enormous underground fortress. Too quiet. Too still.

Dear Clay Reynolds, I type. *Dad* doesn't fit. *Dad* is not a person I know anymore. *Did you know Mary Shelley published two versions of* Frankenstein? *In the original, all of Victor Frankenstein's choices and actions are his own. But in the second version, she made him a victim of fate. I prefer the first one because I believe life is a choose-your-own adventure.*

I guess what I need to know is, Did you choose what you were doing? Did you drive into that tree on purpose? Or did you lose control of the truck? And why did you get behind the wheel? Because even if you didn't mean to hit the tree, you had to know it was a possibility. And Mom did too . . .

"How are you feeling?"

I look up. Graffam stands in the doorway, and I'm overcome with a sudden rush of emotion, my predictable orphan response whenever an adult who isn't Gran offers support or sympathy.

"Dry," I tell her. "Glad to be inside."

"I want you to be careful."

"I don't think I'll be swimming again anytime soon."

She smiles, a little distantly, as she moves to the couch and drops down next to me, so close I can smell her shampoo. Her hair is damp, her face scrubbed clean of makeup. She wears an oversized sweater with the sleeves pushed up.

"I was married once," she says, as if I might not know this. "He was also a writer, but unlike me, he was just starting out. This was eight years after *The Hunt*, after everything blew up in my face and I'd been forced to retreat from the world. So in some ways we were in a similar place. And for a very brief while, it worked."

I blink at her. Unless she's been married multiple times, she's talking about Paddy Eason. "What happened?"

"I wanted him to be more than he was. Stronger, more infallible. Immune to young women and ego stroking, but alas. He had his way of cheating, I had mine. When he told me about Britt, about the affair, I realized I'd lost my way, treating our marriage like that was the most important thing. But it was always the work that mattered most—even then, when no one wanted to publish it. He had this manuscript he was toying with at the time that he documented every lie he'd ever told, to himself and to everyone else—but we both knew he was never going to finish it."

For a second, she's lost in the memory.

"The idea would have been wasted. I changed a few things, of course, made it my own."

"Wait, so that was . . . ?" *No*, I think. *No, no.*

"*The Lie.*" She tilts her head, eyes focused on some spot in the near distance. She has this look on her face—almost nostalgic, as if she's lost in a happy memory. "He was calling it *Confessions of a Galway Fraud.*" She shakes her head. "*The Lie* was less cumbersome, more memorable." She looks at me then, as if I'm coming into focus. "My greatest success has come from writing about things that actually happened. Fictionalizing certain details, but readers know when something is real because it resonates. Have you ever thought about taking those letters you've written to your father and making them a book?"

It takes me a second to change trajectories, from her plagiarism of Paddy Eason to me.

"You mean instead of the short-story collection?"

"Yes. Without having read them, I think they could be compelling. And it would be different. And true."

I feel a lot of things at once. Relief—the letters, so many of them already written, needing only their details fictionalized. Fear—exposing myself and my innermost life to anyone who reads them. A tingling excitement—the urge to re-read what's there *tonight* so I can start shaping it into something cohesive, maybe even powerful.

"Life is a competition, Effy," Graffam is saying. "Don't forget that. When I sold *The Lie*, my husband's reaction was *And what about me?* After all I'd given to our marriage, he couldn't let me have this one thing." She looks at me like, *Can you believe it?* "The writing must always come first. Ahead of romance. Ahead of friendship."

Her words suddenly feel very pointed.

"When Lara died . . ." She stares down at the green of the sofa and traces the buttons there. "When she died, it was devastating, but also freeing. Which, I realize, is a horrible thing to say." She smiles apologetically. "Sometimes the people closest to us will only slow us down. Especially when they aren't as talented. You're a good writer, Effy. But you could be extraordinary. Just make sure that while you're watching everyone else's backs, you don't forget to watch your own."

I assume from the reference to Lara that she's talking about Ness, but then she says, "You may think he wants you here. But he voted to send you away."

"Who?" I ask. "Arlo?"

"Yes. I thought you should know. Especially given your history with him. I would want to know. After Paddy, I never want to be surprised again. I think you and I are alike in that way."

From the doorway, there's the creaking of floorboards. Graffam and I turn to see Drea standing there. I wonder what, if anything, she's heard of our conversation.

"Rumor has it you were a hero today," she calls to me brightly. Then she tells Graffam she's finished the script coverage, if she wants to discuss, and, with that, they are gone.

When I was younger, I went through a phase of wandering into other people's homes. I'd sneak in through an unlocked door or open window and explore. It was a way of being in someone else's life for a while. Before I could be accused of trespassing, I would crawl back through the window and return to my actual life.

But one day I fell asleep in a stranger's bed, and the family came home and the police were called and Gran was angry and the family accused me of trying to rob them. And in a way, maybe I did. Robbed them not of belongings but of safety and security.

As penance, I used to try to put myself in their shoes and feel what they must have felt: a sense of betrayal and intrusion. Now, after today—the island, the lost boat, my swim in the sea, and Graffam's strange warning—this is what I feel sitting here in the Sky Room while a storm rages outside.

Arlo

WEDNESDAY, JANUARY 14

(the wee hours)

Throughout the house, the windows are shuttered, closing us in. I find Effy curled on the couch in the solarium. Her laptop is open and a book lies next to her, but she stares at the darkened windows as if she can see past the shutters to the outside. The wind has picked up, and I imagine the snow coming down and think of water in all its forms—oceans, tide pools, clouds, fog, ice, snow. Water that floods, water that you surf, water that you swim in, water carrying you and holding you up, water pushing you downward until you become a part of it. Our bodies, our earth. Water, water, everywhere.

Just look up.

Out of habit, I do. The skylight is rattling and uncovered, and through it I can see gusts of white. Outside, a storm; inside, warmth and light, the seven of us—Graffam, Drea, Wesley, and we four students—safe and protected.

"Arlo?"

Effy frowns at me. I've learned to read her frowns, which are as varied as other people's smiles. This one says, *Why are you standing there silently staring at the ceiling?* Or maybe, *What the fuck do you want?*

I fish around in the pocket of my jeans and hold out my hand. She looks up again, then sits forward and plucks the button from my palm.

"Where . . . ?" Her expression lightens, a veil lifting.

"Under the dresser, wedged in between the floorboards."

She gazes at the button, tilting it in the light, gently so as not to drop it. For a moment, her frown melts away into a look of wonder. Then she closes her hand around it. "Thank you." Her voice is frosty.

I am not the brightest, most intuitive guy on the planet—that would be my brother. But I do have a built-in system of alarm bells that sound when I enter dangerous territory. Black holes. Standardized tests. Deep-sea volcanoes. This.

"I'm just going out on a limb here," I say, "but is there something going on? I mean, more than the usual?"

She studies me, then shakes her head like she's having an internal dialogue. "I'm sorry you had to go into the water today."

"I'd do it again." For her, I mean. "But hopefully I won't have to."

I want to kiss her right now but then this moment we're having would be over, and it's one of those impossible-to-find moments when you see each other, really see each other. No bullshit. No pretense. For better or worse, just the acoustic, stripped-down version of Effy and me.

Then her frown is back and she says, "Arlo?"

"Yes?"

"I deserve to be here as much as you do." She sounds colder than the water off Brighton's Woe.

"Okay."

"And if for some reason you're disappointed that I'm still here, I don't care."

"Okay."

"Do you want to know who I voted for that night? No one. Because no matter how much I want to win this thing, it's not my place to send someone home."

Her eyes are fixed on mine, and I know she's waiting for a response.

"As God is my witness, Effy Green, I hope you win the whole damn kit and caboodle. I mean it. I swear on green eggs and ham and purple mountain majesties and all the stars in the flag."

And on Ophiuchus and this Lakers hat and my big, foolish heart.

The words work their magic, or maybe it's that behind them my defenses are down. She gets to her feet. "I want to show you something."

We weave through the neighboring rooms, where candles flicker and shadows dance across walls, illuminating the framed, painted faces. A hush has fallen over the Moss and over the two of us. I start to ease into it, like a backyard hammock—Effy and me, no Isaac or Ness, no Graffam, no one but us—when we come to a sudden stop at the foot of a staircase.

"Isn't that . . . ?"

"Graffam's wing," she confirms.

We make our way up, past the horrifically lifelike serpent head—fangs on full display. Each time a floorboard creaks, we freeze. We shouldn't be up here. We've been told to stay out, which, of course, only makes me want to be here more.

"What's in there?" I point to a closed door.

She shakes her head, waving in the opposite direction, and creeps onto the balcony, gesturing for me to hurry. Down below, the theater is dark except for the glow of the fireplace.

"I was up here the day we broke the mirror," she whispers, "and I noticed this."

I peer past her at another door. A light shines beneath it.

She says, "Why would anyone want to seal off a room? I mean, a secret passageway I get. It's secret. But a room?"

"I can't think of any nonterrifying reasons. If you seal it off, you've clearly got something to hide. Or to be more specific, something you want to keep hidden."

"We need to open it." Her eyes are luminous.

"Do we? Any chance it could wait till the bright light of day?"

But she's not listening. She's too busy examining the doorframe and the flat panel where the knob should be.

I say, "You were one of those kids who loved exploring the creepy house down the block, weren't you? The one who always volunteered to fetch something from the basement?"

She smiles up at me. From behind us we hear the distinctive groan of floorboards. Her smile vanishes as we become statues, waiting, not breathing. Another groan, the sound of someone crossing the floor, not below but close by.

Shit, I mouth.

We run, not caring how loud we are as we sprint across the balcony and down the stairs. I miss the last three and go sprawling, but Effy, that traitor, doesn't wait—she's already gone. I pick myself up and keep going, not stopping until I catch up with her in the solarium. The two of us fall onto the couch, inches apart.

And then, even though it's not all that funny, I start to laugh. For a second, she watches me, but then her mouth twitches and now she's laughing and the two of us are covering our mouths, trying to keep from waking the house. The more we try to be quiet, the louder we are, which makes us laugh even harder. And I haven't laughed like this in a very long time. Not since early last summer.

A minute later, we start to wind back down, the laughter fading into the walls and the floor and the corners and the skylight above us.

And then Effy looks at me and says, "Good night, Arlo."

Effy

Wednesday, January 14

Although we can't see the storm, we hear it. Wailing wind and banging shutters, which shake the house and make it sound as if we're inside the subway, trains roaring past. Motion everywhere, even as you sit perfectly still. The power is out and we work by the muted light of lanterns and flickering candles, huddled by fireplaces to keep warm.

Wesley has gone to Parkerton to be with his wife. No one will be coming out here until the storm passes. It's just Graffam and Drea and us.

Not for the first time, I think of Shirley Jackson's Hill House. Of Mrs. Dudley's speech to Eleanor after she arrives: *"We couldn't even hear you, in the night . . . No one could."*

To add to the sense of confinement, I'm nursing a cold and Ness and Isaac are coming down with the flu. We blame it on our swim at Brighton's Woe. Only Arlo seems to be okay.

Dinner is a potluck of leftovers, warmed on the gas stove.

Even though my throat is raw and my head is pounding, I pour soup for Isaac and Ness. Arlo, Graffam, and I move about the kitchen. When Graffam coughs, I say, "Not you too."

"I'm fine," she tells me, although I'm not sure I believe her.

Tonight we eat dinner in the theater, where Drea has spread blankets on the floor by the hearth. We arrange ourselves across them, plates in our laps.

Graffam says, "Dean Booker showed up early this morning—he wanted us to ride out the storm on campus, but I convinced him that moving would disrupt the intensive work we've been doing. He wasn't happy about it." She tilts her glass from side to side, watching the liquid slide back and forth. "But we're perfectly safe here at the Moss. It's only snow."

The house feels vast around us, everywhere dark and cold and quiet except the room we're sitting in. I wish I could look up the weather report to see if Gran is feeling it in Maine. But there's no internet, no radio, no landline, no way of contacting the outside world. The thought is weirdly settling. Like we are survivors together. The Odds against the world.

When we're finished eating, Graffam says, "I have something for each of you."

We glance at one another, at her. Then she passes out four slender envelopes.

"I was going to wait to give these to you next week, but I thought we could all use a diversion. Don't open them until I say so. Before you read the contents, I will tell you that each envelope contains a gift chosen especially for you. Whenever the weather allows, you're going to engage in a competition. There will only be one winner. That person will earn their gift. Any questions?"

The four of us exchange looks.

"Yeah," says Isaac. "What's the competition?"

"You'll find out soon enough."

Arlo raises his hand. "Do we get to choose our weapon, or will it be assigned?"

Graffam smiles at this. "Your weapon is your mind."

"Sucks for you, Noon." Isaac cackles.

"You mentioned the weather," I say. "Is the competition outside?"

"Yes." Graffam's smile grows wider.

Ness coughs, a ragged, rough-edged sound, and I can hear it in her chest. "What if we're too sick and can't participate?"

"We'll wait till everyone feels up to it. Time permitting."

Through her glasses, Ness blinks at Graffam, and I can feel what she's thinking—she has to get better. Quickly.

"We have, what, just over a week? Hopefully you'll be well by then." Graffam reaches for the bottle of wine that sits beside her on the floor. As we watch, she pours some into our mugs. "My father used to add a little brandy to my tea whenever I had a cold. This is the next best thing."

Drea shakes her head, starts to speak.

"The drinking age in Spain is eighteen?" Graffam smiles at her. "That's true of most of Europe. And I don't know about you," she says to us, "but I'm feeling very European tonight."

Arlo's eyes meet mine as I reach for my drink. "Very European," I echo.

"Now"—Graffam turns her head from one of us to the other, eyes luminous—"who's ready to open?"

We respond all at once, too loudly, voices thick with wine and anticipation.

"On the count of three. One . . ."

I slide my finger under the flap of the envelope, ready to jimmy it open, thinking only briefly of the envelope upstairs under my pillow.

"Two . . ."

Her gaze moves around the circle.

"Three."

The ripping of paper. Audible gasps of amazement, including one from myself as I flip through a handful of articles from Virginia, Utah, California, Florida. All of them about fatal car crashes that were later proven to be intentional. As well as a piece on the psychology of accidents, quoting Freud, who believed that nothing happens by chance.

And a note:

If you write it the way I think you can, I'd love to make this film.

xx MG

Arlo

Wednesday, January 14

After dinner, Graffam proposes a game of hide-and-seek to pass the time. And even though it feels a little silly at our age, the wine is flowing and the spirit of The Odds is alive. Isaac is easy to find because of his cough, which acts like a trail of breadcrumbs. But he sticks with the game as if we're being graded on it. And who knows, maybe we are.

I move through the shadows of the Moss, free and awake, my brain fizzing from the contents of my envelope. It takes my eyes a moment to adjust to the darkness, so much darker than the night outside these walls. I feel my way from room to room, listening to the sound of my shoes on the wooden floors, on the tile of the kitchen. I pause, kick the shoes off, and continue soundlessly, even though we are accompanied throughout the house by the eeriest soundtrack of classical music I've ever heard.

I feel liberated. A person of great possibility. In one hand, my shoes. In the other, a tumbler of wine because now we are openly drinking and Graffam doesn't care. It's hard to know which is warmer—the sweet sting of the liquid or the feel of the envelope stuffed in my back pocket.

When we get bored of hiding and seeking, we gather in the theater, where Graffam hands out index cards and pencils and then, settling herself on the hearth, tells us it's time for a different sort of game.

"How well," she says, the fire blazing behind her, "do you know your competition? We all have things we don't want anyone else to find out. But what if they did? It's time to divulge your fatal flaw, your Achilles' heel. Write it down and drop it in here." She holds up the same wooden box that we used when casting our votes.

"How is this different from every other challenge you've had us do?" asks Isaac, tongue clearly loosened from the alcohol. "Ever since we got here, it's 'Tell a personal story.' 'Reveal your biggest fear.' 'Stand in the middle of the fucking—in the middle of the highway and say what's on your mind.'"

"Since when does Isaac Williams hate talking about himself?"

He shoots me a murderous look.

"It's all a part of immersing yourselves," Graffam says.

Isaac continues to grumble. "Yeah, I don't like it."

"You don't have to," I tell him. I pick up an index card and pencil and retreat to a corner.

The rest of them do the same until we are separated from each other, the room gone quiet except for the eventual scratching of pencil against paper and Bach's Toccata and Fugue in D Minor.

I stare down at the blank lines of the index card and think about fatal flaws, specifically my own. I could make something up. I wonder if the others are making something up. I raise my head and peer at them. Everyone in deep concentration. Old

Johann Sebastian, meanwhile, is working himself into a frenzy, and the hairs on the back of my neck prickle. There's a reason this piece is used to score so many horror movies.

Finally I write: *I didn't want to come back here, but I didn't have anywhere else to go.*

When I return to the hearth, Graffam is gone. In her place sits the box. I pick it up, drop the index card into it, and am hit with a wave of nausea. I'm worried I've said too much and not enough. It's not a feeling I'm used to—standing naked for all to see.

The others come forward, wearing varying expressions of unease. One by one, they add their cards to the box.

"Where's Graffam?" Effy frowns at me as if I've done something with her.

"I don't know. She left us this." I wave at the box.

"And this." Ness hands me an envelope.

I tear it open and read:

Remove the cards one at a time and guess who the Achilles' heel belongs to.

I look up. "Oh shit."

For a second, I think Ness is going to be sick all over the rug.

"Well," Effy says. "We've come this far."

She shakes up the box and digs out a card. We watch as she unfolds it, as her eyes move over the words.

I am failing out of Brighton and Hove and have been placed on academic probation. I need this class to graduate.

"Don't look at me," Isaac says, trying to sound breezy.

"Isaac," I say. The others agree.

He's about to respond but then snaps his mouth closed. I can feel the wheels of his mind churning. Finally, in a slow, clear voice, as if he's considering every word, "My grades *may* have slipped a little last year. Do I need to ace this class if I'm going to get out of here? Sure." He shrugs, no big deal. "It's hard to be so good at everything. Means you spread yourself thin." He flashes a grin, one that's meant to both charm and distract. "But 'failing out'? 'Academic probation'? Come on. That's a little dramatic."

"So why did you write it?" I ask him.

"I didn't." He doesn't volunteer what he wrote instead.

"This isn't going to work if we aren't willing to come clean," says Effy, her voice lofty, out of reach.

Once again, she reaches into the box.

When I was younger I used to bully other kids so I could be the brave one and nobody would find out.

She looks at me now like she's waiting for me to confess, but then Isaac goes, "Give me that." He snatches the card from her, eyes darting over it, back and forth. "I didn't write this."

"Is it talking about you again?" Ness asks him.

"Nah, dude. Come on. I wrote about my parents disowning my sister because she's marrying a woman. And about the fact that I didn't stand up for her because I was too fucking afraid that they'd disown me too. And I don't know why I'm telling you all this except that I didn't write these other things. Someone is clearly fucking with us."

Ness says, "There's easily, like, fifteen cards in there." We look at her. The box is open. One by one, she spreads them out on the floor.

I use sex to make sure people don't leave.

I lied on my application to Brighton and Hove.

I didn't want to come back here, but I didn't have anywhere else to go.

I'm afraid I don't deserve to be loved.

I plagiarized someone else's work to get into Jan Term.

I killed my best friend.

On and on, one after the other.

"Did any of you write these?" Effy asks, eyes once again on me. The boy she remembers liked to push buttons and then stand back and watch everything implode, but the fact that she thinks I'm still that boy pisses me off.

"Obviously the one about sex is me," I say. "I mean, who doesn't want a piece of this?" I give her a wink.

In that moment I can tell she hates me again. But then Ness stands on wobbly legs, sending the box and a chair toppling over as she does, and bolts up the stairs. Without a word, Effy gets up and follows her.

Which leaves Isaac and me.

I say, "I know you wrote it, you fucking asshole." My tone is surprisingly calm and even.

I killed my best friend.

The words hang there between us.

He shakes his head at me and laughs. Behind the laughter, though, Isaac is angry. Isaac, who could easily flatten me if he wanted to.

He says, "You shouldn't have come back here, Noon. Nobody missed you."

And then he's gone too, leaving me staring into the fire.

Effy

WEDNESDAY, JANUARY 14

Ness is a lump in the middle of her bed, covers pulled over her head. "Go away, Effy," she says from underneath, her voice muffled.

"Come out from there." I give her leg a shake.

She remains in her cocoon, so I shake her again.

"Ness. Vanessa. Cato."

She doesn't answer. And then, from beneath the blanket, I hear her say, "I have to tell you something."

Gradually she emerges, pushing the hair off her face, reaching for her glasses. She stares past me at nothing. I drop onto the bed and wait because sometimes you have to wait on Ness to formulate her thoughts.

"Have you heard of Lucia Quinney Mee?" I shake my head, and she continues. "She was an Irish poet and teacher. A philanthropist who was genuinely beloved by all who knew her. She died when she was twenty in 1972, I think? She was an organ donor before that was common. An *organ donor*,

Effy." She rubs at her eyes, but it's too late, the tears are already spilling down her cheeks. "She was never published in her lifetime, but about a year after her death a volume of her poetry was released."

"Lucia Quinney Mee. Badass. Got it."

"Her work isn't remembered the way it should be. It's beautiful. My favorite is called 'The Dreamer': 'You came back / a great warm Sun / of love and light / of fire and warmth / of possibility / Cannot say how I love you / and how I am afraid.' Anyway. When I applied to Jan Term . . ." She goes quiet. Picks at a thread on the blanket. Sighs. Stares at the wall.

"Ness?"

"I borrowed it. The poem. I didn't actually mean to, but I guess it was just lodged in there." She knocks on her skull. "This is why I shouldn't read other people's poetry when I'm writing, because if I love something, it sticks around. Which is why I don't feel like I should be here. And then tonight . . . The index card . . ." She huffs out a breath, and for a second I think she's going to throw up. I start to go for the trash can, but she says, "I feel sick, but not like that."

I sit back down. "Who knew about this?"

She sniffles. "No one." But she doesn't sound certain.

"You said you borrowed the poem. What does that mean exactly?" I'm suddenly desperate to make this okay for her, even though I feel shattered and bloodless from the stupid fatal flaw game.

"I changed the words, all except one line—'You came back / a great warm Sun.'"

"So that's still you," I say. "Mostly. You can't think . . .

I mean, Graffam wouldn't have chosen you if she didn't see something—"

"Something that belonged to someone else. Even if I'd changed every single line, it was still Lucia Quinney Mee's idea. It belonged to her."

"I just think . . . I mean, I didn't read it, but . . . you must have had a good reason—"

"To steal the work of another poet? Another writer?" Her voice is sharp, mocking.

"Look," I say. "I happen to think you're smart and talented, way more so than you realize. The Ness I know would never do something like this on purpose. Like you said, it was just lodged in your brain . . ."

Ness holds up a hand. "I know you're trying to make me feel better, Eff, but it's not going to work. Not with this."

"Does it help if I remind you that you're a much better person than I am?" I give her a wan smile, the best I can manage. "The way you agonize about things and people. You make me nicer—"

"That's what you tell yourself. And yeah, I do make you nicer." Her tone is sharp. "But you *like* getting to be the strong one. You pretend that things just ricochet right off you, when we both know that's not true."

"I know that," I say, and this time I sound angry. Maybe because I am. Irrationally, breathtakingly angry. In our years of friendship, Ness and I have never fought. We talk about things. We trust each other. "It's just that you can overreact . . . In the scheme of things, this isn't a big deal. You didn't get caught. Just . . . don't do it again."

"Oh my God, Effy. Sometimes you act like no one else knows what it's like to be upset or sad or afraid. It's like you think all those things belong to you. You don't own the rights to loss." She sighs, letting go of the thread, hands now motionless. "I know a lot has happened to you. I can't imagine what it's like not to have parents in this world. To have them and to lose them in such horrible ways. But we've all got something, and even if that something doesn't seem as big to you because of all you've been through, it doesn't mean it's not big to us."

I need Ness and me to be okay. Because if we're okay, I can deal with just about anything. But if we're not, it'll be as if the ground has disappeared . . .

"I'm sorry," I say. "I love you."

She doesn't say it back, just reaches over and blows out the candle. As I turn, I notice something lying at the foot of her bed—loose papers, an assortment of pens. In our dorm on campus, Ness was always falling asleep under homework or on top of homework. By the end of the semester, it was a wonder she wasn't smothered by the weight of it all. I cap one of the pens, gather the others, and set them on the table by the fireplace. In the light it gives off, I look down and recognize my own handwriting. The piece is short, just a paragraph. The thing I wrote for Graffam pinpointing and dissecting fear.

In red ink, words and lines have been crossed out. Critiques scribbled in the right margin. Unconvincing. Needs more feeling. Expand here. Pedantic. Repetitious.

Pedantic?! I think. *Repetitious?!*

I gaze at Ness, now asleep in her bed.

Then back at the paper, where she has rewritten my paragraph in verse, making it infuriatingly, undeniably stronger.

> The rage in me is the only thing
> that makes me feel safe.
> It isn't destructive,
> but beautiful.
> It protects me against this world . . .

AT THE END of the hall, I climb the stairs to my tower. Inside my room, the windows are—unlike those of the rest of the house—unshuttered, and the green glass glows like the sky beyond it.

I tell myself it's just a paragraph. It was never meant to be anything more than that. It isn't the most personal thing I've ever written, and it's not as if I was divulging secrets. But I am angry. So fucking angry that I can only sit here and think about how angry I am.

Anything but my writing, I think. *Criticize my clothes or my hair or the way I laugh. Don't come for my writing. Especially not you, Ness. Writing is supposed to be hallowed and safe and private. Not to be shared unless I want to share it. One of the few sacred places where I'm free.*

I hear footsteps in the hallway, crossing from one room to another. A knock, which I don't answer. The sound of my door opening and closing, and Arlo appears.

"You okay?" he says. He stands in the doorway looking concerned and sincere.

My former therapist will be the first to tell you I don't like to acknowledge weakness in myself or the people I love. Especially in myself. I don't forgive easily. I'm convinced others will let me down. When they prove me right, I feel vindicated because of course I knew it would happen.

But here is Arlo. Asking me if I'm okay. And in this moment, it feels like everything.

"I want to show you something." I unfold myself from the bed, relieved to feel my limbs—my *branches*—working again, and walk to the windows facing the ocean.

The wind is so ferocious, you can see lights far across the water. Arlo stands next to me and takes a deep, languorous breath, as if he's breathing in the night itself.

"Look," I say. And point to the lights on the horizon, beyond Brighton's Woe.

"What is that?"

"Brigadoon."

"Briga . . ."

"A mythical Scottish village that only appears to the outside world—for one day—once every hundred years." At his expression, I shrug. "Gran loves old movies."

"So we think it's Brigadoon."

"We do."

"And what happens in this mythical Scottish village?"

"A lot of singing and dancing. And Gene Kelly, in the movie, he falls in love with a woman who lives there. But he'd have to give up everything to be with her. His friends. His job. His life. So he goes back to New York, but he can't get her out of his mind. Suddenly all those things don't seem as important as they did before."

And suddenly Graffam's game and Ness's rewrite of my paragraph don't seem important either.

I wait for him to make some flip Arlo comment, but he's just watching me.

I say, "Finally, Gene Kelly decides to go after her, but when he gets to Scotland, Brigadoon has evaporated into the mist."

"He shouldn't have left. Speaking as one who knows, he's going to have some regrets."

"He does."

"So what happens?"

"Gene Kelly stands there in the highlands, in the heather, mourning his lost love, and then—through the mist—Brigadoon reappears. In his world, weeks have gone by, but in the village it's the same night he left. The villagers were asleep in their beds. His being there woke them up. Because if you love someone enough, anything is possible." I look at him then to clarify. "That's what they say in the movie. I personally am not that romantic. I also don't believe that's true." Although sometimes I want to.

Surrounded by all this wild beauty and the sound of the ocean, I feel a sudden candy burst of joy in my chest. I look at Arlo. That riot of curling hair, the dancing eyes, even the rangy, loose-limbed way he moves. A voice in me whispers, *Don't let your guard down. Keep your heart separate. Beware of him. Don't let him in any more than you already have.*

"And that's what you wanted to show me?" he says.

"Yes."

I drop onto the bed. There's no movement except for the rattle of the windows. Arlo's grin fades a little, a ghost of itself.

We go silent, and the silence is charged with all the things we aren't saying.

"What do you want?" I ask him. "From me."

The storm, the promise of the film I might make with Graffam, even Ness's betrayal, have made me bolder than usual, more direct, galvanized with a strange kind of power.

His eyes search for something—the exit maybe, the words to say. They travel around the room and out the window until they come to rest on me.

"I want a second chance," he says. "No bullshit. No pretending. No excuses. I want to show up and I want to be there. I want you."

There is nowhere to hide. I consider running like hell. Deep in the woods where he won't follow.

"You lead," he whispers.

This is what I wanted. To be in charge of the situation and my feelings. *Let him tell Graffam about this*, I think.

"I have to ask you something," I say.

He nods, waiting.

"Did you try to vote me out? That night. Before Peter was sent home."

He shakes his head. "No."

I can believe him or I can believe Graffam, and in this moment I want to believe him.

"Have you heard of the call of the void?" I ask. "It's when you get this impulse. To jump. To just step off the edge. Regardless of the danger."

The meaning of my words is clear. If I do this again, with him, that is the risk I'm taking.

"No one leads," I say. "But if you ghost me again, I will kill you."

"I know."

"I should warn you that I seem to have this cold."

"I'm pretty sure I'm willing to risk it."

His mouth tastes like wine and heat and sex. It tastes the same but not the same. Like I've never tasted him before, like he's never touched me before. I pull him down on top of me and my body presses against his, and we are warm, so warm, and his flesh is goose-pimpled, and then so is mine, and it is a kiss I can drown in. So I do.

I have this need to be closer to him, a need that goes beyond my raging teenage hormones. Beyond the call of the void, beyond him, beyond me. It's like this physical, emotional need for *us*.

"Are you sure?" he asks me a little later.

"Yes," I breathe into him.

The way he touches me, just so—here and here and here. As if he knows my blueprints and all the soft, private seams that hold me together. When we are naked, the green glow of the uranium glass lighting our skin, he whispers it again. "Are you sure?"

I wrap my legs around him.

"Yes." Because it only has to be sex, nothing more.

There is a condom, which is pulled out of his pocket. Still in its wrapper, worn and crumpled at the edges, the label faded so that it simply says *JAN* above the faint silhouette of a man's helmeted head.

"First," I say, "how old is this condom?"

"I bought them last summer in a burst of confidence and ambition. I'd just discovered my fifth chest hair, which for obvious reasons made me feel like a man. A thirty-six-count box, which is still unused."

"Second. The reason it's in your pocket tonight?"

"Always be prepared. If it makes you feel better, I've been carrying old Jan around since June." He says this into my neck so that I can feel the words as well as hear them.

"Oh, for God's sake."

I pull him into me, and it's the feeling of air and helium and wide-open skies and blue and stars and moon and sun and flowers and grass and all the lovely things rolled into one deep inhale.

And then, later, *Yes. Yes. Yes.*

It is better this time because we're older and wiser and we know more than we did then. But it's still Arlo. In a good way. Still funny, quirky, exasperating Arlo, an Odd just like me. We don't make promises, not any I'd believe in the cold light of day. That's my rule, I realize now, as if we're playing a game. No promises. No expectations.

"We got better," he says. "You got better."

"You got better too."

"Considering how low I set the bar the first time, I could only go up."

He doesn't say whether there have been other girls. I assume there have been, but it doesn't matter. They're not here. It's just Arlo and me.

He says, "Our couple name is Arffy."

We start to laugh, and then the laughter gives way to

kissing and at some point he says into my neck, "I'm trying not to let myself get too far ahead."

"Don't. Stay here. In this bed. Right now. With me. It's the only moment that exists."

I don't tell him that, in spite of myself, I'm getting ahead too. *What will it be like tomorrow? Or once we leave the Moss? Or next year?*

In a minute he says, "Do you know what I love about cryptozoology?"

"I can't imagine." My voice sounds dreamy, a happy sigh.

"It believes that there are still parts of the world we don't know. That there's still wonder to be found and discoveries to be made."

His words warm me, and I push Graffam's warnings far, far away. I tell myself we have one day every one hundred years, just like Brigadoon, and we need to live in it. Beyond that, no one knows.

"There are no accidents," I hear myself say. "At least not according to Freud."

"I'm not sure I believe that. Or maybe I do."

"Do you ever worry that your life is already written for you?"

"Sometimes."

"I hope not."

"I hope not too."

"So we write it ourselves," I say. "Our lives."

"And we make it fucking extraordinary."

I kiss him.

He kisses me.

Yes. Yes. Yes.

Arlo

Thursday, January 15

I wake up to Effy in her tower room, hair tumbling across her pillow just like the freckles spill across her cheeks. Her eyelids flutter like she's dreaming, and I could lie here watching her forever. The way her fingers grip the blanket, as if it's the only thing keeping her tethered to the earth. The way she's so peaceful when she sleeps, all her edges blurred and softened.

The envelope Graffam gave me promises college interviews at USC, California Institute of the Arts, and UCLA, as well as a sizable donation to Surfers Healing, a surf camp for kids with autism, in Jonah's name, because his sister is autistic. And while it would be great to have even one of these things, much less all four, I'd give them all up to be able to stay here in bed with Effy another hour or two.

But I get up because I'm too awake to stay still. I go into cat-burglar super-stealth mode, sliding out of bed, gathering my clothes, which are flung everywhere. I throw them on haphazardly, somehow nearly knocking myself out in the process. I pause before the window on my way to the stairs. The sky over the ocean is heavy and low, making me think of the marine layer over the Pacific Ocean. The snow is still falling, but the wind has temporarily died down, leaving us enclosed and shut off from everything but ourselves. If Brigadoon is still there, I can't see it.

"Did it vanish into the mist?"

Effy is propped on one elbow, smiling that close-lipped smile.

"I'm pretty sure it hasn't gone anywhere."

She sits up, draped in the blanket, arms wrapped around her knees. "So now that you've gotten what you wanted, you're—what—sneaking out like a cheating husband? Let me guess, I won't see you again for another two years?"

It takes me half a second to realize she's kidding. But in that half a second my heart does this jerky pinball dance, bouncing off the inner walls of my chest, up into my throat, and down again.

"Books did say no sharing beds," I tell her.

"Then you'd better leave."

I do. Half an hour later.

Arlo

Friday, January 16

Graffam and I are the only two not sick in bed—Effy, Ness, Isaac, and even Drea are sealed away in their rooms with some kind of flu. To conserve firewood, the two of us basically move into the theater. We spend the morning there, listening to the creaking of the house, which seems to shudder with every gust of wind.

The clock in the room chimes ten.

Then eleven.

Then twelve.

Graffam and I alternately talk and write. At some point, I get up to stretch my legs, do some calisthenics, eat some lunch. When I come back, she's still there.

"Can I read you a few lines?" I ask.

"Of course," she says.

"'Here's something I've learned in my seventeen years on earth. You can't live in loss. As much as it takes you over, creating hollows that will always be there, sometimes the sun breaks through, even if it's only for an hour. Because eventually all things end, don't they, no matter how hard you try to hold on to them.'"

Now that I hear them out loud, they're just words. But Graffam is nodding at me.

"Good," she says. "It's honest."

I bloom a little in spite of myself and, feeling emboldened, say, "I'm here to reciprocate if you'd like to share anything you might be writing."

Her expression doesn't change, but there's a subtle shift in the air. "That is the one thing I won't do. I never talk about what I'm working on while I'm working on it." Her eyes hold mine for a beat too long.

BY EVENING, I'VE put my laptop and sketchbook aside and am rereading *The Picture of Dorian Gray* because the Moss—especially the Moss in a storm—is the perfect setting for it. Dorian, on the encouragement of his friend Lord Henry Wotton, sells his soul in exchange for eternal youth and beauty, making a deal with the devil that his portrait will age instead of him. And then he commits every depraved act he can think of, getting away with literal murder as that portrait grows more and more grotesque, a reflection of his wicked soul.

I read the book last year in World Lit when I was a junior at Santa Monica High, and our teacher talked a lot about what makes a monster. Her belief being that Lord Henry is just as guilty as Dorian himself because Henry is the one who corrupts him. Same with Victor Frankenstein—he is the one who creates the monster.

When Graffam sees me reading it, she tells me her production company is considering a film adaptation.

"Wouldn't it be cool," I say, "if Moss Hove really did have a Dorian-style portrait somewhere in this house?"

For a change of scenery, we conduct a search. Cold, dark room after cold, dark room, our shadows enormous by candlelight. And while we find painting after painting of Moss Hove, he remains young and handsome in all of them.

I wait for Graffam to praise me or tell me yet again that I'm her favorite. When she doesn't, I make myself consider the cost of winning. *Would it really be winning,* I ask myself, *if you won Jan Term and lost Effy?*

Not that I have Effy. But I've managed—in spite of my fucked-upness—to get back into her good graces. At least, she doesn't seem to hate me anymore. And even though I've only just gotten there with her, I don't want to revert to where we were when we started Jan Term.

As Graffam and I make our way once more to the theater, I say, "We're on our own." This is me being deep and introspective and the tiniest bit lonely for Jonah, my family, and Effy, up in her tower room.

Graffam manages to give me a smile and then spread that smile over the entire room. A glimmer of sunshine in the gloom, and in spite of everything, I feel myself warming under it.

"Always," she says, and it's clear that she means more than just the here and now.

After she turns in, I light a candle and wander the halls

like a ghost. In the solarium, I stand beneath the skylight and look up, but all I can see is white. Then I wander my way to the game room, where I stand in front of the wall of framed photos, searching for Graffam. I hold up the candle, flame dancing, until I find the Ruler of the Forest for 1995.

The girl in the photo is formal but smiling. Her hair light, not dark. Her eyes blue, not brown. *Lara Leonard*, the plaque reads. Even though they don't look alike, there's something in her expression that reminds me of Effy. *The eyes*, I think. They seem to look through me.

Lara is the only person in all the photos not wearing a crown. *Honorary Winner*, it says beneath her name. The actual winner—Graffam—is nowhere to be found. I wonder if her desire to win started when she was my age or if it was something that came with the public shaming she endured after Timothy Hugh Martin, his name cleared, was released from prison.

I climb down into the reading nook, wishing I could get really, really drunk or, even better, go to the water and feel the spray. Instead I sink onto the daybed and stare at the mural on the wall. If I stare at it long enough, here in this small space, I can almost pretend I'm in the woods.

I set the candle down beside the daybed and pick up my book. I read for an hour, maybe more, until the candle nearly burns itself out. With the faltering light, I have this cold, creeping feeling, like the outside is seeping in through the cracks in the walls.

I get to my feet and collect my things and glance down at the Scrabble board. Where a second word has joined the first:

This is the point when I should get the hell out of Dodge, no looking back, until I'm locked in the safety of my bedroom. The words crawl across and then into my skin, burrowing deep into my bones.

The fuck.

"Okay," I say aloud, just to hear a voice, even if it's my own. "Whoever you are. I'll play your little game." Isaac, most likely, trying to scare away the competition.

Even as my mind is saying, *But what if it isn't Isaac?*

With a shaking hand, I sort through the rest of the letters in the velvet bag until I find an *H* and a *Y* and place these after the *W*. So it reads:

Effy

Friday, January 16

I stay in my room all day and struggle to work. I've pulled all the Dad letters I want to use—263 pages' worth—and have begun the process of arranging them in a sort of order. Not just chronological, but thematic; sometimes a letter written when I was ten relates to something that happened when I was sixteen. Collectively, they form a tapestry of interwoven timelines, flashing forward and flashing back. The first chapter is the letter my father sent me last fall after his release.

Some are hard to read. I was confused and sad at eight, nine, ten. Angry at twelve and thirteen. Alternately defiant and sweet, almost nostalgic, at fourteen. Then, suddenly, at fifteen and sixteen, life got brighter and more expansive—except for Arlo breaking my heart. There are a good dozen letters ranting about the stupidity and fickleness of boys.

As I arrange the puzzle pieces, I can see that Graffam was right. There's something here.

When my head is too heavy to work, I check on Ness, the sickest of us all. Inside her room, she is sleeping restlessly, her breath ragged. She's still wearing her glasses, and I tiptoe across the floor and remove them, setting them on the bedside table next to an unpainted sculpture, just a few inches tall, of a woman. One of Drea's Petunias. I feel this weird sting of surprise, as if I've just discovered Ness has a secret life.

I pick up the statue. Inscribed on the bottom of her feet: *Ness, you are limitless!* I feel a pang—not jealousy exactly, but a kind of envy mixed with homesickness. I think of Graffam telling me Ness is holding me back. And to *watch* my back. It's not a thought I want in my brain. Now that it's there though, I can't shake it.

"You could never hold me back," I whisper to her sleeping figure, and then crawl back to my own room.

Throughout the day, Graffam delivers hot tea, soup, and ginger ale. Before she leaves me, she says, "There's a steadfastness in you that I admire. It's an important quality for what you want to do. Fidelity to yourself, to those who believe in you, is everything."

I'm not prepared for her words, and the backs of my eyes start to sting. I lie there blinking because—no matter how sick I feel—I'll be damned if I'm going to cry in front of Meredith Graffam.

And then she says, "'We know what we are, but know not what we may be.'"

The words belong to the Ophelia I was named after. A Shakespearean heroine who ends up mad and then drowns herself. The reason I go by Effy instead.

"No matter what happens, remember this is only your beginning."

She disappears down the stairs, and I hear the door close. And then, silently, I start to cry.

In a little while, I reach for the tray. The ginger ale is the only thing I can keep down.

Later. Arlo comes. I want to be mad at him, but I can't remember why.

I lie with my head in his lap, and he strokes my hair the way Gran does whenever I don't feel well. I should tell him to leave. This is not just sex. This is not sex at all. But the feel of him is warm and comforting, like a blanket.

Gradually, I drift off. When I wake up, he is curled around me like a fortress.

Arlo

Saturday, January 17

The storm has come and gone, leaving the Moss and the forest and the ocean swallowed by fog. With the shutters open, the house feels awake again. Graffam has prepared lunch for us, and we eat in the morning room, looking out broad windows at a world that feels crisp and new under a flesh blanket of snow. Snow, snow everywhere.

Now we're piled into Wesley's four-wheel-drive truck, heading toward Highway 127. Effy sits up front in the middle, Graffam on her right. Meanwhile, in the cramped back seat, Ness, Isaac, and I are jammed together, bundled in our winter finest. They sniffle on either side of me, and we don't talk.

I watch Effy, her head bent toward Graffam. They are deep in conversation, like old friends. Effy erupts into bright laughter. She seems lighter after her illness, like if someone rolled down a window, she might float away.

My eyes move to Graffam, this person who was brought here to teach us about story in her own—let's call it *avant-garde*—

way. It's unsettling to be riding toward some unknown destination where we could be asked to run into traffic or jump off a cliff or swim the Atlantic till we hit the Irish coast. If this were a regular class during a regular semester, I'd drop it and move on. But I've come this far. For once, Arlo Ellis-Noon is going to see something through.

Even with the snowy roads, it takes us less than an hour to get to the highway. At the northern entrance of Murton, Wesley pulls over onto the shoulder, where I can just see our ghosts standing on that yellow line, Ramon turning toward the woods and disappearing.

"Let the Hunger Games begin," I say. "And may the odds be ever in your favor."

The others—including Effy—frown at me.

"What?" I say. "Get it? *Odds*, like *The Odds*?"

Effy, Isaac, and Ness pile out of the vehicle, ignoring me. Wesley waits behind the wheel, engine idling, as the rest of us join Graffam on the roadside, an ocean dividing Effy and Ness, Isaac pretending the rest of us don't exist. We are four separate countries. The only thing connecting us is the very palpable sense of dread.

I don't know what I'm expecting—another trust exercise? But as Graffam stands by the bed of the truck, I see the four backpacks lying there. My first thought—one I'm not wild about—is that she's going to tell us we're camping overnight in the forest.

"The key to dramatic writing is conflict," she says. "Without conflict you have no action, without action you have no character growth, without character growth you have no story. Look at Isaac. His external conflict is that his parents don't approve of him being here pursuing his art. His internal conflict is the need to do this for himself. Or Arlo, who's conflicted about being anywhere at all. Your characters need to be in opposition to something or someone. The more you throw at your character, the better."

As I listen, I glance from Graffam to the woods.

"Your external objective is to find your way to the Moss. I have a backpack for each of you. Inside that backpack, you'll find an index card listing an additional objective, chosen specifically for you. This may conflict with the objectives of the others. Also inside each bag is a flashlight, a camera, energy bars, and water."

"How long do you expect us to be out here?" I ask.

"As long as it takes."

Isaac says, "So first person back wins the contents of their envelope?"

"Not necessarily." There's an unsettling sheen to Graffam's eyes that reminds me of one of Moss Hove's stuffed birds. "The external objective isn't nearly as important as the internal one. That's usually the case. So while it doesn't hurt to come back first, it's not required to win."

"How do we win then?" asks Effy.

But Graffam doesn't answer her. Instead she says, "Film is collaborative, but writing can be solitary." Her face, within the halo of her hood, looks disembodied, as if it is floating there. "You have to learn to be alone with yourself. The sooner you learn that you are your best, most reliable resource—your only resource—the stronger your work will be."

I don't like the sound of these words. I catch Effy's eye, and her face furrows the way it does when she's concentrating.

Graffam tells us about the film adaptation of *The Lie*. How she didn't trust herself or her story and it turned into something completely different and terrible, nothing she wanted to put her name on. It was a lesson, she says, that she will never forget.

"It wasn't the first moment I realized that you can only count on yourself, but it was the most profound. As we know, people will let you down. They will promise you things, especially as you leave here and go out into the world, but they won't deliver. Sometimes because they never meant to in the first place, and sometimes because things fall through. People will break your heart. But here's the good news: You have you. Don't let yourself down."

It feels like a weird mishmash of graduation speech and sermon, and there's something in her voice that's a little too emphatic, a little too overzealous.

"These will help you on your way." She hands each one of us a GPS tracker. "The main trail here at the entrance branches off into four smaller trails. You will each choose a separate path and follow that back to the Moss."

"Wait, we're seriously doing this?" says Isaac, face frozen in a grin. "You're sending us into Murder Wood?"

"It's going to be dark before long," adds Effy just as I say, "Into the wild, like that guy in Alaska whose body they found in a school bus?" Christopher McCandless. I remember his name from the book.

"Yes, Arlo, but unlike McCandless, you're going to return." Graffam's tone is matter-of-fact, even upbeat.

"What if we get lost?" asks Ness.

"We'll find you if anything happens. That is a promise.

Remember, Ramon made it back to campus in less than two hours—and he didn't have a GPS or a backpack of supplies."

"And if we don't want to do this?" says Ness.

"If you don't participate, you give up your chance of winning. Surely you understand the importance of participation, Ness."

The slam of a car door, and Wesley appears. He opens the truck bed and hauls out the backpacks. Each has a different-colored zip tie. Mine is red. When Wesley hands it to me, he whispers, "Half a mile in, the four trails meet. Wait for each other there so you're not alone."

I look at him, then at Graffam, who is showing the others how to use the GPS.

Wesley passes out the rest of the backpacks. And then we're off. Four of us. Four separate trails, Graffam calling after us in a haunting singsong, "'And into the forest I go, to lose my mind and find my soul . . .'"

A shiver runs through me. I dig the index card from the outer pocket of the bag.

Don't let the others win. Do not stop to help them. Do not stop at all. You alone deserve this. Think of Jonah. Think of everything that brought you here.

Why would they need my help? What does Graffam think is going to happen? I wonder what the other cards say and how in the hell we're supposed to win this little game. I tell myself we've all got the same shot here. Then again, Graffam made us all take separate trails, and that could give any one of us an advantage.

I push the thought away. Focus on the great outdoors. On the fact that I feel energized and terrified. Like I'm in Outward Bound or one of those wilderness shows. The blood pumps through my veins, and my limbs are carrying me forward. I am grateful for my thudding heart and my body and these feet and these legs and these arms and this brain. I am grateful because I'm here and I get the chance to do this.

HALF AN HOUR later, maybe an hour, I still haven't come across any fork in the trail. My head swivels back and forth at every sound. The crack of tree limbs. The snap of underbrush. What sounds like the banging of sticks in the distance. Melting ice, I tell myself.

We have trees in California, but not like this. Our trees are friendlier, more laid-back. Palm trees. California oaks. Bottle-brushes. Jacarandas, which turn the streets purple in spring. Even the giant redwoods. The sky is the important thing out west.

The trees of Murton Wood are humorless and too tall. Cloaked in white, they block out the sky and lean in as if they're listening.

Just look up.

The hoot of an owl, melancholy, lonely. A distant rustling. The high, lonesome cry of a bird. I am not a person who feels at home in nature. There are too many things out there that will kill you because it's what they're programmed to do. Spiders, snakes, bears, mountain lions. And whatever native predators they have here.

I wonder what old Barry the Uber driver's doing right about now and if he'd recognize me in the wild, in the woods.

If they could see me now, I think.

The morning after Jonah died, it felt like waking up in a world I didn't recognize. Just the day before I'd gotten up early, eaten two bowls of cereal, texted Jonah to say I'd meet him at the beach—same as every other day. I couldn't understand how I'd gone from the regular, everyday world to this new one.

Now, out here in the woods, I feel that same sense of disbelief. To find myself alone in this place. To imagine all the possibilities unfurling before me like the Emerald City, if only I can make it out of here first.

I try humming. Whistling. Talking to myself just to hear a voice. I tell myself jokes, which is anticlimactic. After a while I don't bother repeating the punch lines because I already know them. I think of Effy's naked body. The smoothness of her skin. Her leg thrown over mine.

The deeper I go into the woods, the fewer birds I see or hear, which makes me feel like the only life-form, which is both good and bad. I don't venture off the trail, even where it's buried in snow. The fog has turned the trees wet, so that it looks like they're weeping or bleeding. I see the old service gate up ahead, the first stage of walls. Graffam has left it open for us.

A shadow passes above me. Large and black. A crow.

Crows can remember faces. Someone told me this once, or else I read it somewhere. I wonder what kind of omen it is if you see a crow flying over a forest. If movies and books have taught me anything, it's that crows always symbolize something.

I fumble to turn on the camera, slip the lens cap into my

pocket, and press the record button, leaving the strap hanging around my neck so the camera bumps against me as I walk. I imagine the footage—glitchy and *Blair Witch*–ish, my voice in the background, talking to myself, this other version of myself, keeping myself company, reminding myself of this link to the outside world.

"You're okay," I say aloud. "We're just taking a walk. Nothing to see here. Just you. And this unhaunted trail that is free of murderers and predators and, probably, Bigfoot." As much as I'd like to glimpse a Bigfoot one day, now is not that time. "And, somewhere out here, the girl you love. The one you'd do anything for. Even throw yourself on a murderous clown or flesh-eating zombie if it meant saving her life. Because that's how important she is to you."

Oh shit.

My brain is sparking like it's hooked up to jumper cables.

I love Effy.

Oh shit, shit.

I've maybe always loved Effy. Even after I fucked things up with her and went away and didn't see her for two years. I told Jonah about her, and why would I do that? Some girl I knew for three weeks back when I was fifteen. I used to think about her and wonder what she was doing, who she was with, if she thought about me. Whenever I fooled around with someone else—granted, the list is short—I always compared them to Effy Green. Even when I never thought I'd see her again.

It's more than that though. I like the me she sees. Around her, I don't feel like I'm missing some crucial piece that everyone else has. I feel like a sunny day in Malibu with an ocean breeze coming off the waves and a good book in my hand. Like that moment when the tide flips and is starting to come in, and you feel the shock of the water, always colder than you remember, but it's a good shock because it reminds you that you're fully here. And your best friend is alive on the beach and laughing at you and your wet paperback. And you close your eyes under the sun and breathe it all in. That's how it is with Effy.

I look into the camera and keep on talking.

So. Yeah. Apparently I love Effy. If they find my lifeless body in the spring thaw, at least I've said it. I love you, Effy. I've loved you since I was fifteen. And I'm pretty sure I will still love you at the end of my life. Which hopefully isn't today.

A vibrating sound that I feel as well as hear. I go still. The vibrating again.

It takes me several seconds to realize it's me.

Not me, specifically, but something on my person.

I check my coat and then pull off the backpack, slinging it around to face me. I search the pockets. Emergency blanket. Flashlight. Protein bars. First-aid kit. So many pockets. I set the backpack on the ground, bend over it, and dig.

I find it in a small zipped pouch in one of the inner compartments. My cell phone. Fully charged. And, wonder of wonders, I have service. I swipe to the home screen and check my notifications. Texts from Aaron. My parents. As the phone comes to life, the notifications pop up one after another. And a number I don't recognize. The text was sent this morning.

> Hey. If you see this, call me. I'd rather talk live. Sorry I didn't say goodbye.

And then, right after, a second text.

> This is Ramon by the way.

Effy

SATURDAY, JANUARY 17

I love the world like this—the gloomy melancholy of winter. I drink it in, the stark white snow contrasted with the black-brown trees, the rawness of the wind. A temporary deadening of the earth until spring comes again.

Murton Wood is 11,000 acres. It's tradition for upperclassmen to scare the absolute shit out of first-years with stories about people who've been lost in these woods and the girl who was murdered here. Most are just stories, but Lara Leonard is not. So who's to say what's fact and what's fiction?

I take a swig of water and check the GPS to see how far I've gone, how far it is to the fork in the trail. If it actually exists. I don't need to look at my index card again to remember what it says.

Don't let the others win. Do not stop to help them. Do not stop at all. You alone deserve this. Think of your mom. Think of your dad. Think of why you're here.

The fog is spreading, filling the gaps between trees so that the world fuses together like a great, endless wall. I walk faster, hating the fear that's gnawing at my brain. *You don't get scared*, I remind myself. But I can't shake the feeling that I'm not alone.

I stop walking.

I turn around.

The trail behind me is empty.

I keep walking.

But the feeling remains—something or someone is following me.

"Arlo?" I call. "Ness? Isaac?"

When no one answers, I tell myself it's all in my head.

The fog is rolling outward. I watch as it swallows the trail and then me, so that I can only see my foot when it's directly below me. The moment I step forward, it disappears with a crunch of snow.

Before he crashed into that tree, my father had never even had a speeding ticket. He grew up a farm kid, driving ATVs and four-wheelers from the age of twelve. This is what he told the police, as if to prove the accident was a fluke, something that happened *to* him, as if that made him less culpable for killing his wife.

"The accident was my fault," he said at his trial. "But I never meant to hurt anyone. I'm going to live with this for the rest of my life."

The *snapping* of a branch from somewhere nearby. Or maybe in the distance. Out here it's easy to lose your bearings, to feel like everything is close and far at once. My mind is as foggy as the air.

I turn, even though I can no longer see the trail. I remind myself that Ness is somewhere nearby. And Isaac. And Arlo. I could shout or scream and someone would hear me and come.

Somewhere to my left—*snap*.

Somewhere to my right—*snap*.

Something rustles in the brush.

Something whistles overhead, in my ear, fluttering my hair.

And then there's a crashing of branches. I can't tell where it's coming from. I turn around and around, but I can't see anything, only the white mist, only myself.

"Arlo!"

"Ness!"

"Isaac!"

My voice bounces off the fog and back to me. Like me, it is trapped in here. If I didn't know better, I'd think that Graffam had staged the fog and the sounds, or summoned them like the great and powerful witch she is, to illustrate her point—we only have ourselves. I glimpse fragments of things. Sky. Trees. Snow. Snow. Snow. God, there's so much snow.

And then—from somewhere in the distance—a gunshot. A single deafening *crack* that shakes the ground and the trees and the sky and me. A *crack* that scatters the birds and stops time.

I've heard that sound before—in the Maine woods during hunting season.

I start to run. I hear only the pounding of my feet and my breath, ragged and shallow. And the echo of that *crack*.

I tell myself, *You're safe, you're fine, you're not alone.*

I run, I run, I run.

I don't know if anything's chasing me—if anything ever was—but I run until I come to the walls surrounding Moss Hove's water garden, now little more than a swamp.

So many walls. Walls locking in the forest, walls locking in the Moss, walls locking in the swamp. A shooting pain in my shoulder, and I am cold, so cold. My head is heavy, like a stone, as if the fog is pressing in on it.

I turn right, walking the perimeter wall. I have to get warm, find some sort of cover, because the temperature will drop as it gets darker, and if I don't get moving, I might as well just give in to the fog and the cold.

Another gunshot rattles the trees and my teeth and my pounding heart.

Five minutes, ten minutes—I keep going. The world tilts. When I don't fall over, I turn to look behind me. I know without seeing them that the trees are out there, tall and dark—like an army—stretching in all directions. For the first time, the thought of them is almost comforting. Unlike this fog, which has erased everything, the trees are solid and real and familiar.

If the GPS is accurate, I've lost the trail and—worse—I'm heading away from the Moss. I feel butterflies stir somewhere deep and distant. My mouth goes dry. So dry I can't talk or scream, not that anyone would hear me. I'm no longer thinking about winning. I'm thinking about getting out of these woods.

Another thing I've lost track of—time.

The trail disappears and reappears. Now you see it, now you don't. I strain my ears for the sounds of the sea. I walk for what feels like miles. My feet ache. My limbs ache. My mind aches. And so does my heart. Because no matter what Graffam says, sometimes it gets exhausting to only have yourself. Sometimes you want more than just you.

Arlo

SATURDAY, JANUARY 17

In the distance, I hear the sharp, unmistakable explosion of a gunshot. I freeze and send up a prayer to you, my best friend, to watch over me and make sure I don't get my head blown off.

I have to scramble back the way I came, north toward the highway, to get a cell signal. I go as far as the old service gate, which is now closed and padlocked. I pace back and forth along its periphery, the phone to my ear. After three attempts, it finally connects. As it starts to ring, the time is 4:22. I can already feel a chill in the air from the waning daylight. I have ground to make up, which means I'll be getting back well after dark now.

He picks up on the third ring. "Hello?"

"Ramon? It's Arlo."

"Hey. You got your phone."

"Yeah. It was in my backpack. I don't know how it— Jesus.

It doesn't matter. I'm sorry about what happened with Graffam. Sorry we didn't get to say goodbye—"

"I was in the woods for almost two days—"

"Okay, you old jokester. You almost got me—"

"Two fucking days. No search party. Nothing—"

"But. Wait. You're serious—"

"Yes, I'm serious. Christ—"

"But you weren't missing. You were in the dorm. You walked back to campus Monday and told Books. You made it there in under two hours."

"Who told you that?" His voice goes higher, louder.

"Graffam."

"Graffam." It sounds like a four-letter word. "She told you I was okay? That I was, what, safe and sound?"

"Something like that."

"Yeah. Of fucking course. Listen to me, Arlo, where are you right now?"

"Murton. The woods. We're doing this challenge. She kind of turned us loose in here and was like, *Good luck to you, try not to freeze to death in there*. Well, not those words exactly, but the meaning was very much the same, and I'm pretty sure someone is hunting me—"

"Arlo! Shut up. Just shut the hell up." His voice is sharp and loud. "Graffam isn't who she says she is. You can't trust her. The guy she sent to prison—the one she said killed her friend during the—"

"*The Hunt*," I say. "The Wild Hunt. That was the thing that precipter—that precipera—that started it all." My brain feels sluggish, slushy with cold.

"My mom, she has a fixer, this guy who makes problems go away like they never happened." He's talking faster now, as if we're running out of time. "My first year at school I cheated on a test. He dug up info on the teacher, and instead of me getting expelled, the teacher got fired. *No one* knows about that. But Graffam does. I don't know how—"

"Wait—" The call drops. *Fuck. No, no, no.* I eye the service gate then start to climb. At the top, I hold on for dear life with one arm and wave the phone around with the other. The last thing I'm thinking about now is winning some stupid competition. I just want the bloody phone to work and not to fall to my death. I'm not all that schooled on hypothermia, but I'm pretty sure this is how it starts—racing heart, disorientation, bodily functions shutting down. Above me the sky is darkening. Night is coming. Which means colder temperatures and a trail that's harder to find.

Three minutes later, we're back on the line, Ramon talking like the call never dropped. "So I had him look into Graffam. I didn't like her from the start, especially not after what she told us about her friend, about her story. That story that launched her career. He was the one who told me about Timothy Hugh Martin. The guy's dead now, but he wasn't the only one to claim he was innocent at the time. The family of Lara Leonard, the girl who was killed, they believed it too—"

"Believed what?"

"That this Martin guy, the one she ID'd, didn't do it."

"We know that. The world knows that. What does that have to do with us?"

"Graffam was the only witness. There were other students in the woods that night playing that game, but Graffam was the only one who saw anything. It was her word against his. She may have been only eighteen, but she went after the guy hard. Adamant that he was the killer."

"So maybe he actually—"

"You're not listening. He had an alibi. But she said she saw him there, when we know he was somewhere else."

"So, what, she pinned it on him?"

"Yes. And, Arlo, she knew him."

"Timothy Hugh Martin?"

"He worked at the doughnut shop in town. I guess she worked there too for a while. Their time there overlapped."

I don't say anything because I'm trying to make sense of it all.

"Arlo?"

"Yeah, man, I'm here. I'm just . . . This is a lot, and I'm pretty sure I'm dying of exposure—"

"Where are you right now?"

"You were really lost in the woods for two days?"

"Yes, and she didn't tell anyone. When I got to school and told Books I'd been lost for forty-eight hours, he went out to the Moss to make sure everyone was all right."

"She said he came to the house because he wanted us to go back to campus, you know, to wait out the storm . . . So why would she tell us that you were okay—"

The call cuts out again. This time I don't bother calling back because I know enough. Even though I feel like I know nothing.

As if I'm watching a film of my own life, I suddenly see the aerial view of this scene—the earth blacked out from the forest to the ocean, the Moss and the lighthouse the only lights for miles. And on the outside of all that darkness, Ramon. Safe in his dorm at Brighton and Hove after being lost for two days in the woods. No one looking for him. No one even aware he was missing.

Effy

SATURDAY, JANUARY 17

I am still running. Sound shifts and moves like refracted light, bouncing toward me, then away. In the darkness, the only sign of the trail is a slender break in the trees, and I skate along it until I smack into something. A tree blocks my way. I shove it with all my might and it falls backward, and then the tree shouts my name, its breath ragged and swift. "Effy," it calls, reaching for me. It crawls along the forest floor, limbs outstretched like spider legs. It swipes at me, and I smell sulfur and earth and blood.

In the fog, I know it is a false tree, one that is only pretending to be a tree so that it can catch me, and I dash away from it fast as I can until the forest grows thicker, darker, more tangled, and I can no longer see the sky. The gravity of the earth holds me up, but it feels like any moment I could go hurtling away into space.

"Dammit, Effy."

Arlo shakes my arms until I see him there, a bloody nose

from where I elbowed him. "There was a gunshot," I say. I can smell him—the fear, the adrenaline—and I know right away something's wrong. His expression has gone strange and hard. His easy smile is nowhere to be seen.

WE FIND NESS up ahead at the fork. There is a scratch on her cheek, but otherwise she looks like herself. Good old Ness. My best friend, regardless of the thousand little paper cuts we've inflicted on one another. She throws her arms around me, and I bury my face in her shoulder. And I can't remember why we ever let things get weird or strained between us.

She starts chattering about the gunshot. Did I hear it? Where do I think it came from? Who do I think it was? She was terrified, so terrified, that whoever it was would come for her, that for some reason they were tracking her.

Arlo interrupts to ask if she's seen Isaac.

"He was ahead of me," she says. "I caught a glimpse of him through the trees."

"He might be back already, at the Moss," I say, but Arlo just pushes on like he has a homing device. He doesn't use the GPS, just follows some inner compass that's telling him where to go.

"What's wrong?" Ness asks.

Without a word, Arlo holds out his phone and then tells us to check our backpacks. Ness and I dig around in them until we come up with our own.

"How did they . . . ?" I start. "Did Graffam put them in here?"

"Ramon is fine," Arlo says. "I talked to him. He was

missing for forty-eight hours in the woods. No one searched for him. He had to find his way out. He's on campus now."

"But Graffam said he was okay." Ness sounds as confused as I am. "Why would she lie to us?"

"Because, Ness, that's what people do," he says a little too harshly.

He shows us the text. Then he shows us the outgoing calls. He tells us that this is why—according to Ramon—Dean Booker came out to the Moss on Wednesday. Not to persuade us to go back to campus to wait out the storm. To find out why Graffam didn't report one of his students missing. Arlo clicks his phone on, off, on, off. A nervous habit. When he sees me watching him, he shoves it into the pocket of his jeans.

"Look," he says, "what we know is that she lied about Ramon being okay when he wasn't. And she kept that from us. We just don't know why."

Ness says, "She's an actor. I mean, in addition to being a writer, director, and all the rest. Maybe she's lied about other things."

There's this poem by Sylvia Plath:

I shut my eyes and all the world drops dead;
I lift my lids and all is born again.
(I think I made you up inside my head.)

That last line has always made me think of my parents. But now I think of the past ten days. Of Meredith Graffam. Of the way she understands and listens and inspires and cares. Of the film we might make. All of it real.

Right?

Because it has to be.

"Ramon isn't exactly the most reliable person," I say, hating the way it sounds.

"I don't know," Arlo says. "I don't know."

The three of us decide to push on. I feel brutally, painfully awake now. I can feel the salt air, the way it nests in my hair and starts to frizz the ends. A pang because all of it—the air, the waves, my frizzing hair—reminds me of home and Gran, and even though I'm nearly eighteen, I miss her and our rambling house with its jumbled garden of flowers. Every kind of flower you can imagine because Gran loves color. I miss the warm, bitter smell of the coffee she brews in the morning and again in the afternoon when she's working on a deadline. I miss the sound of the sea outside my bedroom as the waves dash against the rocks. I miss the way Gran hums to herself, songs from a long time ago, back when she was my age.

I lose myself in the thought of her because it's a better place to be.

I think I made you up inside my head.

Gradually the path narrows, and the ground rises up on either side of us. The air here is thick with sulfur, and the earth beneath the snow is soft. We scramble up the embankment to get our bearings.

"What is that?" Ness wrinkles her nose at the swamp below.

"The water garden," I say. It disappears into the horizon, encircled by a stone wall at least six or seven feet high. "It must run for miles because I crashed into that wall earlier."

One by one, we slide back down the hill to the path below.

Under the canopy of trees, the ground slants at precarious angles, and our feet become tangled in the undergrowth. No one is talking now. I bang my foot on something—a stone greened with moss, followed by another, this one nearly as tall as I am. *What if we can never leave the forest?*

The walls are wild with moss and ivy. We can't see above them or beyond them, and it's either keep going or turn back.

"Why would they block it off?" Ness trails her fingers along the wall.

Arlo and I don't answer because we are out of answers. Minutes later we come to a moss-covered door. I've heard the expression *My heart was in my throat*, but for the first time I know what it feels like. My heart feels as if it's literally in my throat as a voice from inside the walls shouts "Hey" over and over. *Hey hey hey.*

"Isaac?" I pull at the door, which is wedged shut and overgrown with lichen, as if it hasn't moved in decades. Ness and Arlo move in to help me, Isaac banging on the other side.

We pull and pull until the door gives enough for a body to slide through. When Isaac doesn't come out, we go in.

Inside, there's an eerie stillness. I've seen photos of the water lilies, the paddleboats that looked like swans, the flowers blooming on the banks in its glory days. Now the garden is just a dead, murky place.

Isaac is bent over his backpack, contents strewn everywhere. "Did you hear the gunshot?" He starts shoving things inside, then swings the backpack over a shoulder. "I felt like I was being hunted."

"Did you see the shooter?" Arlo asks.

"No, but I could hear them." He's out of breath and furious, his voice too loud. "The only thing that kept me from going after them is that Murder Wood is the last place I want to die."

Before we can tell him about Ramon, Isaac disappears through the door. His words lingering in the air, we rejoin the path and find him standing still, looking left and right, lost.

Arlo takes the lead. "This way." The rest of us fall behind him, single file.

We march in silence. After a few minutes, I hear a high, earsplitting cry, and catch sight of a seagull soaring above us.

"Arlo," Ness calls, as if he's our captain. She waves at the bird.

He looks up. The four of us start to run after it, hoping it will lead us to the sea. We tumble over roots and other unseen obstacles, and it feels as if the forest is trying to stop us, like it wants to yank us down into the earth.

And then—suddenly—we emerge from the wood.

The trees are a dividing line. Inside Murton, a heavy fog. Outside, the mist all but disappears. I pause for a second, taking in the sudden openness of the world, watching the gull fly away.

"Wait," I say before we go any farther. "What were the instructions? On your cards?" One by one we produce them, out of pockets, out of the backpacks. Four cards. Four messages.

Don't let the others win. Do not stop to help them. Do not stop at all.

Each one the same with only slight variation.

Isaac swears under his breath. Without a word, Arlo holds out his hand, and I place my card in his palm. Ness and Isaac do the same. He adds his to the stack and then slides them into his coat pocket. "For my scrapbook," he says, not smiling. And then he tells Isaac about Ramon.

No longer single file, we traipse through the snow in the direction of the sea cliffs. The windows of the Moss are illuminated, which means the power has been restored. The house materializes ahead of us like a beacon. In that moment, I'm grateful for its solidity and the strength of its walls, built a century ago.

My muscles ache, my bones ache. I am cold and wet and scratched and scraped. I can't feel my fingers or my toes. I want to take a hot bath and crawl into bed. I want to sleep for days.

Then—"Graffam," Isaac says.

A figure stands on the edge of the cliff, surveying the vast night sky.

She turns, raising a hand. We don't wave back.

The hand lingers in the air for a second or two. And then she's walking toward us—beaming, I realize. She hugs us, one by one, and I'm startled by the contact, by the realness of her. I breathe her in—her strength, her sturdiness, her earthy, feminine scent.

"You worked together," she says. She starts to laugh, and it sounds like music.

In spite of everything, I want to join her. But the four of us remain quiet and restrained, and I know we are thinking the same thing: *Can we trust her?*

Graffam tells us to rest, shower, eat, get warm, take care of ourselves. No mention of who, if anyone, has won today's challenge.

We, in turn, don't bring up Ramon. Instead we head toward

the house, and as I start to walk away, I feel a hand touching my sleeve.

"Effy," Graffam says. "A word?"

Arlo hesitates, but I wave him onward. I watch as the others disappear inside. And then, before she can say anything, I suddenly feel this surge of energy.

"How did you get through to Dean Booker when he told you Ramon was back on campus? I tried making a call the other night, but the landline was dead."

"Dead?" She looks startled.

"Yes."

"I didn't use the landline. I called on my cell." As if offering proof, she pulls her phone out of her pocket. "I had to walk a long way from the house to find service."

I study her, head tilted. She tilts her own head and studies me in return. In this moment I wish I could step into her skin and see what's there. I want so much for this woman to be genuine, to mean the things she says. For some reason it's vitally, urgently important.

"Effy?"

"Sometimes it's hard to be cut off from everyone," I deflect, the surge of energy disappearing as quickly as it arrived.

"I know," she agrees. "I forgot how remote this place can feel."

She sighs, a clearing of the air. We both look out at the sea.

"What I wanted to tell you is that I'm proud of you. I see something in you, Effy. It reminds me of myself at your age. In complicated ways, good and bad. We're a lot alike, and I'm not going to pretend that's strictly a compliment."

I don't smile, but she has my attention.

"The difference between you and me is that you know who

you are in a way I never did, not until much later. I suspect that's a product of your generation—you're a lot more self-aware. But it's also because of you. All you've been through and who you are. As Freud says, there are no accidents. Only tragic mishaps that are, on some level, purposeful. Your father knew what he was doing. Deep down, you know that, and you don't owe him forgiveness."

A strange thing happens when she says this. As often as I've thought this exact thing, it sounds wrong coming from her.

I carry her words upstairs with me, down the hallway, past Arlo's room and Isaac's and Ness's. Past Ramon's room. I want to shake off everything Arlo told us about their conversation, all the doubts it raised. I want to shake off this day in the woods and live a while longer in Graffam's belief in me.

In my bathroom, I shed my clothes and any thoughts of Ramon and the hunters in the woods and my father's motives and what may or may not be up Graffam's sleeve.

All I have is this moment. This is all there is.

I let the hot shower pour down on me like a cleansing, like a baptism, washing me clean.

Arlo

SUNDAY, JANUARY 18

The index card under my door the next morning reads: *A picture is worth a thousand words.* That can mean only one thing: class photos. We spill out into the brick courtyard to find the sky an impossible shade of blue, the air unseasonably warm. Drea has found a trunk of old hats, and we wear them as we pose for the camera, Graffam at our center—like the sun—our own version of The Odds.

Looking in the viewfinder, back through the shots, we are gold in the daylight, Graffam's shine extending to us all. You can't tell how stilted we were, how hard we were trying to look natural and easy, as if nothing had changed.

Once the photo shoot is done, we linger outside. I lounge in my T-shirt, jacket under my head like a pillow. Graffam is leaving tonight for a day or two. She doesn't say where she's going or why, only that Drea will be accompanying her, leaving Wesley to babysit us. My word, not hers. I, for one, am glad she's going away. It will give us time to breathe and work and try to wrap our minds around *Meredith Graffam* and just who the hell she is.

For now, we soak up this moment. Today is a reminder that winter won't last forever. That someday spring will come again.

Overhead, a gull swoops toward the ocean. Graffam follows it with her eyes.

"Your envelopes," she says to the horizon. "I was thinking about them. I've never been a fan of window-shopping, of seeing what I can't afford. I'm only interested in what I can have." Her gaze settles on us. "I don't want to be one more person who shows you what *might* be possible someday. 'Do this, do that.' You get enough of that at this school. So I've decided . . . you each win what's in your envelope."

"You're not—are you serious?" Ness looks at us, her voice wary. Like Effy, she wants desperately to believe in Graffam.

"Yes. Provided you stay to the end."

Ness takes a deep breath. Lets it out. The only one who makes a sound.

"That's it. That's all I ask." Graffam inclines her head, considering a small white cloud moving past. Several seconds pass before she speaks again. "Think of yourself in a garden, locked away from the rest of the outside. You can sit there and write about the world you see, a sliver of sky, the flowers and plants within the walls. But think of how much you would miss. Omission is a vital part of film. What you leave out can be just as important as what you put in."

She seems lost in thought. I shift, suddenly cold, and her eyes fall on me.

"Everyone here has, at one time or another, for whatever

reason, withheld information from someone. It is easy to be terrified by this dark thing that sleeps inside us."

"Sylvia Plath," Effy says.

"Sorry?"

"What you said. It's from the poem 'Elm' by Plath: 'I am terrified by this dark thing / That sleeps in me.'"

Graffam stares out at the ocean. "We all have dark things that sleep inside us. Anyone who claims they don't is lying."

It seems like the perfect moment to ask her about Lara Leonard. *Ramon says you knowingly framed an innocent man. That the only person confirmed at the scene of the crime was you.*

But Graffam is suddenly on her feet, looming over us. She says, "I have a confession to make. Ramon was missing for nearly forty-eight hours. He's fine now. I should have told you, but I didn't want you to worry."

No one speaks. We are too busy staring at her and at one another, wondering which of us confronted her.

"I'm sorry. I've never been in this position before. In charge of students like this. In a place"—she waves at the Moss—"like this. I thought it was best not to worry you while Dean Booker and the police and the Park Service were working to locate him."

"I talked to Ramon," I say. "He told me no one came to look for him. He said you didn't report him missing."

"Is that what he told you?" She looks angry and hurt at the same time. "He disappeared on my watch. He was my responsibility. I was ashamed because I felt like I failed him, not just with the whole woods debacle, but as a teacher. I failed to guide him past the walls that were suffocating his creativity.

The fact that he didn't want to stay is on me. And the fact that I didn't tell you that he was missing till now is also on me. But I absolutely promise you that they searched for him. As soon as he didn't return Monday, I let Dean Booker know."

I catch Effy's eye, and she shakes her head, as confused as I am. I sit on the brick wall kicking one heel against it over and over. *Thump. Thump.* I'm thinking of Ramon and how he never liked me. How he never liked any of us, including Graffam. I wouldn't put it past him to screw up our chances here now that he's gone. *Thump. Thump.*

But.

But . . .

My brain pounds in rhythm with my leg.

Graffam says, "I'm grateful Ramon is safe. He is bright and talented. But to succeed in this industry, you have to be more than talented. You have to want it more than anything. And even then there's no guarantee. I realize, though, I should have been honest with you. I have my reasons for doing things a certain way, but my methods aren't for everyone. So thank you, Arlo, Effy, Ness, Isaac, for sticking it out."

UPSTAIRS IN HER room, Effy and I undress in the glow of the uranium glass. We take our time because we can. Because here in her room, there's only Effy and me. I lose myself in the feel of her, the taste of her, the scent of her. And afterward I work up the courage to show her the portrait I've drawn of her—Effy in motion. Then we stand in front of the windows and stare out at the sky.

"Ophiuchus," she says. A breeze, soft and sweet, ruffles her hair.

She remembers, I think, my pulse fizzing like champagne. Tenth grade. Behind the field house. The first time we'd ever been alone.

"Home to Kepler's supernova," I say, soft as the breeze so that I'm part of the moment, not outside of it. "The last massive star explosion ever observed by the naked eye. Hundreds of years later, the debris can still be seen."

"Gosh, you know a lot about stars." She bats her eyes at me.

"I know a lot about a lot of things," I say into her neck.

I wrap my arms around her and rest my chin on her head and then her shoulder. We stand like this, quiet for a long time, until I feel my uneasiness about Graffam return.

As if she senses it, Effy says, "She told me a story. It was a lot like the story she told Ness. Only in this one she used Visine to drug a producer she was working with. He made a pass at her and then, when she said no, demoted her to running his errands."

My brain and body tense. I think of *The Picture of Dorian Gray* and the discussion over what makes a monster. By all accounts, Clay Reynolds didn't mean to kill his wife, but the suffering he caused Effy makes him a villain in her eyes. Graffam meant to poison the shitbag producer and her ex-husband—as arguably deserving as they may have been—so does that make her a villain too? Maybe not to me specifically, but to someone.

"Huh," I manage.

"Yeah."

Here's what I know: Meredith Graffam is all-powerful and prepared to grant our wishes. Somewhere along the way I started thinking of her as a mentor. Maybe even a friend. An adult who gets it. Who gets me. At least in ways that matter.

"Arffy," Effy whispers.

"Arffy," I echo.

Here's what else I know: Something is wrong here. But if I leave now, I risk whatever this is between Effy and me. I burst the bubble we've created, and there won't be any third chances. We haven't talked about what happens when Jan Term is over. The next semester is coming for us. Dorm life. Classes. Eight hundred and twenty-four other students. Final exams. College acceptance. Graduation. University. Life.

"I can feel you thinking," she says.

"Sorry. It's this overactive, unstoppable, cat-café brain of mine."

I kiss her neck and breathe her in one last time before slipping away.

In the dark, I wander toward the kitchen. I forage in the pantry for something to eat and grab a bottle of water to take upstairs. *Look at me*, I think, *finding my way through this old labyrinth of a house. Braving the solitude and barely flinching at the countless creaks in the night. The next thing you know, Arlo, old boy, you'll be fighting monsters.*

What was it Nietzsche said? My English teacher quoted it last year. Something like, "Be careful when you fight monsters that you don't become one yourself."

I detour toward the game room. The fireplace smolders and the moon glows through the window. From her picture frame, Lara Leonard's eyes follow me as I cross to the window seat and descend into darkness.

The air inside the secret room is still and calm. I stand

there letting my blood warm again. Everything is just as I left it—the cushions on the daybed, the playing cards, the copy of *Dorian Gray*. The only thing that's changed is the Scrabble board. The tiles have shifted and the ones I added have been removed. Now it reads:

week three

Immersive Storytelling

Monday, January 19 – Thursday, January 22

SESSION THREE

- Bleed on the page, but guard your mystery and protect your true objectives from others.
- Never let them see you sweat.
- Safe gets you nowhere.
- Pick the places you don't walk away from.
- Embrace the dark thing that sleeps inside you.

If indeed sometimes I do happen to tell the truth,
I hide it among so many lies that it is hard to find.
—**Niccolò Machiavelli**

Arlo

Monday, January 19

Graffam's absence is like an unexpected drought. She and Drea have gone to New York City on sudden mysterious business, leaving us to fend for ourselves. Even though I'm happy for the reprieve, the Moss without her seems dull and ordinary, not made of magic and light after all, but merely a collection of old bricks and boards.

I sit outside on the wall of the courtyard, laptop balanced on my knees, and read through everything I've written since Barry dropped me off in his Uber. Then I pull out my Moleskine and thumb through everything I've drawn. What started as a story about you, Jonah, has gradually been taken over by the Moss and the people in it. Effy. Ramon. Graffam. Me. What happened to you, that's your story. Without realizing it, I've started writing mine.

So I get rid of the things that belong strictly to you and I begin writing down what I know from experience. A teenage boy, emerging from the depths of grief to find the world has gone on without him . . . trying to mend the bridges he burned, and understand himself—the good, the bad, the ugly—a little bit better.

Whatever I may think of Graffam, she gets the creative process. This version of the story may not go anywhere, but at least it'll be mine. For every written chapter, there are ten pages of art. I make notes on the laptop about which images go where and keep writing forward until the sun dips and the sky turns golden.

After dinner, I help Wesley clear the plates. There's no dishwasher in this place, so he washes and I dry. It reminds me of a house we lived in when I was ten or eleven. A bungalow in San Diego that had a really old fridge and a built-in booth in the kitchen but no dishwasher or microwave, which meant young me constantly complained about doing dishes and having to eat cold leftovers.

When I'm finished drying, I return the plates to their cabinets. Then I pull off the Lakers cap, making a show of shaking it out, molding the brim, fluffing the inside of it. Wesley watches me—it's quite a production—and when I'm done, I hold it out to him.

"What's this?"

"Let's be honest," I say. "My hair is far too glorious to be covered up."

"What? No. I can't take your . . ."

He tries to give it back, but I wave him away. "Seriously, man. It's just a hat. I don't need it to remember . . ." As I say it, I feel a sharp pang of loss that has nothing to do with the baseball cap. "I want you to have it."

He searches my face, trying to see if I'm serious. And yes,

Wesley, I am. Deadly serious. I need to move forward and stop looking back.

His entire face lights up then, a kid at Christmas. Reverently, he affixes the cap to his head like it's the crown jewels. I feel another little pang, but my hands are steady. I use them now to grab a bag of Oreos from the pantry and begin shoveling them into my mouth, eating my feelings, trying to keep the emotion at bay.

I'm going to miss old Wesley when I go back to campus. I tell him this now, my words punctuated by the shrapnel of Oreo crumbs. "You can come visit," I say. "You and the hat. Don't be a stranger. Not that you want to be hanging out at a high school."

"Thanks, man. Truly. This is . . ." He coughs, clears his throat. Wipes his hands on his jeans, takes a drink. Clears his throat again.

"I hope you're not coming down with the croup," I say. "That was some nasty bug they had. Me, I've got an iron constitution. My mother attributes it to my tenacity. Or, as she calls it, my extreme pigheadedness." I shrug. "Tomato, tomahto."

"Arlo?"

"What?"

"I need to show you something."

"Show me what?" I'm seeing how many Oreos I can shove in my mouth at one time. "How much you'll miss me when I'm gone? Because I get that a lot."

He doesn't answer me. Instead he takes another drink, and then another. Giving me the time I need to chew and swallow and take a drink myself.

"Still waiting," I say.

He glances at the door. Then he opens one of the lower cabinets and pulls out a familiar peacock-blue bottle. "Come with me."

THE BASEMENT IS accessed by a secret panel just below the service stairs that lead up to the staff wing. As I duck in behind Wesley, he reaches past me to close the door tight. He flips on a light, and I follow him into the earth, the air growing cooler and drier the deeper we descend.

At the bottom we stand in darkness until there's a *click* and lights flood on—fluorescent strip lights that are so harsh I actually raise my hand to shield my eyes. I blink. Wait for my vision to adjust. And take in the deep and cavernous space that seems to span the length of the house.

In that space—the size of an IKEA—is a pirate's trove of treasure. Make that several pirates. Long aisles of sculptures, vases, paintings, tapestries, picture frames of various sizes. Cabinets of jewelry and trinkets and gold. So much gold. Shelves and shelves of leather-bound books locked away behind glass, and even cars—Duesenberg, Rolls-Royce, Bentley—polished to a shine.

"What is this place?" I ask, my voice muffled, small in all this vastness.

"Moss Hove was a collector. For years he traveled the world and brought back souvenirs. Some of these things came from his travels, sometimes through The Odds or through companies that charged double to track down items and ship them back. Some he displayed, others he stored down here. Almost as if the joy was in the procuring, not the procured."

"Jesus." I whistle, long and loud.

"Back when they first started letting people stay at the Moss, they made high-quality imitations so you could see the house as it was when Moss Hove lived here. They removed everything priceless and replaced it with replicas."

He starts down one of the aisles, and I trail behind him, my head swiveling like Linda Blair's in *The Exorcist* as I try to take it in. This aisle consists mostly of artwork. Hundreds and hundreds of frames. Some draped with cloth, some wrapped, others exposed, color-coded cards attached to each one.

Wesley leans over, consulting one of the labels, and then carefully removes its wrapping. It's a huge gold mirror. The shine of the gold is practically blinding. So blinding that it takes me a moment to see the decoration that adorns the frame. Birds. Not just any birds. A mythical version of the phoenix.

"Those are ho-ho birds," I say.

From under the Lakers cap, Wesley stares at me with something like sympathy or maybe pity.

"They look like the same ho-ho birds . . . Well, actually the whole thing looks like the same—"

"Mirror you broke?"

"Yeah."

"That's because it is," he says.

"So Moss Hove loved it so much he had two? Please tell me he had two."

"This is the original."

"The original," I repeat. "So the mirror we broke . . ."

"Is worth about two hundred dollars. Maybe less."

"We should tell Graffam. If she hasn't already spent the money to replace it."

Even as I utter the words, I realize how naïve I sound.

Wesley says, "Graffam knows."

"But she sent Leela home . . . that was why Leela was kicked out."

"Listen to me." He glances quickly over his shoulder toward the stairs. "You can't let on that you know. That's why I put those cell phones in your backpacks. She cut the landline. Graffam. I saw her do it."

I wait for him to tell me he's joking, my mouth hitched into a partial smile, ready to bust out a laugh as soon as he yells *Gotcha*.

But instead he goes, "I need money, but I don't need it that badly. Not when it . . . Look, I get that this class is supposed to be immersive. And she's eccentric. A lot of them are—there's a reason they're artists, that they come here to teach Jan Term but they're not part of a faculty somewhere. But I don't trust her. When she found out about the blizzard, she took the master key without telling me. The one that opens the gates. She shut off the internet, changed the password. She wanted to isolate you."

Feeding us info about the others, trying to turn us against each other. It's as if I see the different puzzle pieces and am just starting to put them together.

"And then earlier today I found this." He holds up the blue bottle, the one I'd forgotten about. "I do the errands, right? I buy everything for the kitchen. When we first went over what Graffam needed, for her chef, for you all, she made a big point of saying she had the wine all covered. I remember thinking it was weird because what teacher serves wine to high schoolers?"

I watch as he peels back what's left of the label, revealing another label underneath.

"I noticed this the other day. The blue glass is unusual and it's pretty, so I thought I'd keep one of the empties for Kaya. As I was washing it, the label starts to come off."

He hands me the bottle. Instead of *Whittier*, it reads *The Mixture (as Recipe). Containing Laudanum.*

"Laudanum?"

"It's made from opium. Poppies, basically. It can be used as a sedative, but also a painkiller. It can make you sleepy, give you wild dreams, cold sweats, hallucinations. Make you lightheaded. Dry-mouthed. There are dozens of empty ones and a dozen or more full ones where that came from. All containing varying percentages of the stuff."

"Who needs that many bottles of laudanum in the twenty-first century? Wait—you can buy laudanum?"

"If you're famous and have a shitload of money? You can buy anything." As proof, he looks around us at this giant treasure vault.

"But why bring so much of it? The laudanum?"

"She has wine at dinner, right? That's how you drink it. You can drink it straight. Or you can mix it in. But not just wine. You can put it in any liquid. Really, you can add it to anything."

My stomach flips. "Hot tea. Juice. Soup. Stew . . ."

"Sure."

I think of everything we've eaten since we've been here,

all those meals prepared by Graffam's personal chef and, after she left, the ones Graffam made herself. I think of how sick Ness, Effy, and Isaac have been.

"Can it make you feel like you've got a cold or even the flu?"

"Oh yeah. Depending on how much you ingest, it can make you feel like complete and utter crap."

And then, for some reason, this makes me think of something else, like my mind is playing a frenetic game of connect the dots.

"That's why you wrote *Run* on the Scrabble board. You were trying to warn us."

Wesley shakes his head, frowns, looks utterly lost.

I say, "The word *Run*. And then *Now*. And then *Run* over and over. You left me a message. Left us a message."

"No, I didn't."

"You're saying Graffam did it herself. Trying to, what, scare us?"

"I'm saying I didn't do it."

I SEARCH THE house for the others, as if I'm seeking and they're hiding. I feel like I'm deep in this game that I didn't know I was in, and suddenly the Moss is shrinking—walls closing in, ceiling dropping, floor raising, nothing more than a suffocating box shrunk down to dollhouse size. Every portrait I pass, the eyes are watching.

I find Effy, Ness, and Isaac scattered throughout the dollhouse rooms like children's toys. I tell them to come with me, just come on, and when they want to know why—*I'm in the middle of something, just leave me alone*—I tell them to come the *fuck* on.

I lead them upstairs, then into my room because I feel the need to put a closed door between us and the rest of the Moss.

"What's so important?" Isaac asks, dropping into a chair. Of the three of them, he seems the most annoyed by the intrusion.

I hold up my phone. They lean in to see the photo of the original gold mirror.

"That looks like . . ." Ness begins.

"Arlo?" says Effy.

I set the bottle down on my desk. The one that says *Laudanum*. And I tell them what Wesley told me.

Effy

MONDAY, JANUARY 19

I break away from the others because I need to clear my head. I return to the solarium and open my laptop. My eyes scan the words of the manuscript that's coming together, the one Graffam pretended to be interested in. But was she really ever interested? Does she actually care about our work, about our stories, about us?

My mind is racing. *Why would she lie about the mirror? About Ramon?* Was it just to feel better about herself? She's always talking about using your own material to fuel the writing. Taking the anger and pain and feeding it into the work, which is something she knows about firsthand. I imagine her at twenty, her first novel an overnight sensation, the accolades, the immediate fame. The thrill of it all, especially so young. I imagine myself, three years from now, the whole world at my feet.

And then—a few years later—everything imploding. The public shaming, the cancellation. Who's to say she's not still angry?

But that doesn't explain why she lied to us. *If she lied.* A tiny part of me holds out hope that she'll come back tomorrow and explain it all away.

I stretch out on the half-moon sofa. Close my eyes. Open my eyes again. I rub at the headache that's been forming over the past half hour, ever since Arlo told us about the mirror and the laudanum. *Laudanum.* I pull out the letter from my dad. Turn it over in my hands.

They sentenced him to the New Hampshire State Prison for Men in Concord, where he became a model prisoner, eventually graduating from the character development program 'Choose Love,' which promotes self-empowerment and teaches inmates how to act with kindness.

While my father was busy learning these basic human qualities, I was lying in bed at night wondering why I was the only one at school without parents. And across the country, a woman named Meredith Graffam continued to capitalize on a story she wrote about a dead girl she once knew, becoming ever more famous—and infamous—when the lies she'd built her career on were exposed.

Whatever happened that night on the road, my dad, monster that he is, claims he didn't mean to kill my mom. It was, according to him, an accident. A horrible, reckless, stupid accident that could have been prevented.

It occurs to me, for the first time, that maybe he's not a monster. That maybe he's only a monster to me.

IN MY ROOM later that evening, Arlo and I are too consumed by our own thoughts to have sex, both of us in a state of suspended animation. I rest my head on his chest and he strokes my hair and I listen to his heartbeat.

Tomorrow, tomorrow, tomorrow, it says. Graffam will be back tomorrow.

There's this feeling of dread, of waiting, of something outside trying to get in. No. Of something outside that has managed to get in and is now in the house with us.

I say, "I used to complain to Gran that life was unfair. Because that's how it felt. This terrible thing had happened to my mom. To me. She said, 'It is. But it's also impartial.' That made it worse. And also better."

He says, "If that's true, then it doesn't really matter how good we are or whether we atone for things we've done."

"I don't think the universe can be bribed."

He lets out a breath, one he seems to have been holding for a long time. "The last thing Jonah said to me was 'Just look up.'"

"As in don't forget to look for Ophiuchus?"

"As in literally look up. When I did, I saw there was a place in the ceiling of the sea cave that jutted out, almost like a nose or a chin. He was telling me to grab it and hang on. Because he was trying to help me before he helped himself. But I couldn't hold on. I'd inhaled so much ocean by that point. I tried to grab it, but it kept slipping out of my hand."

Below my cheek, his heart beats louder and swifter.

"And so they saved me. And now my hands shake sometimes. It's this reminder, like I need one, of my fallibility."

I try to come up with a response that won't sound hollow

or false or like I'm trying too hard to make him feel better. The silence stretches between us.

And then I say, "What do you think happens when we die?"

Visions of his friend Jonah, of my mother, of Graffam standing on the roof threatening to jump.

He doesn't answer right away. He's taking his time, even though I'm sure he's contemplated the subject a thousand times before. There's a tiny part of me hoping that Arlo might actually know. *You will get your mom back. You will get to know her one day. She will get to know who you've become.*

Finally he says, "There's got to be something. Otherwise, what's the point?"

Yes, I think. "Yes," I say.

I listen to the rhythm of his heartbeat again, to the chug of blood in his veins. The fear in me wants to pull away. Because what if his heart suddenly just . . . stops? And I hear it stop?

But in this moment it tells me he's here and breathing and warm and alive. *Tomorrow, tomorrow, tomorrow.* My head starts to swim the way it does when I'm standing on the cliff looking down at the sea, when I know I could just step off.

"Maybe *this* is the point," I whisper.

And I mean all of it. Him and me—us, the cliff, the fall, our beating hearts.

"Effy Green?" His voice reaches through the dark.

"Yes, Arlo Ellis-Noon?"

"I think I love you."

I feel the words as well as hear them, the way they vibrate through him. I've never told anyone other than Gran and Ness—and, once upon a time, my parents—that I love them. The idea of saying it to someone new is petrifying. But then I think of the ache I felt when I thought I'd never see him again. Of his lips and the deep gray of his eyes when he looks at me—not just looks at me but *sees* me. Of the hammer he's taken to the walls I've built. Of him. And I decide it's time to start accepting the good.

I whisper into his chest, "I think I love you too."

Arlo

TUESDAY, JANUARY 20

The morning and afternoon are calm and blue. Like Massachusetts in summer after the rain. The scent of earth and flowers and fresh, clean air. Just a perfect sunlit day.

Drea is back from New York without Graffam. She seems subdued, far away, distractedly telling us to work on our projects before disappearing into her room. Instead I meet Effy outside on the cliffs.

She waits for me, sitting cross-legged on the rock, Stray's Chasm to her left, eyes fixed on the horizon. As I approach her, she says, "When Graffam gets here, I think we should confront her. Give her the chance to explain herself."

"Hmm," I say.

She squints up at me. "What does that mean?"

"It means—hear me out—we're two days away from leaving

here. Two days away from fifteen thousand dollars and the contents of our envelopes. I don't know about you, but I need that scholarship and—as much as I hate this about myself—I want what she's promised. College interviews. A donation to Surfers Healing."

I offer her a hand, but she ignores it. So I drop beside her on the rock.

"So you're saying, what, let's just ride it out? Let's sit back and pretend we don't know that she left Ramon out in the woods for two days without alerting anyone? And that she sent Leela packing over a mirror that wasn't even valuable? And—I don't know—whatever the laudanum means?" Little sparks are shooting off her. "People like Graffam, they're allowed to go through life running over everyone without ever being held accountable . . ."

And now I wonder if she's thinking about Graffam or her father or maybe both.

"And you were going to love her forever," I tease.

"I can't believe I fell for it, for her."

I watch as she deflates, a discharged firework, all burnt out.

"Have you ever heard of prosopometamorphopsia?"

She gives me a look that is equal parts *Really?* and *Now is not the time for one of your weird facts* and *What do you think, asshole?*

In spite of this, I charge bravely onward. "PMO, as it's otherwise known, is a rare neurological condition that makes people see monsters. They look at a human face and see distortions that aren't there. This one guy I read about—he said if he looks at someone for longer than three seconds, their face starts to transform. Their teeth elongate, their features bulge, they grow snouts, pointy ears, a vortex where the eyes should be, reptilian skin—"

"This is a real thing?"

"Yes." I hold up my hand. Cryptozoologist's honor. "This other woman I read about says it looks to her like people are melting. She can't even stare at her own face in a mirror because it morphs and contorts in front of her until she resembles an old-fashioned movie monster. She says it's like every day is Halloween."

"Why are you telling me this?"

"Because most of us look at people and don't see those distortions. So we can't be hard on ourselves if we miss it. And maybe the key is to not look too closely because it's only when you do that you see the monster there."

Effy is quiet, and for once in my life, I am quiet too. From far off, I hear my name. We turn to see Isaac and Ness coming toward us from the Moss.

"We don't need to bring them into this," says Effy.

"They're already in it," I remind her. "We're all in it. Look, worst-case scenario, Graffam's like, *You caught me. I lied. Again.* And we spend the next two days going through the motions and finishing the term. Best-case scenario, she has a reason for Ramon, for the mirror, even for the laudanum. I mean, I'm the last person to defend her, but maybe it's all part of her plan. A cockeyed, off-the-beaten-track, fucked-up-but-still-means-well plan."

I get to my feet, careful on the wet surface of the rock, and offer Effy my hand again. This time, she lets me pull her up. I see her face soften a little. "Sorry," she breathes.

"Love means never having to say that."

She rolls her eyes, and for a second the earth's gravity is restored. I wrap my arm around her and pull her into me, and let myself pretend that there's nothing in the world to worry about except standing here on this frigid, wet cliff with Effy Green.

I start telling her about the *Velella velella,* painting her a picture of bright blue discs washing up onto the sand. How each one is a colony working together.

She looks up at me, then out at the ocean as if she's waiting for the *Velella velella* to appear. "And you're telling me this because we're like tiny shipwrecked sailors?"

"I'm telling you this because, one, I thought you might enjoy a good nature story and I wanted to impress you with my array of knowledge on rare but fascinating topics." The ends of her hair lift and dance in the wind. "And, two, I think we need to channel the *Velella velella*, not the going-along-for-the-ride part, but the part where we, the four of us, put all differences aside and work together."

Effy doesn't react, but I can tell by the way she's gone still that she's listening.

"So she's been trying to undermine our relationships," I say. "Well, there's strength in numbers."

We fall quiet again, and this time it's me who can feel her thinking.

"Is this a private party, or can anyone join?" Isaac without the smile, without the swagger, is almost unrecognizable. I kind of miss the old him.

Through chattering teeth, Ness adds, "After we leave here, I hope I never see the ocean again."

In the sky, a flock of birds soars past in a V formation. The four of us look up and watch until they disappear. Then, over the sound of the waves, I say to Isaac and Ness, "Have I ever told you about the *Velella velella*?"

Effy

Tuesday, January 20

By evening, Graffam still hasn't returned. As a fire crackles in the fireplace, the four of us and Drea eat dinner to a soundtrack of big band classics, festive and upbeat. The table is set like a blooming garden. But tonight something about the music and the fire and the candlelight and the flowers is too much noise.

At first Drea attempts to engage us in polite conversation.
Can you believe it's the last week of Jan Term already?
No.
Are you all looking forward to your last semester at Brighton and Hove?
Sure.
Do you know where you're going to college yet?
We've applied, but none of us have committed to a school.
We're supposed to be acting like everything is normal, but we don't have it in us, not even Arlo. We eat or push the food

around on our plates and act like the sullen, angry teens we are—only not for the usual reasons.

Eventually Drea falls silent too, as if she doesn't have it in her to try any longer. When I ask her to pass the water pitcher, she doesn't seem to hear me. I stand up to get it myself. A few minutes later, she makes her excuses and starts to leave.

In the doorway, she turns back to us. "I know I work for Meredith, but I don't tell her everything. So if there's anything going on that you need to talk about or for some reason don't want her to know, you can come to me."

And then, without waiting, she's gone.

"I think we broke Drea," Isaac says.

"She may be broken, but not by us."

We look at Ness. She dabs at her mouth with her napkin, then drops it onto her plate. It misses by a mile and lands on the floor instead. "While they were in the city, I guess Meredith had meetings and Drea went to the gallery where her opening is supposed to be next week. But they'd never heard of her. There was never going to be an opening."

"'Meredith'?" I echo.

Ness barely glances my way. "Sorry. She, um, asked me to call her that."

I shift in my chair, as if shifting will somehow change the fact that my best friend is now apparently best friends with Drea *and* Graffam. Graffam, who is still *Graffam* to the rest of us.

"So what," says Isaac. "Maybe the person she talked to just didn't know about it."

Ness shakes her head. "The guy she talked to was the

owner. He told Drea he knows who Meredith is. I mean, of course he knows who Meredith Graffam is, but he doesn't *know* know her. As in they've never actually met. They've never even spoken."

"Huh." Arlo leans down to pick up Ness's napkin. He sets it absently beside her plate.

"Also? Meredith told Zoe, who told Drea, that she has an idea for a new film, something to do with 'resurrecting The Hunt and exposing the real villain.'"

I sit perfectly, rigidly still now, flooded with the need for someone to tell me it's all going to be okay, everything is okay, and nothing bad will ever happen to me. Even if bad things have already happened and will still happen today, tomorrow, years down the road. I just want someone to lie to me for a little while.

As if reading my mind, Arlo goes, "We can't borrow trouble. Not until we know more."

AS SOON AS Wesley clears our plates, we go off to separate corners of the house to work. Instead of the solarium, I seek out the sanctity of my room. But when I sit down at my laptop, I fill an entire page with *I think I made you up inside my head.*

When I hear a knock on my door sometime later, I'm grateful for the interruption. I open it to find Ness. "Can I come in?"

"Of course."

I perch on the end of my bed, and she stands in front of the fireplace, arms wrapped around herself as if she's trying to get warm.

"I'm sorry," she says.

"For what?"

"For 'Meredith.' When she asked me to call her that, I assumed she was asking everyone."

"No. Just you."

She nods, then shakes her head. "You don't know how much I want to trust her."

"I do." I can hear how robotic I sound. And because she's making an effort, I try to make one too. "We all do."

Ness drops down beside me on the bed. We stare out the windows at the sky beyond.

"It's right there," she says. "I can see it. The future I could have. The one that makes it all—everything—worth it. You know what's in my envelope? A letter from an anonymous benefactor, offering a full four-year scholarship to Brown. So that I can go and study poetry on a beautiful campus and be inspired and blossom like constellations . . ."

A line from one of her poems: *My round cheeks, thrones where dimples blossom like constellations . . .*

"I think Meredith—Graffam—has made me a better poet. It's like she knows the way to pull things out of me. She just reaches in and—more than that, she knows how to talk to me about my work." She tugs one of her curls out straight and flat against her palm, then sets it free to spring back into place. "She's helped me learn to trust myself. Which is somehow the key to me writing."

"That's all— That's why we're here."

"I know. But, Eff?" She looks at me now, her eyes wild behind her glasses. "If she isn't who she says she is . . . if she really promised Drea something huge and spectacular but never planned to give it to her . . . if all that is true, how can we believe her when she makes promises to us?"

"I don't know."

I should tell her that all is not lost. That—no matter what happens—she won't ever lose what she's learned here. That she's part of my *Velella velella* colony—not *my* colony, *our* colony, Ness's and mine. But before I can say any of this, there's a sound from outside. A car in the drive.

Ness and I freeze.

Doors are opening and closing. Voices from below.

Graffam is back.

Arlo

Tuesday, January 20

Even though it's past nine o'clock, Effy, Isaac, Ness, and I wait to be summoned. We wait in the kitchen. We wait in the theater. We wait in the Hall of Oddities. Together we move from room to room, but there's no sign of her.

When the hour comes and goes, and then another hour comes and goes, it's clear that Graffam isn't planning to see us until the morning.

Just before midnight, the index card arrives under my door. Class will be held in the Octagon Room at ten a.m. At the bottom, Graffam has added a handwritten note.

Our last class of Jan Term. Please come prepared for a surprise.

x MG

Effy

Wednesday, January 21

At ten a.m., we gather in the Octagon Room for class, composed and calm, our best manners on display. I was awake all night imagining this moment when we see her again. There's the smallest part of me that hopes she'll breeze in with explanations and apologies. Instead she's already there when we arrive, draped in her chair, elegant wrists dangling off knees, looking like a languid society girl.

She turns glittering eyes on the four of us, no hint that anything is amiss. In fact she seems different—lighter somehow. As buoyant as a pool float. She asks how our work went while she was away, as if she's been gone for weeks. *Good*, we say like robots. *Great*.

Then she says, "I posed a question on our first day of class. Free will. Does it exist? I'm interested in hearing if your opinions have changed."

She scans the room for a reaction but we remain silent.

"For centuries, we've been taught that we alone are responsible for our actions. That we have the option of choosing between right and wrong. Our civilization depends on it. Our dreams depend on it. No matter where we begin in life, we can make ourselves into whatever and whoever we want." A scraping sound as she pushes her chair back and stands. "But," she continues, "the American physiologist Benjamin Libet thought differently." All eyes are on her as she starts to roam the room. "His research proved that the electrical impulses associated with decision-making peak in our brains before we make a conscious choice."

A hand on the back of my chair, and I look up. Her face is bathed in morning light. It occurs to me in this moment that the magic of Meredith Graffam isn't her ability to change shape. It isn't her ability to lie effortlessly and assume different roles with each of us. It isn't that, on-screen as in life, she is small and big and sometimes both at once. Sometimes Brunhild the warrior and other times that wounded girl who nearly died her senior year at Brighton and Hove. It's that she is always Meredith Graffam.

Herein lies her power, I think as she talks to us about the biological code that defines who we are and what we do. The illusion of choice. Accidents that aren't accidents at all.

She settles by the window, one shoulder leaning against the glass.

"Do you believe in free will?" I ask, my voice chilled but also tinged with wonder. I genuinely want to know her answer.

"Yes," she says thoughtfully. "But not for everyone. I believe in it for myself because, in my own case, I've been able to overcome my upbringing and my past and do things no one ever believed or expected I could do. I did it because of and in spite of. And I still do. To this day. Over and over again."

Me, me, me. How did I never notice it before? Meredith Graffam is only interested in Meredith Graffam.

"Do you believe in it for us?" To my own ears, I sound like an impatient parent, trying to refocus my child.

There is a lift to her eyebrows, a shine to her eyes, as if we are playing a game. And maybe that's what this whole thing is to her—one big game.

Finally, she says, "I believe everyone has potential, some more than others. But that's something you have to figure out for yourselves."

"The mirror," Ness blurts out, curls trembling. "The mirror we broke was a fake. But you sent Leela home. And you lied about Ramon too. And what were you giving us to drink? *Laudanum?*"

Graffam stares at her.

"I can't tell what's real and what's not and what to believe and what to count on."

And then everything spills out of Ness in a rush. I know her well enough to know that once she starts she can't stop, not until she's empty.

"All I've done since I got here is try to do my best. I've participated, I've gone way, way out of my comfort zone. I've exposed myself and been open and honest." She stumbles on this last word. "I've stood in traffic and jumped off a cliff and frozen my butt off in the woods, even though I was sick as a dog and I don't like the woods—I've never liked the woods, even though I'm from here. I've tried to give you everything, but I'm not sure that matters now. Does it?"

My eyes go from Ness to Graffam, and I see it as it happens—the switch. Like something flicking on or off inside her.

"What the hell is going on?" Graffam stands, hands on hips, dark hair spilling over her shoulders like wild smoke, eyes black with anger. "Anyone other than Ness?" She doesn't wait for us to speak. "Okay, I'll go. I wasn't aware the mirror was a fake. Not until I tried to have it replaced. But that wasn't why I sent Leela home. I sent her home because, once Joey and Peter left, it was clear to me that she wasn't as strong as the rest of you. Not as talented and not as mature. I thought I could better serve you"—she points at each one of us—"if I had fewer people to concentrate on. I've already explained what happened to Ramon. Yes, he got lost. And then he found his way back. It's not as if he's dead. And as for the wine, you're not supposed to be drinking anyway."

I sit very still. This is not the apology I hoped for. We've gotten all of it—gotten *her*—so completely wrong.

"It's time to get over yourselves," she says. "As harsh as that may sound. You've been coddled and handheld by your families and this school. They've handed you the world on a silver platter and told you that you earned it. But you won't be here forever. And then what? What happens when you leave?"

She looks at Isaac, at Ness, at Arlo, at me.

"There's a reason I did my research and had you vetted before I chose you. I needed to know who you are and what you're running from. Because we're all running from something. The things you don't like about yourselves? Your fatal flaws? Those are the reasons you're here. Not your talent. Don't you see that?"

She says this like it should clear everything up, like this is good news.

"Isaac. Your failure to live up to the family name. Your desperate need for something to set you apart from all their expectations. It's not just that you don't want to follow in their footsteps. It's that you can't. Because you don't have it in you.

"Effy. Your inability to love or be loved. Which has nothing to do with your father killing your mother but has everything to do with you.

"Ness. Your crippling insecurity and desperation to go to college, something you can't afford without help. Your willingness to do anything to get there and your fear that you don't belong.

"Arlo, your therapist was the one who suggested you start writing, and you've discovered you're good at it. But writing isn't about making yourself feel good. It's about telling the truth. And the truth is, you made sure you were the one who was rescued when your friend drowned. So own it. Have the courage to tell *that* story."

You can hear a pin drop. I feel out of my body, like a ghost trapped in this dimension, drifting among the living but unable to communicate. *I'm right here*, I think.

When Graffam speaks again, it's as if the fight has gone out of her. Her eyes return to their regular brown, her hair just hair, not smoke at all.

"The danger of places like Brighton and Hove is that they program you to think you can do anything, but what happens when you leave? What I'm trying to do, for better or worse, is prepare you in a way this school can't and won't."

I've never once made excuses for why my father did what he did. But for some reason I make excuses for Graffam. Even now I tell myself she is not a cruel person. She is a person who has been through hard things. She is a survivor.

As we leave the Octagon Room, the world around me looks like the usual, regular world, but it feels different, as if there's been a shift in the earth's gravitational pull. My father feels very far away. It's hard to remember why I wanted to write about him or to him in the first place.

Arlo

WEDNESDAY, JANUARY 21

In my postclass daze, I wander into the pantry—always hungry, even in a crisis. As I tear into a bag of chips and try to wrap my mind around the past hour, I hear noise in the laundry room. Music first, followed by a clattering and a splashing. My instinct is to hide and keep eating, here in the solitude of the pantry.

But something makes me set down the chips and investigate. I expect to see maybe Wesley. Instead I find Drea at the enormous sink, rinsing her paintbrushes.

"Arlo," she says, blowing a strand of hair off her face. "Do you mind turning that off for me?" She nods at her phone, on the counter beside her, and then down at her arms, up to elbows in sink water.

The screen of her phone is lit up, a video playing music. I stare down at it. "You've got service."

"Not cell service, although I will tell you, not having it has been really peaceful. When I get back to LA, I'm thinking about doing a kind of regular digital detox. It's pretty incredible what you can get done without the interruption."

She might say more, but I don't hear it because I'm focused on the curved bars of the Wi-Fi signal. I watch as she dries the brushes with a towel and lays them out side by side.

"So how was the trip to New York?"

Drea continues laying out the brushes, as if she hasn't heard.

"Drea?"

"Meredith doesn't exactly keep me in the loop on everything. There's another storm coming, by the way. It sounds brutal. I think they call it a northeaster? I heard a report, they said it was shaping up to be as bad as the one in 1991. I guess there's a book based on it?"

"*The Perfect Storm*," I say. But back to New York. "How was the gallery?"

She keeps her eyes on the brushes, ordering them and reordering them as if it's the most important task in the world. "Did you need something, Arlo?" Her tone is polite, but it also says, *Go away*.

"I thought the Wi-Fi wasn't working."

"Meredith brings a hot spot, just in case. Not the fastest I've ever used, but if you think about how far we are out in the woods, it's kind of amazing we have it at all." She seems grateful for the change in subject. "Sorry, I thought she'd given it to you. The login is 'PhyllisDietrichson.' All together, the first letter of each name in caps. That was Barbara Stanwyck's character in *Double Indemnity*."

"And the password?" I look around for something to write on.

"You don't need to write it down. It's so easy. 'TheLie.' Capital *T*. Capital *L*. The rest lowercase. That's it. She uses the same one for everything. Zoe's been on her about changing it up and using computer-generated passwords, but she says she has enough to remember."

"'TheLie,'" I repeat.

"'TheLie.'" And then she straightens, her expression changing. "You know, actually—let me write it down for you. Just in case."

She pulls another bunch of brushes out of her overalls and drops all but one into the water. She disappears through the door into the kitchen and then reappears just as quickly, her movements suddenly hurried.

She lays a Post-it on the counter, coppery hair spilling across her face as she bends over and, with the paintbrush, makes a few quick strokes. She hands the Post-it to me.

"There you go."

And then she glances past me and upward toward the ceiling. I follow her gaze to one of Moss Hove's stuffed birds, high up in a corner, perched on one of the shelves that holds various cleaning supplies, looking as if it's about to swoop down on us.

There's something about it—one eye dead, the other too bright—that reminds me of the bird in the Hall of Oddities.

A splash as the paintbrush joins the others in the sink, and like that, I feel it—we're done here.

I don't remember the Post-it until I'm halfway to my room. I unfold the square of paper, where Drea has written: **RUN**.

IN THE HALL of Oddities, I stare up at the crow with the mismatched eyes. As I do so, my heart and pulse remain steady, my breathing calm. It's my skin that changes—slowly turning cold until it feels as if ice is being shot into my bones.

I reach up and pluck the bird from the shelf, turning him over in my hands. He's heavier than I expected, and his feathers feel too stiff, his body too cold. I examine his eyes, the dead one and the glinty one, and then I pop the glinty one out of the socket. I don't even have to pry it. It just falls right out.

I hold it up to the light. It's no bigger than a button. A camera.

BY AFTERNOON, I'VE discovered seven more. I take the narrow stairs to the staff floor and find Wesley in his room at the end of the hall. The rooms here are smaller, the furniture simpler. A bed, dresser, closet. The floors and walls crisp and clean, the antiseptic feel of a hospital ward.

Wesley sits on his bed, textbook open, wearing the Lakers cap I gave him. He looks up, clearly surprised to see me. "Arlo?"

I open my palm and hold it out so he can see.

He sets down the book. "What am I looking at?"

"Cameras."

He's up now and peering at my hand. "Okay . . ."

"I found them around the house. I assume they were installed by the school or maybe even the Park Service?"

He studies them, then looks up at me, shaking his head. "The only cameras are visible. Here, let me show you."

I follow him until we're down the stairs and in the kitchen. He points at a small rectangle, roughly the size of a phone, mounted to the ceiling in one corner. "All the official Moss cameras look like that. They're old-school, but Brighton and Hove wants you to be aware of them. Given the value of the house and its objects, they like to maintain a presence."

My heart goes cold, calcifying like bone. "I wonder if you could do me a favor?"

His eyes meet mine. "Sure." I feel this rush of gratitude at the way he doesn't even need to think about it.

"Can you ask Graffam to help you with something, maybe in the kitchen or outside, for half an hour? Longer if possible? Or get Drea to distract her? Keep her away from her wing?"

"Yeah, man. Of course. I'll stall her as long as I can."

As soon as I hear *Yeah, man*, I'm halfway out the door.

Effy

Wednesday, January 21

Arlo leads the way up the back stairs to Graffam's rooms. "Fucking cameras," Isaac mutters, as if these are the only words remaining in his brain. When he repeats it, I tell him to stop talking, for fuck's sake, just *stop fucking talking*. I don't mean to snipe at him, but we have just learned that, in addition to lying and—possibly—drugging us, Meredith Graffam is recording us with hidden cameras all over the house.

At the top of the stairs, the air is sweet and pungent. Arlo, Ness, Isaac, and I move through the passageway that opens onto the gilded balcony over the theater.

Arlo pushes open the door to Graffam's room, revealing the coral-painted walls. The sharp, fresh scent of flowers makes me lightheaded.

"It's like a funeral home in here," he says.

We step inside. Drea is downstairs on the sunporch, but

just in case, I close the door behind us. I was in the solarium when he found me, showed me the cameras, barked at me to *Come on. No time to ask questions.*

"What are we searching for?" Ness asks.

"I don't know," I tell her.

The thing that takes up the largest space is the desk in front of the window. It's relatively neat right now, considering Graffam has been here longer than us. It's mostly just stacks of magazines and books—novels, a couple of film biographies, a collection of photographs taken by Moss Hove, a book on secret societies. The four of us sift through the drawers, which are barely wide enough to hold anything other than paper clips and pens.

We open the wardrobe, look under the bed, and in the bedside tables. But there's nothing unexpected. Nothing that seems out of place or rings alarm bells.

We move as a pack into the adjoining bathroom that connects to another bedroom beyond this one. There's not much to see in here except the sort of stuff you'd expect a celebrity to travel with—acres of beauty products and makeup, razors, shampoo, conditioner, and various beauty tools I recognize from Gran's bathroom back home.

The second bedroom is decorated in hues of violet. It feels like springtime, smaller than the other, with a canopied bed, a dresser, a single bedside table, an ornate wall-sized mirror, and an enormous window overlooking the water.

There is a stack of scripts on the bedside table. An expensive-looking lip balm. A couple of pens. The top drawer is empty, but as I open the bottom drawer, something rolls around in the back. I sift through Post-it notes and various other office supplies, a vape pen and cartridges, more lip balm. And there, behind it all, is a doorknob.

It's heavy in my hand. A bright polished gold. I hold it up at the same time Arlo holds up a thick paperback. *Power Play: Directing for the Theater and Screen.* I watch as he starts to flip through it, eyes skimming the words. From the floor, it's hard to read his expression.

"'Establish a hierarchy. Don't leave any doubt as to who is in charge. Delegate tasks that are beneath you to the assistants and gofers of the world.'"

He turns the pages.

"'Bait the hook, but always leave them hungry.'"

More turning pages.

"'Keep the wheat, but cut the chaff before the stink of failure rubs off on you or others.'"

"What is that?" I stand immobile, doorknob momentarily forgotten.

"'Scatter confidences and compliments like breadcrumbs, giving them just enough to feel they are truly special.' And this one—'Pose as an ally against a common enemy—up until the moment you must cut them off.'"

Isaac takes the book from him and begins to read. "'Subordination is key.' 'Never underestimate the element of surprise.' 'Do not be afraid to make them afraid.'"

"Let me see that." The book is in my hands now. I stare down at the page it opens to. "'Remember that people crave belonging and purpose. If you can fill this need, they will worship you as a Messiah. But first, you must cultivate the illusion that they are choosing this path of their own free will.'"

There are fifty "power plays," and she's highlighted at least half of them. More disturbing than that are the details she's marked and underlined within the text:

> Once you break down their defenses, you have the power to build your vision.
>
> Withhold your approval (and, sometimes, your presence) to leave them wanting more. It will only heighten their fear and respect.
>
> Switch the script and keep them guessing. If they can't predict your next move, they will lose trust in their own instincts, relying on your direction all the more.
>
> Leverage emotional weakness to tighten your grip. Their deepest fears and greatest ambitions can serve as tools of manipulation.
>
> One bad apple can spoil the whole barrel. Swiftly remove any troublemakers who threaten your vision.
>
> Everyone has a fatal flaw—an Achilles' heel—that leaves them vulnerable to

```
absolute control. Find this flaw, and
twist the knife until they bend to your
authority.
```

My eyes meet Arlo's. "Where did you find this?"
"In here."

He moves to the painting on the wall opposite the bed. Arlo pushes the button that blends into the green of the painted trees alongside the River Thames. It swings open to reveal an empty space. He takes the book from me and slides it into the empty space and closes the panel.

The four of us stand blinking at the painting, at Big Ben, at the Thames.

"But why would she have that book, let alone hide it?" Ness asks, and I can hear the edge in her voice. She doesn't really want to know, just like I don't really want to know, and I'm sure the boys don't either.

I look down at my hand. I hold up the doorknob.
"I found this."

Ness and Isaac stare at it, at me, lost, their minds still on the book and its hiding place. Only Arlo seems to understand what it means. "Why would anyone want to seal off a room?" he says. "Unless you've got something to hide."

Arlo

Wednesday, January 21

The four of us move to the door at the other end of the balcony. With the help of a letter opener found in one of the desk drawers, we are able to remove the panel that covers the hole left by the missing doorknob. It's pretty anticlimactic, really. The thing just pops right off, which means we could have opened it much, much sooner.

Effy slides the doorknob into the hole and turns it. Like that, the door swings open.

I don't know what to expect. A dead body. The mummified remains of Moss Hove. Windows shattered or missing and a thousand dead birds lying beaks up.

What we see instead is a small room with a single window. A couple of old trunks sit in one corner. The walls are blank, the wallpaper sprigged with pale flowers, the floor bare. The only furniture is a square table and a wooden chair.

The surface of the table is covered in papers. A camera similar to the ones we've been using. An enormous monitor.

On the floor, below the table, sits a hard drive and a backup battery like the one my dad uses when he's home.

For a long moment, we stand in the doorway, Effy, Isaac, Ness, and me. No one moving. No one speaking. *Back away*, I think. *Shut the door. Return the doorknob to its hiding place and get the hell out of here.*

Then Effy crosses to the table. She bends over the papers. She glances at one, then another. She starts to shuffle through them, faster and faster. Her mouth falls open.

"What are they?" Isaac asks. "Let me guess—our grades?"

She looks up. Her expression is hollowed and ghostly. Her lips are moving but nothing comes out. Finally, she simply holds out a handful of pages.

I take them from her. Illustrations, like a comic strip. Heaps of them, one after another. Not a comic strip. A storyboard. Drawings of scenes. Each one numbered. Each one labeled with the location, the time of day. I look at them out of order, and at first they don't make sense. Scenes of snow. The woods. A wide expanse of ocean. A rocky shoreline. A house.

A scowling girl with a long fringe and unsmiling eyes.

A broad-shouldered boy with a cocky tilt to his chin and an enormous smile.

A large, heavyset guy with a baseball hat and an orange parka.

A tall, full-figured girl with glasses, half in the shadows.

A lanky boy with a riot of hair, mouth open in every frame, as if he never shuts up.

I flip past Leela. And Peter. And Joey.

The only one missing is Graffam herself.

"What the fuck is this?" I hear myself say.

Isaac swipes the papers from me, and then Ness grabs a handful, and Effy again. All of us staring at what are clearly storyboards for a film shoot. Here's a close-up of Effy with a title written across: *The sad-sack orphan, bad-girl suck-up.* Here's a close-up of Isaac: *The privileged asshole with a massive chip on his shoulder.* Here's one of me: *The overtalkative nerd who doesn't realize he's a bargain-bin Wes Anderson trope.*

"What the fuck," Isaac echoes.

There are thousands of images. At least that's how it feels. In reality, there are probably sixty or eighty frames, but it seems as if they're everywhere, as if they're dropping from the fucking ceiling, from the fucking sky, as if there's a blizzard of them trying to flatten us.

Effy presses a button on the computer keyboard. A buzzing and the monitor powers on. I'm suddenly seeing this scene from one of Graffam's storyboards—the four remaining students inside the locked room, discovering their teacher's dark secret, faces lit by the glow of the screen.

The computer wants a password. Of course it wants a password. And unfortunately I am not the kind of overtalkative nerd who can hack into mainframes. Everyone starts throwing out ideas, Isaac's fingers hovering over the keys. *Birth date, the name of her first film, the name of her ex-husband, the name of a pet she had. Does anyone know if she had any pets?*

"Hold on," I say. I lean in and type *TheLie*. "Drea says she uses the same password for everything." I press enter.

Denied.

I type it again.

Denied.

I'm typing feverishly now, a third time, but Effy yanks me away before I can enter it. "You're going to lock up the computer."

And then Ness goes, "Wait."

In the movie version, this would be where she remembers something Graffam once told her that will magically grant us access to her computer. But instead she picks up a thumb drive, lost beneath the mountain of pages, and holds it up for all to see.

NESS'S LAPTOP HAS the most juice, so she hurries off to get it. Isaac and I pace the floor, bitching and moaning—just endless hot air—while Effy stands at the window, eyes far away. When I join her there and lay my hand on her arm, she doesn't seem to notice. She just continues staring out in the direction of Brighton's Woe.

A few minutes later, we hear the sound of footfalls and Ness is back. She sinks into the chair, takes the thumb drive from Effy, and plugs it into her laptop. We gather around, all eyes on her screen, and wait.

When the drive appears in the menu, Ness clicks on it.

Instantly a file appears.

Untitled Graffam.

Ness clicks on this.

Inside there are just three folders. *Footage*, *MKUltra*, and *Rough Cut*.

She opens *Footage* first.

Within it, eight folders, one for each of us. In alphabetical order: *Arlo, Effy, Isaac, Joey, Leela, Ness, Peter, Ramon.* And inside those, the same five folders: *Video Journals. Stunts and Games. Gaslighting. Scare Tactics. Everything Else.*

The files render. Hundreds of them. Film clips of various length, divided by location—the woods, the beach, the south side of the house, north side of the house, Brighton's Woe, first floor, second floor—and within those folders, more folders labeled by room.

Ness opens one randomly. It's Isaac. He looks into the camera. For a long time, he doesn't speak. Then he says, "Do you ever feel alone? I mean, I guess we all do." On camera, he sighs, rubs both his hands over the stubble on his head, from the back of his head to the front, over and over. "But I mean the kind of alone where you're shouting into a vacuum and you don't even hear an echo? Like not only is no one else there, you aren't even there either. That's how it feels to be Isaac Thelonious Williams III."

Isaac reaches past her and stops the video. "That's from my video journal," he says without feeling, or maybe with too much feeling, it's hard to tell.

"But . . ." Effy begins.

She's interrupted by another film clip. Ness this time, talking to the camera. "And then I wonder if she isn't kicking them out *because* of me. To see what I'll do, if I'll confess. Like each time I feel worse because that's another person's place I've stolen. Because I appropriated—"

This time Effy is the one to press stop. She leans over her friend's shoulder and maneuvers to the file icons as Ness looks on as if in a trance. And now we start clicking through. Peter talking about what a bunch of pussies we are, how he's got the scholarship in the bag. Me talking about Effy, how she needs to just get over it and herself. On and on. And then, in another clip, me talking about Jonah. Then Effy again, staring out at us from the computer. "I love her. I just get tired of carrying her. I want to shake her sometimes, and maybe that's not fair, but I'm like, *Come on*. It's not like I feel great about myself all the time, but the alternative is to be Ness."

Ness herself stops the video. "I'm sorry you have to carry me," she says in this short, angry voice. She doesn't look at Effy or at any of us. Her eyes stay fixed on the screen.

"It's not like it sounds," Effy says. "Ness? You have to believe me. I was in a shitty mood and—I didn't mean those things. I was just bitching about everything and everyone." She turns to Isaac. "That was in my video journal too. On my camera. The one Graffam gave me." Her eyes find mine. "My account—I never shared it."

We echo her: *I didn't share mine either.*

Ness scrolls through the library of clips. I see all of our faces go by. But there are other things I don't recognize from the thumbnails. We point out this one and that one, another and another. The eight of us in the water on that first day with Graffam. Peter swiping the bottle of wine. Badminton. The shattering of the mirror. Graffam writing out the index cards of our darkest secrets. Graffam throwing away the remnants of the mirror.

Ness quickly closes *Footage*. She hesitates and then opens the other folder. Inside *Rough Cut* there are six different files. Each labeled *RC*, followed by a date. We open the most recent one. From yesterday.

She presses play. Expands it to full screen.

A brief pause and then the images flicker to life. Footage cobbled together, raw but in chronological order, the sound of wind and ocean—spare, haunting—playing beneath scenes of us jumping into the frigid ocean, shouting in the middle of Highway 127, playing hide-and-seek. Me telling the camera that it was my fault, that I killed Jonah. Me with the joint, on the cliffs. The five of us drinking wine. Ramon walking into the forest. The four of us in the woods, separated, lost. All our confessions and revelations. The house shuttered and locked, the four of us hiding within.

Image after horrible image. The entire rough cut lasts maybe three minutes, and I can't tell what it's supposed to be, what the story is, what the point of it is. Except to show the world how fucked up we are. Just your average overprivileged fucked-up kids. No redeeming qualities. Nothing good or worthwhile. And so easily manipulated, so easily influenced, so easily, pathetically led. All in the name of, what, success? Power? Winning for winning's sake?

Maybe that's the point, to show that we'll do anything to win. But if so—why?

We go back to the first *Rough Cut* file and view the videos in order. We can't seem to stop ourselves, can't look away.

"Is this real?" Ness whispers.

And then, once again, we play the file from yesterday. The time stamp reads *22:03 p.m. 1/20.* Which means she worked on this after she returned from New York while we were downstairs waiting to be summoned.

"Oh my God," Effy says, her voice just a breath.

Something scratches at the back of my brain. I tell Ness, "Go back to the first screen."

She navigates back to *Footage*, *MKUltra*, and *Rough Cut* and looks up at me. Effy and Isaac protest. They've seen enough. They don't want to see any more.

I point to the screen. "That one."

"Here." Ness hands me the laptop, clearly done with it.

I click on *MKUltra*. It contains a single document, pages and pages long and broken into sections: *MKUltra. Laudanum. Tetrahydrozoline. Psilocybin. Microdosing. The Effects of Psychotropic Drugs on Teens.*

I skim through it while Effy, Isaac, and Ness watch. I stop when I come to a list. All of us are there, including Joey, Peter, Leela, and Ramon.

Only now—in this moment—does it all catch up with me. A gut punch that leaves me sick. My right hand starts to shake, so I set the laptop on the table. Run my fingers through my hair, fast and furious. I look up. All their eyes on me.

"I recognized the name. In the 1950s the CIA approved this thing called Project MKUltra. The US was scared that North Korean agents were trying to brainwash our prisoners of war. The whole purpose was to develop techniques that could be used against our enemies to control human behavior. It went on for decades. I think they officially ceased operation in, like, 1973. I know this not because of my own encyclopedic knowledge of world events—"

"Arlo," Effy snaps, focusing me.

"Right. But because my parents are in the military. Anyway, these tests were conducted at universities, prisons, hospitals—they recruited prostitutes to lure men in. Most of the people being experimented on had no idea."

"Dude," Isaac groans. "Experimented on them how . . . ?"

"Lysergic acid diethylamide. LSD. The whole purpose was to learn how to control people's minds. To make them commit unspeakable acts. Get them to do things they might not normally do. A mind on acid becomes confused. Perception is distorted. There can be euphoria or panic. Your identity can get lost. But it's not just MKUltra."

I scroll through the document again, pointing out the various headers.

"She's been researching other instances where people were dosed without their knowledge. Tetrahydrozoline, that's the active ingredient in Visine." I tap the screen. "Laudanum is basically opium. Psychotropics are Adderall, Ritalin, mood stabilizers, antianxiety meds, that kind of thing. Psilocybin is mushrooms—"

"Wait. Arlo." Ness's voice falters. "You're saying . . ."

Effy sways where she stands, or maybe it's me that's swaying. Or maybe it's the room, or maybe it's all of us.

"I'm saying it looks like Visine isn't her only drug of choice." And then I show them our names on the screen, followed by dates and amounts, the exact drug unspecified.

Isaac grabs for the computer, scrolling backward and forward and backward again. Then Effy, then Ness, each taking a turn reading and rereading, scrolling and scrolling and scrolling, trying to understand.

I think back to Graffam turning us loose in the woods. To the day we stood in the middle of the highway, traffic rushing by. To every fucking moment where I felt blurry or out of it, impulse control lowered, paranoia heightened, inhibitions freed.

The others are doing it too—Isaac aloud as he paces, practically wearing a groove in the floor. Effy and Ness silently, eyes darting as they, like me, add it all up. The dates we felt sick or tired. Effy, Ness, and Isaac bedridden with what we thought was the flu. Chef sent home suddenly. Graffam stepping in to prepare the food.

"But why?" says Ness, her voice small and scared.

We sit and stand, the four of us side by side. Not speaking. Not moving. Each of us trying to grasp what the fuck this is and what the fuck it means. And why, why, why.

Effy

Wednesday, January 21

Arlo raises his eyes to meet mine. They are darker than usual, a deep storm gray, filled with anger and pain and confusion, all the things he must see in my own. Time just . . . stops.

And then Isaac is gone and there is a crash from another room, and I can't tell whether it's upstairs or downstairs. Arlo turns toward the noise. Another crash, a smashing sound, a howl of pain.

"Graffam," I say. Meaning *Make him be quiet before she comes up here and finds us.*

Arlo says, "I'll go. We should all get out of here though."

As Arlo disappears after Isaac, I turn back for Ness, who sits perfectly, unnervingly still.

"Ness? We need to leave this room. We don't want her finding us, and we don't want her knowing what we know. Not yet . . ."

From the chair she says, "Even when I'm talking to myself, whether or not someone is eavesdropping on me without me knowing it, I never bitch about you. Not for who you are. Not for who you aren't."

"What about my paragraph, the one you rewrote?" The words burst out before I can stop them. "The one you said was 'repetitious' and 'pedantic'?"

"Graffam said it was extra credit. I was looking for a way to make an impression. The rest of you make one just by walking into a room, so I felt like I needed something extra because . . . I'm not like you."

"And you didn't think that was weird?"

"No," Ness says simply. "She said it's always good to dissect the work of other writers. That's what I thought I was doing. I wasn't rewriting you because I felt like you needed it. And I wasn't bitching about you behind your back."

"I'm sorry," I say. "Let's go to your room and we'll talk about it. We just need to get out of—"

"All the things she said you said—she told me not to trust you."

"Who? The same woman who's been *filming* us? Who's been essentially telling me the same thing: *Don't trust anyone, no matter what?*"

"We believed in her." Ness starts to cry.

Don't cry, I want to tell her. *Not now. Not yet.* I want to shake her and drag her out of this room. But why shouldn't she cry? What she's doing is perfectly normal in this un-normal situation. I should be crying too. What does it say about me that I'm not?

Then, from somewhere down below, I hear Graffam's voice.

"Ness," I bark. It comes out too sharp, too loud.

She flinches like I've slapped her.

"Let's go," I hiss.

She gets to her feet, her movements labored and plodding, and shuffles out the door, gone, leaving me to collect her laptop and return everything to its rightful place. The last thing I do is remove the doorknob, but as I cross the landing of the catwalk toward Graffam's rooms, I hear her voice again, louder this time.

I freeze.

My heart beats harder than any drum. I consider jumping over the balcony railing into the theater below. But then I catch sight of her head as she strolls to the piano and begins to play a song. Her fingers dance across the keys with skill and grace.

*"Oh who sits weeping on my grave,
And will not let me sleep?"*

Her voice is low and throaty. Not a beautiful voice, but hypnotic just the same. The meaning of the words hits me for the first time—it's a dialogue between a woman who died and the man who loved her. His grief so deep that it keeps her from eternal rest.

*"Tis I, my love, sits on your grave,
And will not let you sleep;
For I crave one kiss of your clay-cold lips,
And that is all I seek."*

I slip down the stairs, trying not to breathe. There's no sign of Ness. I send up a prayer to Moss Hove and my mother and the universe to help me pass soundlessly, invisibly. *Please let me get back to my floor and the others.*

When I reach the very last stair, I exhale—too soon. As I set my foot down, the wood lets out its own breath, a quick, defensive creak.

Graffam stops playing.

"Hello?" she calls.

I don't answer. I don't breathe. And then I hear the sound of her footsteps as she crosses from the rug to the wooden floor. The serpent's mouth is open wide, and I slip the thumb drive deep into its recesses.

Just in time, I tuck the laptop under my arm and change direction so that it looks as if I'm coming from the Sky Room.

She appears in the doorway of the theater.

"Effy?" She glances past me up the stairs.

"I didn't know you played," I say. My own voice sounds surprisingly normal, if a little louder than usual. "That was beautiful."

She studies me. Then, after a few seconds, she smiles—closed mouth, the way I do. "Thank you."

"Well." I tap the laptop, hoping she won't notice its pink cover, so obviously Ness's. "I guess I should get back to work. Only one more day and there's still so much to do."

I give her a regretful smile and turn away, heart hammering in my chest.

But then something compels me to turn back, to open my foolish mouth.

I say, "You never saw Timothy Hugh Martin in the woods the night of The Wild Hunt."

She looks surprised, almost flattered. *Tell me I'm wrong*, I think. *Tell me I'm wrong.*

"No," she says matter-of-factly. Then she glances at the laptop. When her eyes meet mine again, her gaze is clear and untroubled.

As I cross through the theater and back toward the other side of the house, I wait for her to stop me, to tell me this is all just a fever dream. But instead I hear the song resume, her voice ringing brightly through the halls.

IN MY TOWER room, Ness, Isaac, Arlo, and I assemble like the cast of a low-budget slasher film. The sad-sack orphan. The overtalkative nerd. The privileged asshole. The anxious wallflower. In here, at least—as far as I could tell from the footage—there are no cameras. *How nice of her*, I think. *To grant us this one privacy.*

Outside, the wind is gathering force and the ocean is swelling like a creature being fed. Already more powerful than the last blizzard. Something bangs against the window, and all of us jump. And then we begin to talk at once, over each other, not listening to anyone but ourselves.

"We need to find and disable the remaining cameras in the house."

"We need to pretend like everything's normal until we figure out what to do."

"We need to confront her, give her a chance to explain."

"There's nothing she can say to explain this away."

"We need to find a way to break into the cloud and her computer and delete the footage."

"We need to retrieve the thumb drive from the serpent's mouth."

"We need to talk to Drea and see what she knows."

"Maybe Drea can help us delete the originals. She might have the computer password."

"But what if she's part of this? After all, she works for Graffam. How much does she know about the cameras, the drugging?"

"But she warned us, she told us to run."

"We can borrow the gate key from Wesley, get him to drive us back to campus."

"We need to call our families. We need to talk to lawyers."

"We need to tell Dean Booker what she's done."

"Is this really happening? How is this happening?"

Around and around until my head is splitting. The four of us together but apart, unable to agree until Arlo says, "It's time to blow this pop stand. No good can come of staying. We'll think better when we're out from under this roof."

Arlo

Wednesday, January 21

We make our way down the grand stairway as quietly as possible. With every groan of a floorboard, we freeze. Listen. Wait.

When we reach the landing, something scratches at the glass, and I jump. Just a tree branch. Just the wind. Effy lays a hand on my arm, and I go immediately calm—or, at least, calmer.

We cross the wide expanse of entryway. The hall is vast as a river, the front door, on its opposite shore. I take Effy's hand in mine, and we entwine our fingers. The feel of her skin anchors me.

And then, suddenly, we're there. I let go of Effy's hand and try the doorknob, which is cold to the touch. I look down and realize the key is missing.

I turn the knob anyway, pushing on the door, but it doesn't budge. I tell myself the key just fell out of the lock. It's here somewhere. It's got to be here. I back away, scanning the floor.

"What's wrong?" Effy asks.

"The key's gone."

Isaac rattles the doorknob, the door itself, then Effy tries it, then Ness, then me again. All of us hoping against hope that somehow it'll open. When it doesn't, we spread out, searching the floor. Bent over, on hands and knees, until, overhead, there's a sound of footsteps.

"There are other doors," Ness whispers.

We explore neighboring rooms, trying any door that leads outside. Every single one of them is missing the key that opens it.

Isaac whirls on Effy. "Did she see you?"

"I told you no."

"She must have seen you coming down."

"You were the one making all the noise . . ."

"Shut up," I tell them.

Another corridor. Another. And then the last. Until we've tried all the doors but one.

The four of us head for the library. We skulk past the solarium, a passageway lit with uranium glass, a room wallpapered in flowers so thick and heavy they feel suffocating.

"You don't think . . ." Effy starts, then stops herself. She almost laughs. "You don't think we need to be afraid, do you?"

No one answers her because we have entered the library, right beneath Graffam's rooms. And suddenly the French door is there, within reach. My heart flips when I see the key in the lock.

Effy's face is as anxious and hopeful as my own. I hear the softest *click* and the creak of the door swinging open. Isaac grins back at us, takes a step forward, and disappears.

It takes Effy, Ness, and me one long, heart-stopping second

to realize what's happened. As we rush forward, a frigid blast of wind hits me in the face, and I see Isaac clinging to what remains of a deck. At one time, it must have been large and grand, but all that's left of it is a narrow ledge of buckling and rotting wood. His legs dangle over the rocks and the ocean below.

Ness moves first, gripping one side of the doorframe with her left hand and grabbing for him with the right. I catch hold of the other side, and Effy yells at him to stop thrashing. The more he moves, the harder it is to hold on. I watch as the last of the deck gives way beneath him, and for one horrible moment, it threatens to take Isaac—and Ness and me—with it.

But then I think of you.

You didn't die so that I could survive, only to follow you a few months later. That would mean you gave up your life for nothing.

I dig into the doorframe with my fingers, arms, legs, melding myself to the floor. I dig into Isaac's flesh so hard I bypass muscle and feel the bone. I feel Effy grab one of my legs, anchoring me as Ness counts: *One... Two... Three.* And we pull.

Gravity tries to drag Isaac downward. I start to lose my grip and shout at him to help us, to use momentum to wrench himself up and away so that we can haul him back to safety. For a moment, I'm not sure he hears me. Then I feel him suck in a breath, and his other hand claws at the wood of the threshold. Ness and I jerk him toward us with superhuman strength. All four of us tumble across the floor, chests heaving, breath rattling above the wind and the waves. My hand is still on his wrist, and I'm sure he can feel the rapid-fire beating of my pulse.

Ness whispers to the ceiling, to all of us, "She left the key, knowing we might open it."

Yes, I think. *Yes, we need to be afraid.*

WE FIND WESLEY in the laundry room, pulling clothes out of the dryer. His expression darkens when he sees us. It goes even darker as Effy asks if he has a key to the front door, to any door. She tells him the keys are missing. All doors locked, all keys gone.

He gestures for us to follow him. We pass from laundry room to kitchen to a utility room I've never seen, narrow and spare except for cast-iron hangers on the wall by a back door, which is also keyless. Hanging there are umbrellas, raincoats, winter coats, scarves. One hook is empty.

"I have a ring with all the keys to every door and window. My spare." Wesley rests his hand on the empty hanger. *Gone.* "Graffam . . . she confiscated the gate key, said she'd feel better holding on to it herself. But I didn't know she took the others."

"You can call Books," I say.

He shakes his head. "Not without a landline. Not unless I can get outside to use my phone."

"Does that mean we're locked in?" Effy asks, even though we already know the answer.

Wesley lowers his voice, as aware of Graffam as we are. "Yes," he breathes. "You're locked in. We all are."

Effy

WEDNESDAY, JANUARY 21

Silently we wind our way to the staircase that leads to our wing. We climb them in single file. We pass the stuffed birds of prey and the dead landline and arrive in our hallway.

"Before dinner," Isaac says. "We find her and confront her. One way or another."

I don't want to know what he means by this.

Inside my room, I drop onto my bed and study my limbs, expecting to see the blood from this new wound seeping into the bedding, the walls, the floor, the trees, until the sea turns red and the Moss and everyone in it is carried away.

When did she start drugging people? When she was a child? When she was a student at Brighton and Hove? Or did the poisonings come later?

I open my arms wide on the mattress and let it all in, a

flood of thoughts and memories. All the hope and promise and excitement when I found out I was accepted to Jan Term, when I found out who would be teaching us. The first time she sought me out to talk to me, to tell me she believed in me. The electric thrill that I, Effy Green, was chosen as a protégé of the one and only Meredith Graffam. Because she saw something in me that was good and valuable.

Or was it that she saw in me something weak and malleable? Something that reminded her of Lara, her former best friend? Something broken that would make me a good test subject for her experiment?

The sting of the betrayal spreads through me like venom, filling tissue and bone, settling into the part of myself I keep hidden away.

We let her in, I think. *I let her in.*

I see something in you, Effy, she said.

This is only your beginning.

We trusted her. The worst betrayal of all.

Then a montage of images and feelings replays in my mind—of Arlo and me. How much of it was real, and how much of it was drug-induced?

I feel drugged right now as I try to sort through the wilderness of my emotions—everything I've felt for him, everything he feels for me. For the past couple of weeks, for better or worse, I've felt like I was a part of something. Not just Arffy, but all of it, everyone. *How do I know I can trust it?*

I think about Arlo's fascination with Bigfoot. His desire to see one for himself, to know that they're real. His belief in things unseen because we all need to believe in something outside ourselves, even if it's a fantastical creature. Suddenly I get it, that need. For a while, I believed too. In the mythical Meredith Graffam, who didn't become real to us until it was too late.

Arlo

Wednesday, January 21

Two weeks ago, I dreaded the end of Jan Term, knowing it would mean leaving the Moss and Meredith Graffam and Effy and having to figure out the rest of my life. It's strange how everything can change and nothing can change all at once. Isaac and I still need this class to graduate. Ness needs the scholarship money. Effy needs . . . the validation, I guess? The closure?

The four of us find her in the kitchen, preparing our dinner like the witch from "Hansel and Gretel." Music plays softly from some unseen source. She floats from refrigerator to stove—where various pots are simmering—gathering ingredients.

"Ness," she says without looking up, "see if there are more potatoes on the shelves."

Reflexively, Ness starts toward the pantry, but Effy lays a hand on her arm. "We need to talk to you," she tells Graffam.

"Oh?" Graffam finishes stirring something on the gas

burner, winds the old kitchen timer that sits on the counter, wipes her hands on a dish towel, and faces us. "I hope this isn't about the cameras."

It's the last thing I expected her to say. Effy, Ness, Isaac, and I stare at her like four stunned little birds that have flown into a window.

"Actually, it is the cameras," I begin. Of course she knows we found them. They must be everywhere.

She nods, and now she's smiling like a proud parent, like we, her exceptionally unathletic children, have just earned Olympic medals. "Well done." As if we're all in on a big, juicy secret.

She lifts the lid of one of the simmering pots and inhales. Stirs the contents. Covers it again. Checks the timer. Turns back to us.

"But because each of you signed a waiver—a legally binding contract that gives your consent to be filmed during this three-week period and grants me full control over all the footage . . . because of that, there's nothing to talk about. At least not on that subject."

She looks from Isaac to Ness to Effy to me.

"I hope you can see—if not now, at some point—that this isn't personal. None of it is."

She is still smiling, but her voice has iced over like a pond in winter.

"Now. I need to make dinner. Drea and I will meet you in the dining room at seven."

WE SIT AT the table, Graffam and Drea at either end, Ness and me across from Isaac and Effy. Graffam chatters happily, our last conversation seemingly forgotten. Drea lifts an eyebrow at me, almost expectantly, but I'm not up for whatever silent message she's trying to communicate or whatever silent question she's asking. And so I stare down at my plate, at this meal so lovingly prepared by my teacher. I twirl my fork in the mashed potatoes, the butter soaking it, the chicken smothered in sauce, so much liquid. *All the better to dose you with, my pretties.* I push the food around the way I used to when I was younger and didn't want to eat my vegetables, trying to make it look as if I've had some.

I glance at Effy, who isn't even pretending. Her fork lies on the table, her meal and her drink untouched.

Meanwhile, Graffam rattles on about New York, the weather, the traffic, yada yada yada. Pretending to complain, but her eyes are shining. I stop listening until Drea says, "I've been hearing about the call of the void."

My head pops up. Isaac and Ness are staring at Drea, at Effy.

For a second, Effy merely blinks, over and over. But then she says, "Oh. L'appel du vide. Yes." This is a flat and toneless version of Effy, but no one else seems to notice.

She describes it the same way she has described it to us, and then Drea says, "In Spanish, there is no exact translation, but there's something called la atracción del vacío. It means *the attraction of emptiness.* Although yours sounds more positive, more exhilarating."

Graffam takes a sip of wine, cradling the glass with one hand. If I were lighting this scene in a film, it would look exactly like this. Our villain by candlelight, her shadow looming above us on the wall at her back.

She asks, "Is it the same urge you have when you're in a quiet movie theater and you suddenly feel a scream rise in your throat?"

"That's more of an intrusive thought," Effy says. "The call of the void is literally the urge to hurl yourself into a void. It's also known as high-place phenomenon, even though it doesn't always have to do with high places. You could think about jumping into deep water or sticking your hand in a garbage disposal or jerking the steering wheel into oncoming traffic."

Effy delivers each word crisply, as if she's picturing these things happening to Graffam.

"Like a death wish?" Our teacher tilts her head, trying to grasp the concept.

Effy shakes her head. Her eyes have come alive again. "Actually, it's scientifically proven to be life-affirming. Something you think about because you want to live. And it's totally normal. We all experience it to some degree."

"The call of the void," Graffam murmurs. "What a great title."

She nods at Drea, a gesture I take to mean *Write this down.* But Drea doesn't.

Graffam frowns and then leans forward, as if we're all conspiring. "During The Wild Hunt, when I was a student here, I hid in the hardest spots. In the creek. Up a tree. At the edge of an overlook. Places I didn't think anyone else would search because they were too afraid. But I wasn't. I liked the feeling of peril. Just out of reach. But within reach if I wanted it."

"That's exactly it." Effy smiles now, catlike.

Graffam sits back in her chair, surveying us. When her

eyes lock with mine, she is somehow looking beyond me, at something only she sees.

Suddenly there is a *click* in my brain, as if the solution to an equation—one I've been wrestling with for years—has just appeared, and all this time it was *right there*.

"It's the last night of Jan Term," I say to Effy, Ness, and Isaac.

Graffam starts to laugh. "And you're only remembering this now? I hope you have your project done, Arlo. It's due tomorrow before you leave the Moss."

But I'm not talking to her. "The Wild Hunt. Isn't it always played on the last night of Jan Term?"

"Yeah. It is." A light dawns in Isaac. "It's tradition."

Drea says, "This storm's supposed to arrive by morning, maybe earlier. It's meant to be bad. Far worse than the last. High winds. Ice. We might be stranded out here."

But no one is listening. And if Graffam is concerned, she's not letting on. I imagine our bodies discovered with the spring thaw. Everyone dead but her.

Without meaning to, I meet her eye. Her head is tilted to one side, and she is studying me. I wait for her to ask what I'm up to. Then she says, "What was it I told you on that first day?" She takes a sip of wine as she pretends to think. *Ever the actress.* "You can choose to be safe. Or not. 'You have to pick the places you don't walk away from.'"

My eyes flick from the peacock-blue bottle on the table to Graffam herself. She is quiet, still pretending to think. Then she just . . . smiles. An enormous, too-bright, red-carpet smile.

"Tonight, then. The Wild Hunt." Her voice trips lightly across the room. Like her smile, it's impossible to read.

"Tonight," I echo.

"You'd better eat up," she says, a singsong. Her eyes move from Isaac to Effy to Ness to me. She is waiting. And so—not wanting to give ourselves away—we eat.

BACK UPSTAIRS, THE four of us flee to our respective bathrooms to throw up our dinner. Minutes later, teeth brushed, faces washed, we meet again in the hallway.

Effy hisses at me, "What was that about? Are you serious about playing The Wild Hunt?" She looks back and forth between Isaac and me.

Ness pokes me and then Isaac like, *Yeah*, and I can't believe they don't see it.

"That," I tell them, "was about the *Velella velella*."

Effy goes, "Are you trying to tell us in your vague, asinine way that all is not yet lost and good can win?"

"Yes, Effy, that is exactly what I'm saying."

"More literal please, and faster." Ness glances over her shoulder.

But it's Isaac who explains. "I had a bully when I was in grade school. This was before I hit my growth spurt. He used to beat the shit out of me during recess, and no one—not even the teachers—would do anything. I came home looking pretty rough one day, and my father said, 'You need to hit him back,' I was like, 'Yeah right.' But he said, 'What you do is take a rock and wrap your hand around it and then you hit him, but don't let anyone see the rock.'"

"What happened?" asks Ness, momentarily swept up in the story.

"I broke his nose and gave him a black eye. I got a lecture from the principal and a two-day suspension. His parents called my parents and threatened to sue, so I had to apologize. I told him, 'I'm sorry you're such an asshole.' But that kid didn't touch me again. The trick is to disguise the rock so no one suspects anything."

"So the rock isn't a rock." One by one, we look at Ness. Her eyes shine like fireflies. "The rock is a game." It's not a question.

"We hit back." The corners of Effy's mouth begin to lift.

"Yes," Isaac says. "By scaring the shit out of her."

"And the way we do that," I say, "is by threatening to destroy her. And the way we do *that* is by letting everyone know who she really is. And I mean everyone."

They look at me, questioning.

"Peter," I say. "We call up Peter."

"Peter." Isaac nods. "Whose parents own more than a few magazines."

"Magazines," I add, "that would probably love to hear what kind of person Graffam really is, not to mention the shitty things she's done."

Ness is shaking her head slowly. "But what about the NDAs?"

"Who gives a shit?" I tell her. "I'll be the one who does it, who breaks whatever contract we signed with her back when we didn't know what she was planning. I don't care."

"I don't care either," Isaac says. Of all of us, he has the most to lose. He knows it, and we do too. But just like the *Velella velella*, we're all in this together. "Quid pro quo. She deletes the footage and we keep quiet."

"And if she doesn't?" Effy is frowning, still not convinced. "If she keeps the footage and we *can't* destroy her reputation? In case you all forgot, she rebuilt herself once. She'll just do it again."

No one speaks for a long moment.

In a quiet voice, Ness says, "Then we find a more permanent way to destroy her."

We stand as still as statues, unwilling to disturb the moment. When something bangs against the windows, we jump, breathless and on edge. The wind. It's just the wind.

Rules for The Wild Hunt

The Hunt takes place in the month of January, Perchta's feast month.

The Hunter, Perchta (or Percht) the Undead, is chosen. A volunteer is allowed; otherwise, the Hunter will be designated by straws. (The shortest equals the Hunter.)

Those who are not hunting are the Living, also known as the Perchten.

The Living must hide in the woods or cliffs surrounding the house, no farther than the perimeter walls. (Refer to map for specific boundaries.)

The goal of the Hunter is to collect as many souls as possible. The goal of the Living is to outlast and evade as many Hunters as possible.

If the Hunter is unable to find more than one member of the Living within thirty minutes' time, a new Hunter will be chosen. With the choosing of a new Hunter, the Living must leave their hiding places and choose new ones.

The Hunter has three "calls" at their disposal. They may use these calls to summon their prey. The Living must respond if called.

The Wild Hunt continues until every player has had a chance at being the Hunter.

Ruler of the Forest is awarded to the Hunter who collects the most souls. The Ruler of the Forest will be crowned and celebrated and allowed to escape death for another day.

Effy

WEDNESDAY, JANUARY 21

The forest is immaculate in the snow. Everything feels at once hushed and alive—not just the birds but the trees themselves. A rustling, a humming, the hypnotic cadence of waves on the shore. The calm before the storm.

I take it in, knowing that nothing will be the same after tonight. Not sunsets, not the sound of the ocean, not the Moss. Not me.

It's a rare starless evening. The five of us are masked and hooded, separated by the trees. We are reminded of the boundaries: *The woods, the grounds, the cliffs. No going down to the water. We must, at all times, be able to see the house. If we lose sight of it, we've gone too far.* We are reminded of the rules, and one of our own: *We must strike fear into the heart of Meredith Graffam.*

A breeze blows my hair into my eyes, and I brush it away, holding it in place. From somewhere nearby, I hear Ness's laugh, and then I hear Arlo begin to sing some long-ago song I've forgotten the words to.

Hello?
Is it me you're looking for?

I can't see the others, and I assume they can't see me. We blend into the forest. But it's enough to know they're there.

And then I hear Graffam's voice from somewhere deep in the trees, in the undergrowth: "'The night is chill; the forest bare . . . / The moon shines dim in the open air, / And not a moonbeam enters here. / But they without its light can see.'"

"'But they without its light can see,'" we echo from our places among the trees. "'But they without its light can see.'"

A figure moves, wraithlike, in and out of darkness, and I begin to follow. Into darkness. Out of darkness. The forest closes in: the cracking of tree limbs, the rustling of brush, the howl of a distant animal, the sight of red eyes glowing somewhere off the path, the sulfuric stench of the swamp. It feels as if the entire planet is nothing but trees and moss and undergrowth and phantom sounds and the dark, dark sky.

"The Wild Hunt has begun," someone calls. And we are off.

I AM ALONE. Moving in the shadows. In the distance, a glimmer of light, a reminder that it's only a game and I'm within running distance of my green room, my mom's nightshirt, my dad's letter, my books, my earthly possessions.

From far away I hear a singsong: "Ready or not, here I come . . ."

I pull deeper into the shadows. We are hiding at the same time we are seeking because we must find her before she has the chance to find us. Not seeking. *Hunting.* Because it is The

Wild Hunt. A night steeped in folklore, in which the dead hunt the living and the door between worlds is opened.

I secretly wish the myth was true so I could see my mother, even for a single night. I would memorize her voice, the way she moves, the way she smells, every little gesture, so I could repeat them and make them my own. A part of her I could keep with me when she was gone again.

The air is thin and close. In spite of my pounding heart, I am invisible, protected by the trees, which grow up into the sky. I feel drugged, but I'm not drugged, just alive in every sense of the word. All my senses firing at once. Dizzy with power and focus. Terrified by Graffam and what she might do to us. At the realization that she's someone who will stop at nothing, who's killed before and could kill again.

I should be afraid.

I am afraid.

I can feel the pulsing of every tree, of every living creature. I stare down at my feet, dug into soft green moss. The moss is a living thing. I can feel it throb beneath my shoes and realize I'm killing it as I stand there. I jump back, but the ground is covered in moss, moss everywhere.

A voice sings, "Come out, come out, wherever you are . . ." It seems to originate from the earth, the sky, to the left of me, to the right of me. My heart hammers within my chest. Graffam embodies the role of Perchta. The goddess with two sides, one true, one false.

I bat at cobwebs as I slip from tree to tree. I remember to look for the house, which is just right there even though it feels like it should be farther away.

"Come out, come out." The voice is faint, like an echo. "You can't hide forever . . ."

No, I want to call back. You *can't hide forever.*

In the thick of the woods, I lose sight of her, of my fellow Odds. It feels as if she could be anywhere. I spy something moving in the distance. Then a body crashes toward me, the face contorted. It takes me a second to realize it's a mask. A ghoulish animal. I tell myself it's just Ness or Isaac or Arlo. But—out here on my own—my mind plays tricks in the gloom, and we race away from each other, away from Graffam the Hunter, who has somehow vanished.

I will not, cannot scream. I run and I run until I am the air and the wind, until my feet no longer touch the ground but are carried over it and above it. I spread my arms wide, as if I can embrace all 11,000 acres, or the earth itself. I twirl until everything begins to tilt, and then I start running again, taking big, bounding steps, playing hopscotch across the woodland floor.

I lose track of time. The world in here is shadow and stillness. When I hear a trumpeting cry in the distance, it takes me a few seconds to respond. The others answer the cry from various points in the wood, voices faint and haunting. They are far away, and I wonder how we let it happen. We were supposed to work together like the *Velella velella*.

We need to gather ourselves, remember our purpose. We are hunting her, not the other way around. But minutes later there is a wild shriek, which tells me Ness has been caught. And then the sound of the old bell splits the night in two. Drea, ringing it from the courtyard of the Moss. Which means half an hour, already gone. Ness becomes the Hunter, and Graffam will, like the rest of us, try to hide. Before she takes off, I need to find her, follow her, see where she goes. We are losing time.

I start to move in their direction. For a minute or two, I manage to track Graffam—or the figure I think is Graffam. But then she seems to evaporate. She has played this before, and she knows how to be invisible.

Suddenly I hear my name. "Effy," it calls, and I imagine claws reaching for me, a creature crawling along the forest floor, limbs outstretched. But then I hear my name again and it's her, it's Graffam. She's supposed to be hiding, not hunting.

Something swipes at me, and I smell sulfur and earth and my own blood from where it tore at my leg. *What the fuck.* I dash away until the forest grows thicker, darker, more tangled, and I can no longer see the sky. I am a tiger outrunning it—her. A tiger with teeth and claws, capable of tearing flesh with a single swipe, a single bite. But when I look down, I have hands, not paws, and I realize my mind is playing tricks on me. *But we threw up Graffam's drug-laced food.*

I glance behind me, searching for her, and this is when I trip and fall.

I pick myself up, but she is closer now, within arm's reach. For her mask she has chosen the swan, beautiful and deadly. In that now-familiar singsong, she repeats a word over and over. A word that doesn't make sense.

She is behind me, running hard, earth vibrating beneath her. And that's when a voice inside me says, *Turn around.*

But before I can turn, I feel it—the moment the rock comes down on my skull.

As I start to fall, the gravity of the earth spinning violently, I spread my arms and legs and grasp for something to hold me steady, suddenly afraid of spiraling off into the universe.

And as I drift away, watching the snow turn red, I think, *The index card—during the fatal flaw game—the one that said,* I killed my best friend. *It wasn't about Arlo at all. Graffam wrote it about herself.*

Meredith

JANUARY 18, 1995

When I emerge from the woods, the night is clear, the stars are bright, and my skin glows beneath them. For tonight, just tonight, the Moss is ours. You and me. Drew, Eytan, Colin, and the shiny girls—which is what we call them. You could have easily joined them, but instead you chose me.

You and I hide together even though it's against the rules. But then I lose sight of you, Lara. Suddenly you're up ahead with Colin Cho, the two of you like a John Hughes movie couple—complete opposites who somehow found each other last year. Holding hands in the rain, walking to dinner, watching meteor showers and gazing at the stars, writing love notes, him standing beneath our dorm window blasting your favorite song—R.E.M.'s "Everybody Hurts"—on a boom box. You were going to marry Michael Stipe because he knows the human heart. I was going to marry Bono because he is a fighter like me. Until you decided you wanted to marry Colin instead.

You should write about us, you said. *Immortalize us.*

And stupid me, I thought you meant you and me, not you and him.

The Wild Hunt. The last night of Jan Term. We are supposed to be playing the game, but you are too wrapped up in Colin, masks pushed back, bodies moving together to music only you can hear. Something by R.E.M. most likely because Colin pretends to understand why they speak to you the way they do, making you feel seen in a way he could never. In a way your family can't. In a way no one can but me.

You waited until tonight to tell me your news: *After graduation, Colin and I are moving in together.* No Michael Stipe. No Bono. No us. Just you and Colin. You thought I'd be grateful to hear it first, before anyone else. You thought I'd be happy for you, maybe even excited that this is how you plan to spend your life—as a wife, a mother, Mrs. Colin Cho, your identity erased, in spite of all the opportunities you've been given. *This* is what you plan to do with all your many talents.

I said nothing, but you didn't notice because you've stopped noticing lately. I just sat inside the Moss listening as you talked about the plans the two of you have made.

And now in the woods, in this moment, watching you with him, I realize where I belong, which is on the outside, a place I believed to be reserved for the shiny girls. Over the years, you and I have created our own secret language of looks and stories and things only we know, but none of it, none of it, comes close to the way you and Colin move together—without effort. In his face I see none of the *trying*. The constant *trying* that I feel even when I'm at my very best, which is rare, even around you, who can bring it out in ways no one ever has.

I am standing there watching when I feel arms around my waist and Eytan the Hunter lifts me off the ground and gives a sinister laugh, and instead of hating him, I love him because his time is up and now it is my turn to hunt.

I call out so that everyone will know to hide. I am the Hunter now, and only then do you and Colin break apart, dice thrown and scattering in different directions off the game board. I watch you run through the woods by yourself—so strange to know you are still capable of moving independently of him—your legs long, feet barely touching the earth. I give silent chase, a part of the woods. The trees are my friends. They are on my side. They shield me and shade me, and you are the last to know when I find you and bring the rock down upon your skull.

The jolt of it is a shock. A surprise to me as much as it is to you. The look on your face as you turn, hand to your head, the blood already pooling and streaming, a dark stain—black, not red, in the shadowy light. I imagine a similar look on my own face. Incredulity. The impossibility of such a thing.

I begin to sing another R.E.M. song, just for you. "'This one goes out to the one I love . . .'" Which manages to sound menacing, my voice thin, no more than a whisper, as I stare down at the rock in my hands, wondering how it got there, and then let it fall to the earth beside you.

You don't cry or scream, just stare at me, at the blood, and say, "Mere, why?" Like it is one word—*Merewhy*.

So plaintive, so heartbreaking. I reach for you then,

realizing what I've done, thinking maybe I can change your mind and remind you of the impact you can make if you'll just ditch this idea of Mrs. Colin Cho. But you start to run again, a wounded animal, no longer graceful and swift, but faster than you should be with a head injury. Leaving me behind—*again*.

Technically I've found you, which means I should be hunting for someone else, but you won't stop running. I need to tell you it isn't like that—whatever you secretly believe. It isn't that I want to *be* Colin. I don't love you like that. I love you more than that, a love that goes deeper than sex or desire or want or need, a love that is like night swimming on a summer evening, the bright colors of leaves in fall, the purest laughter, Holy Communion, a kind of sanctuary, a place where I can be myself in you.

You won't stop long enough for me to explain, you just run and run and run, and so I run after you until the ocean is below us, the forest at our backs. We stand on the cliffs, and you give off this phosphorescent glow that comes from somewhere deep down—the loving parents, the big, beautiful house, the generations of smart, good, beautiful people, the ones who passed down to you all these same qualities. The intrinsic goodness that makes you *you*. That enables you to befriend someone like me, with nothing to my name but sheer determination.

I feel a sudden upswell of gratitude and hatred, which knocks me senseless for a moment, until a gust of wind brings me back to the here and now. Life can be unfair. It gives some people everything and others nothing, but the ones who have everything don't always appreciate what they've been given. A terrible, horrible waste. At the same time, life is fleeting and the earth can disappear from under us in the blink of an eye. Which is why I need to be more than I am and more than my parents are and more than anyone has ever been. If I were to disappear tomorrow, I need to be remembered, to prove that I was here.

"Here, let me take a look at that cut," I say. It is meant to be a peace offering, an olive branch, but instead you spit at me and call me crazy, say Colin is right, the shiny girls are right, everyone is right about me—I am *insane. Trouble. Trash. Nothing.* Words so ugly, so cruel, I feel my heart wither and die.

You are on your feet as you shout at me, and Stray's Chasm is behind you, but you aren't thinking about the precariousness of the cliffs and the rocks below and the churning ocean and the distance from here to there. As usual, you are only thinking about yourself.

I say, "Everybody hurts." Even though *you* never have, not as long as you've been alive. Not once in your seventeen years. Not until now. I push you into the chasm and watch you fall down, down, down, Alice in the rabbit hole, feet no longer touching the earth or needing the earth because you are flying. Leaving me alone, the way you'd always planned to do.

At some point I hear voices in the distance.

The game, I think. The game.

It's like waking from a long, nightmare-filled sleep.

I descend the rocks, slipping and falling until I am at the water, and there I dive without looking. The surf pulling me under. The pain of the impact—something sharp and hard puncturing my ribs, my leg, the soft flesh of my stomach. I close my eyes and stop fighting and think of the story I will tell if they find me.

An attacker in the woods. Disguised to blend in with the Hunt. Targeting the privileged. Lying in wait. Killing Lara. Trying to kill me. He—this myth I create—will become as legendary as The Wild Hunt, something to be whispered about and feared for generations to come. When all along it was me. *How brave she was*, they'll say. *Willing to risk her own life in order to defend the life of her friend.* How, in spite of everything, I survived.

Effy

WEDNESDAY, JANUARY 21

I open my eyes to a face. "Effy." The face is worried. "Effy." The voice is worried.

"Arlo?"

"Yes."

"Is it you?"

"It's me."

I want to ask him again and again, *Is it really you?* and have him tell me a hundred times, *It's Arlo. Arlo. Arlo.* He's pushed up his mask, and I see the wild, messy curls, the generous mouth, the dimples. I throw my arms around his neck and nearly fall back from the weight of my head, which seems to be stuffed full of cotton and moss and the heaviest stones. I am still wearing the tiger mask, moldering and damp, and beneath it a headache is forming at the base of my skull.

"We've been drugged again," I slur.

"Yes," he says. I feel his fingers in my hair, so tender I

want to live in them and that tenderness. I close my eyes and he goes, "Effy." He holds up a rock. In the moonlight I can see the stain. I press my own finger to it, and the stain is wet.

"What is that?"

"This is what Graffam used to knock you out." His eyes are the eyes of a wild thing, and I wonder if mine look the same. "I'm guessing your head feels like the inside of a neutron star."

I try to push past the cotton and moss and heavy stones to make sense of what he's telling me. *Was Graffam trying to kill me or only scare me? And where is she now?*

"I know where she's hiding," he says, as if he's in my brain.

"Where?"

In answer, he takes my hand. Together we run, a lurching, staggering half run. My head throbs, and my eyes keep closing. A concussion probably. Threads of cobwebs brush my skin, and I bat them away. I don't look up, because if I do, I will see the branches reaching for each other, trying to block out the sky. I don't look ahead, because I will see only the bottomless black of the swamp, waiting to drag me down into its depths. I keep my eyes on the trail, on Arlo's back. In my mind I hear the nonsense word she kept repeating—*mairwy*.

The path grows twisted and disappears in spots. Each time I think we've lost it for good, I feel a frantic, scrabbling fear rise in my chest and throat. But then the trail reappears, and I breathe. I follow him through the trees on and on for what feels like miles. And then—all of a sudden—he stops hard, and I bang into him.

"Where did she go?"

At first I think he's asking me, but then I see the others—two cloaked, masked figures blending into the underbrush and the leaves and the snow. Ness and Isaac.

"That way." Isaac points as Ness reaches for me like she's checking for a fever.

She turns to Arlo as if I'm not there. "What's wrong with Effy?"

"Graffam." Arlo holds out the rock. Then he makes me turn around so he can show them the wound, and Ness says something about the hospital, and they are all talking at once, and I want to tell them it's making me hurt so much worse. I need them to be calm so *I* can be calm. But then Arlo says, in this soft voice, "Like Lara."

Everyone falls quiet. I shake my head as if this will shake the pieces into place. But the movement of it causes the world to tilt. I find his hand and use it to steady myself.

"Like Lara," I repeat. "She killed her . . . The index card during the game . . . Why me?"

"Maybe," says Arlo, "because power play number one in *Power Play* is 'Never upstage the director.' And she doesn't see you as her student, she sees you as competition. Or—who the fuck knows?" He runs his hand through his hair. Again and again until it's a wild creature all its own.

"Or," says Ness, "it's because you remind her of Lara. Ever since we got here, she's been telling me, 'I understand you because I was also the scholarship student, never at the top of the class, having to fight for what I wanted.' Sometimes it felt like she was talking about someone else. She kept saying, 'It's impossible to keep up when others have every advantage, no matter how close you are. Especially when you're close.'"

Ness's eyes meet mine. "She was talking about you, but she was also talking about . . ." Her voice fades off.

Herself, I think. All the things Graffam said to me—how I shouldn't let myself be held back by anyone, not even my best friend.

"What did she do?" I ask Ness. "When she found you?" I scan her face for signs of blood or bruising.

"Nothing. Just grabbed my arm."

We fall quiet. The wind howls and my head throbs in harmony. Something cold and wet brushes my cheek, and I look up. It's beginning to snow.

In the distance, there is movement. We turn to see a shadow appear then disappear, and it hits me what the word meant. Not one word. Not *mairwy*. Two words. *Mere. Why?*

Isaac whispers, "She's heading for the cliffs."

Arlo

Wednesday, January 21

We emerge from the forest, hovering at the tree line, eyes adjusting to all this open space. Brighton's Woe is just a black smudge on the horizon. In the dark I can barely make out the angles of the Moss, much less the ghostly silhouette of Graffam moving swiftly across the cliffs.

"She's changing the rules," Isaac says, his voice carried back to me on the wind.

"So we do too," I say.

The four of us move as one, letting ourselves be swallowed once again by the trees, using them for cover as we head toward the house.

The thud of my heart grows louder as we come around the back of it, out of sight of Graffam. Staying low, we leave the woods and run for the Moss, feet pounding against the earth, breath coming out in ragged huffs. Effy's hand is in mine. She sways, and I try to steady her.

We disappear inside its shadow, staying close as we creep

from one end to the other, toward the cliffs. I peer around the corner of the house, eyes straining, but Graffam's no longer in sight. She could be anywhere, I think, and a shiver runs through me.

"If we all go together, she'll definitely see us coming." For a second, I don't think they hear me, because the closer we get to the water, the louder the wind howls, trying to blow us back toward where we came from.

"So we split up," says Isaac. "Ness and I can wait here."

Effy nods, her eyes moving to the horizon. "Arlo and I can . . ." She rubs at her head. Not the back of it, where Graffam hit her, but a spot between her eyebrows.

"We can go down the rocks," I guess. "By the dock. And come up again, scaling the ledges, the rock stairs—whatever you want to call them. If she's still there, we'll find her. As soon as you see us or hear us yell," I say to Isaac and Ness, "start closing in."

"We surround her," says Isaac, "so that she can't run."

The four of us separate, breaking off two and two. In the distance, there's the *hoo hoo* of an owl. The snow is starting to fall in clouds, buffeted by the wind, swirling in all directions as if we're inside a snow globe. The ocean heaves and churns, a giant witch's cauldron.

"There," I say.

A figure appears atop the cliffs. Almost as if she's waiting for us. Then, just as quickly, she disappears again.

Snowflakes dot Effy's hair and cheeks, making her look like a winter fairy. She manages a smile, and I feel something lighten in my chest, like spring has come. The author Ray Cummings once said, *Time is what keeps everything from happening at once.* But every day here feels all at once, and I wonder how we're expected to go back to the real world and live in regular, dutiful time. Suddenly I want to run away with her, away from Graffam and the Moss and Bullshit Prep and the forest. Just run and run until we get to California, where we can live on the beach and find jobs that will pay us enough to take college classes and rent a little place just our own. Every night we'll sleep tangled together, and it'll be like Meredith Graffam never existed.

But if we do run, eventually there will be a film, and in that film will be the four of us in our most vulnerable, incriminating behind-closed-doors moments, out there for my parents and my brother and Jonah's family and the entire world to see.

Effy and I move toward the cliffs. We pick our way gingerly down one level of rock face to the next, heading for the waterside ledge we jumped off the first day of Jan Term. Just a little farther, a little farther.

We're near the bottom when a crash of heavy spray leaves me damp and shivering. *High tide.* I pull Effy back with me so that we're standing beneath the overhang of the rock above. I'm numb and wet and my hair is plastered to my face and the tide seems to be coming in instead of going out and this is a stupid game.

I push the hair back out of my eyes. In the black, black night I search for the path we took down here. Not an actual path: a tiered wedding cake of rock upon rock descending or ascending, depending on where you stand. Only my eyes must be playing tricks on me because the rocks look like great, hulking giants, crouched and waiting, and there is no way up. It has been swallowed by the darkness.

Here in this temporary shelter it's just the two of us. I blink down at Effy and she blinks up at me.

"Whatever happens," she says, "I'm not sorry."

I barely hear her over the sound of the ocean. The waves crash just feet away like they're reaching for us. With the next crash, we flatten ourselves against the face of the overhang and rise on tiptoe to avoid the water. I picture myself swept out to sea, eventually floating ashore, where someone will find me and wonder who or what I was. My heart pounds, so hard I feel the vibration of it everywhere, because I'm thinking about you, Jonah Maguire. The water surges toward me again, and I remember this about the tide—that sometimes it gets one last burst of energy before it flips.

Then, like a magic trick, the moon appears from behind a cloud. Effy and I look up at the same time, for only a moment. I look long enough to find Ophiuchus. The sight of him immediately makes me breathe out, breathe in, as if he's helped me remember how.

Just like you, I think.

And then I see her on the cliff, maybe fifteen feet above us. I flash back to that day she jumped into the water, when we followed her lead and did what she told us because we didn't know any better.

She hasn't seen us yet. Effy and I replace our masks, covering our faces once more, the tide threatening to sweep us away every time it thunders in. We shrink from it, fingers clawing at the rock wall, trying to latch on. A wave rushes in and drenches us. I wait till the water recedes and then launch myself forward. My feet immediately slip out from under me, and I land, belly first, on the rock face. The force of it nearly knocks me out, and I cling there, burning with shock and anger.

I scramble upright again, and Effy and I crawl-walk along this tier of the wedding cake, teetering and shivering, but managing to hold our ground. Suddenly I'm ten years old again, barreling down the twisting roads of our neighborhood on my bike, no helmet, speeding around turns. I remember the feeling of sailing over the handlebars, weightless and free, before I crashed into the ditch or the roadside or the road itself. At first, it was about rebelling against my parents. They had all the power, while I had none. They decided where we lived and when we moved, and I didn't have a choice in the matter. But gradually it became about something else—those few seconds, weightless and free. I became addicted to that feeling. I wanted it all the time.

"Arlo!"

The second I raise my head, I lose my grip and go sliding off, waves dragging me with them. My body goes limp as my ears fill with thunder, as my lungs fill with salt, as my eyes close.

Effy yanks me back, breaking the hold of the waves.

"Up that way," she calls, her words nearly lost in the wind and the wet.

She picks her way forward and then starts the climb upward to the next tier and then the next. I follow her, pausing briefly to catch my breath and look to see where we are, how much farther we have to go.

And that's when I see Graffam staring down at us.

Effy

WEDNESDAY, JANUARY 21

She glides away beyond our reach, cloak billowing in the wind, long hair blowing around her. I wonder how she can see where she's going. Some of the cliffs are more precarious than others, some more stable. Some have a sheer drop, while others slope down into the sea. Stray's Chasm, with its plunge of sixty feet, is the most dangerous of all.

I have a moment—in spite of the dull ache of my head—to think about what we're doing here on our last night of Jan Term. I should be sitting in front of a fire polishing my work, not prowling the forest and the cliffs. But then I think of what we discovered in that locked room, and the bloody knot on the back of my skull.

I'm nearing the top of the cliff when I see her move away. "She saw us," I call over my shoulder, hoping Arlo hears me.

I start after her again, faster than I should, so I don't lose sight of her. I have no idea if Isaac and Ness are coming. Graffam moves quickly, with purpose. I catch my breath as a figure appears in front of her, and she is caught—Graffam is caught! But then she swats the figure away like she's swatting a fly. The figure tumbles, nearly falling off the edge of the chasm itself. But Graffam hurries on without a backward glance.

"Hey!" I shout. She turns. I whip off my mask and throw it to the ground. "You've lost. Just give up."

And then I see Isaac within arm's reach of her. She's fast but he's faster, and now he has the element of surprise. He's shouting something I can't hear, and I make my way to them. Even up here, atop the cliffs, we feel the spray. Or maybe it's the snow that's making everything slick. I slip and then right myself. I glance behind me and see Arlo. To my left, Ness crawls away from the edge of the abyss.

Graffam stands rooted now, no longer moving. We are all maskless, our faces revealed. The wind carries most of her words away, so I hear only: ". . . you have betrayed my trust."

The expression on her face says that we have wronged her somehow, that *we* should apologize to *her*. We've momentarily forgotten that we're supposed to be hunting her. It feels more like she is hunting us.

"You set the boat loose," I say as it dawns on me. "When we were on the island. And you drugged us. You made us sick."

Isaac echoes me. "You drugged us. Like you drugged your former boss, like your ex-husband. Only, we never did anything except come here to learn from you and let you read our work—"

"*Let* me read?" Graffam roars at this.

I reach down and help Ness to her feet. "People are more

than one thing," she shouts at Graffam. "We are more than one thing."

"We want to know what you're planning to do with it," I add. "The footage of us."

I don't know what I expected—maybe shock, outrage. "Why?" she asks.

"Because we're in it. Because it's our lives."

"Oh, but, Effy. There's something powerful there, far bigger than the four of you." Instead of running away from this moment, Graffam is relishing it. "It's raw and unexpected. It's truth, and no one deals in truth anymore. I'm giving you the chance to live outside the box you've been living in your whole lives. To be immortalized."

Her tone is patronizing, as if we are very small, stupid children. *She actually believes what she is saying. She believes it. It's no use . . .*

"Nothing about this is for us. It's for you," Ness cries.

"At first," Graffam continues, "I thought it would be a fuck-you to Brighton and Hove—this incubator for worthless nepo babies—and all it stands for. And the things people are willing to do to win—walk into traffic, jump off a cliff, wander alone through the woods. But somewhere along the way, it became more than that. It became about you."

She perches on the clifftop, the snow whirling around her, the yawn of the chasm beyond, and gives us this look of genuine pity—that's the only way it can be described. I don't know how we ever thought we'd scare her. The woman has no fear.

"It's time you learned that life isn't always what you want it to be. No one handed me anything. Everything I've ever done, good and bad, is mine." She looks at us with wide, bright eyes.

"And the drugs?" Arlo says. It's the first time he's spoken since we climbed up here.

She tilts her head, her wild hair like seaweed. "I've always thought places like this brainwash you. They make you forget who you are and what's important."

"Is that what Lara did?" His voice is cool. He doesn't shout the words, but I watch as they land, like an arrow finding tender flesh.

"Lara never knew who she was. She played the role she was told to play. But when she spoke, people listened. She didn't even need to have a good story. I was faster and smarter. I was the rightful winner of The Hunt. I was Ruler of the Forest, not her. But after she died, they took my crown and gave it to her."

Graffam pulls her hair back and starts to braid it, the way I've seen her do before. She laughs, a hard, cutting sound, but it's the braiding of the hair—that simple, everyday act—that makes me think, *What if we don't get out of here alive?*

"No one cares what the scholarship student has to say." She smiles then, gazing straight ahead. "But the sole survivor of a tragedy? Suddenly everyone wants to hear from you."

"'If you don't have a story, create one,'" I say faintly, but my words vanish into the wind.

"Delete the footage or this time *we* out you," Arlo shouts. "More specifically, Peter Tobin's parents break the story in their many, many publications. Not just what you've done here, but what you did to Lara."

I wait for her to beg for mercy, to apologize, to go speechless, even for a moment. Instead she laughs. *Laughs*, a tinkling sound like breaking crystal. In spite of our plan, in spite of all we have on her. The earth below me tilts again, and my stomach lurches into my throat. In the distance, I hear the bell begin to ring.

She turns away from us then and moves across the rock face, quick and sure as a seabird. Out of the corner of my eye, a movement. Drea rushes toward us from the house.

When I wheel around again to look for Graffam, she is gone.

Where did she go?

She just disappeared.

How could she disappear?

We are shouting at one another. And then Drea is there too, shouting something over the wind and the waves.

"Her head," Arlo is telling her, his voice hoarse. He turns my face, so, so gently. Drea holds on to me as I feel fingers once more on my skull, poking at the wound.

"She did it." I wrench my neck to look at Drea. There on the cliffs, we all lean into each other as if seeking shelter from the gale. Drea is breathless, her voice barely audible. "It was her. Meredith killed Lara Leonard. Zoe overheard Paddy Eason—this was when they were fighting over the divorce. She had to sign an NDA. But when I told her about New York . . . Meredith was the one . . ."

A wave crashes against the rocks, drowning her words. Drea shifts, arm still tight around me.

I don't tell her that we know, we already figured it out. Drea is still talking: "She did it to take her story—no, not to take it, to create a story. To build her platform."

My head throbs in confirmation. Arlo shouts something about rogue waves, and I know this from Gran—extreme storm waves, also called storm surges, monster waves, sneaker waves, and killer waves, which can snatch people off the shore and end their lives in the blink of an eye.

The wave slams into the rock we're standing on, reaching us all the way up here, forty feet above the sea. The five of us go sprawling, half submerged in water. Another wave follows, and I feel it pulling my body with it, a great suctioning force. I cling to the cold, hard surface, fihgers scraping and digging.

Vaguely, I register Drea, red hair wet against her face, dragging me to safety and shouting something.

And then—from nowhere—Graffam lunges for me. She has crept her way back to us, and I feel myself being pulled into another wave, larger than the first. She is taking me with her until we are both under the water, and I feel the sharp sting of salt water in the wound on my head. I do the thing you should never do—panic. My breath is uneven as the sea fills my throat and my nose, my ears and my eyes, my hair tangling with my hands, which are struggling to loosen themselves from Graffam's grip. I hear my grandmother's voice: *Trust the power of the water.* The words she told me when she taught me to swim, me fighting against the water with every stroke. The more I fought, the more I sank. *Your body wants to float*, she said.

Graffam pushes me under, and I begin to fight—Graffam, not the water itself. I fight with all I have because I am not dying like this. Not here. Not now. I feel her on top of me, using me as a float, as something that will save her. She is using me as leverage, pushing down on the back of my skull where it's open and bleeding, a way to hoist herself from the sea.

I wrench myself free but it is too late. Everything goes hazy and then black.

When I open my eyes again—seconds, minutes later—I see sky.

And this is when everything slows down.

Sound stops.

Time stops.

I lose track of everyone else.

In my mind I hear a song, and an energy, intense and otherworldly, courses through my body. Like I'm a puppet, and the melody is pulling my strings.

"The wind doth blow today, my love,
And a few small drops of rain;
I never had but one true-love,
In cold grave she was lain."

Somehow I get away from Graffam. And then I see Ness's hand reaching for me. My vision is off, everything blurry, as if I'm looking through a fogged-up lens. I swing my own arm outward, and suddenly I feel the contact—her hand grasping mine.

Ness heaves me toward her, closer to the rock ledge. She falls back hard, and I break my own fall with my cheek. Through the spray, I see Isaac, crouched low, and Drea on her back, red hair like blood.

"What is this?" I manage.

"The perfect storm," Ness chokes, coughing up water.

I search for Arlo then, my heart pounding. I am unable to move. I see him a few feet away, pale and shaky and soaked through, chest heaving, breath ragged. I think of Jonah, his best friend.

"Arlo," I call, but the word is drowned out. "Arlo." Louder this time.

His eyes slowly focus on mine.

"I need you. Hang on."

He blinks. Then again. He nods, barely. Then more emphatically. "Hanging on." The words blurred beneath the wind and the thunder of the ocean. "Hanging on," he repeats, his voice stronger.

We scramble upward—Arlo, Ness, Isaac, Drea, me—instinctively going for higher ground, until we once again reach the relative safety of the clifftops. From up here I can see only snow and waves, the sea thrashing and crashing after us. The world lists. I close my eyes. And then I open them again.

"'Tis I, my love, sits on your grave,
And will not let you sleep;
For I crave one kiss of your clay-cold lips,
And that is all I seek."

Arlo reaches for my hand, or maybe I reach for his. Our fingers twine together, warm in the cold. Together, we hold on—holding each other, trying to root ourselves to the rock face. A sound behind us and we turn. She has followed us up here. Meredith Graffam.

"You crave one kiss of my clay-cold lips,
But my breath smells earthy strong;

*If you have one kiss of my clay-cold lips,
Your time will not be long."*

It's then I see where we are—at the edge of Stray's Chasm, the drop below us pitch-black and bottomless. A few inches closer and we would have fallen fifty, sixty feet, our bodies crashing to the earth far, far below.

All of a sudden I'm overcome by the call of the void, that urge to jump, to soar, to fly, to pitch headfirst into the unknown.

I sway in the wind and the wet, the sleet slicing my skin like the sharpest razors. The abyss *right there*, too close.

I think about my parents. About the impact that took my mother's life, a meteor strike, its reverberations still felt all these years later. If I could bring her back, I would. I would shock her to life like Frankenstein's monster. But she isn't here. I am. And I have a choice. We all do.

I turn my head to look at Arlo, Ness, Isaac, and Drea here on the edge beside me. Our eyes meet, and in that instant I see it. A decision made. All for one. I don't want to live in a world with Graffam, knowing that she can and will expose us—our most tender, fucked-up selves. Never sleeping, being always afraid, not knowing when she might come for me the way she did for Lara.

I turn my head again.

Meredith Graffam looms before us, eyes glittering, a smile that says she's won, her back to the chasm.

I hope you know this isn't personal, I think.

Slán go fóill.

Goodbye for now.

And then we push her.

Oscar winner Meredith Graffam identified as woman who died after being pulled from ocean; no foul play suspected, DA says

BY GWEN THOMAS (AP)

The woman who died after she was pulled from the ocean in Parkerton, Massachusetts, has been identified by authorities.

Meredith Graffam, 48, was found unresponsive Thursday afternoon in the water near Stray's Chasm, a large rock fissure in the shoreline of Murton Wood, according to a statement from the Essex County district attorney's office.

Her body was reportedly floating face down in proximity to the chasm around 4:14 p.m., the statement said.

Graffam was pulled out of the ocean and taken to Reid Hospital in Parkerton, where she was later pronounced dead, according to the statement.

Foul play is not suspected, the district attorney noted. Wednesday night saw the largest storm in the area since the Halloween nor'easter of 1991, with 80-foot waves that caused widespread flooding and left some 75 homes destroyed.

Graffam was in Parkerton to teach writing as part of the renowned Jan Term program at Brighton and Hove Preparatory Academy. The winner of two Oscars and a Tony Award, Graffam was—in addition to being an actress, director, playwright, and screenwriter—the author of *The Hunt*, a *New York Times* bestseller published when she was 20 years old. In a career marked by both controversy and acclaim, Graffam was admired for her tenacity, resilience, and ability to reinvent herself.

five years later

BRIGHTON AND HOVE
PREPARATORY ACADEMY

Parkerton, Massachusetts

September 1

Dear Effy Green:

First and foremost, huge congratulations on the success of the movie! I am sure it will come as no surprise that your family here at Brighton and Hove has followed the blockbuster trajectory of *When We Were Monsters* with enormous pride and excitement. It is alumni such as yourself and your distinguished film colleagues Vanessa Cato, Arlo Ellis-Noon, and Isaac Williams who inspire and reaffirm what we do and why we do it. You and your fellow Jan Termers are exemplary models of what we at Brighton and Hove strive to achieve.

On that note, we would like to cordially invite you to return to Brighton and Hove to teach the next session of Jan Term. We cannot imagine a greater inspiration for our students than to be mentored by four of this school's most accomplished graduates. In addition, honorary Brighton and Hover Drea Garcia will be joining as well.

We understand and appreciate that you are in demand. Your presence will be required from Wednesday, January 8, through Thursday, January 23. You will, of course, be living in the Moss. All travel will be paid for, and once we hear from you regarding your interest and availability, we can discuss remuneration and further details. Please reach out with any questions!

I look forward to hearing from you. We hope to see you in January!

Sincerely, your old friend,

Scott Booker
Dean of Students

Effy

WEDNESDAY, JANUARY 8

I gaze up through the sunroof, tilting my chin toward that calm blue sky, admiring the way the light splashes through the treetops. I chase it, that magical, dappled light. I am technically behind the wheel, but it feels almost as if I'm flying, no pedals, nothing touching the ground. Weightless.

This is my first time in Massachusetts since I graduated from Brighton and Hove five years ago. When the invitation arrived from Dean Scott Booker, I thought it was a joke. But then Ness called and said, "You'll never believe this." And then Arlo got one too. And Isaac. And Drea.

Gran said, "You don't have to go." She's never forgiven the school for leaving us in the "care" of Meredith Graffam. A word Gran always emphasizes as if using air quotes. If she only knew the half of it. No one knows except for the five of us. And no one ever will.

The film we made reveals many of the sordid details, but we've never claimed it's factual. Only that it's "loosely inspired by a true story." Arlo's novel, the one we based the film on, is closer to the truth than anyone can imagine.

I pass through Parkerton and its idyllic small-town main street lined with boutiques and cafés. And then, suddenly, I'm at the gates of Brighton and Hove. I almost turn around, but I don't. Because that's what we do. We don't turn around. We keep going forward.

The campus hasn't changed. It is blanketed in white. Students cluster outside the classroom building and library. They hurry down sidewalks, this way and that, like I once did, always rushing to get somewhere. I feel a stab of homesickness, but I'm not sure for what.

Past the dining hall and the dorms, I wind through the trees until I reach the gated access road to the Moss. Gone is the elaborate gate. In its place, a guard in a booth.

"Effy Green," I tell him.

He consults his list and says, "Right. You're here for Jan Term." He is young, with a pleasant face.

"Yes."

"Did you work on the movie too? The director just arrived." Admiration in his voice, pride that he's met Isaac Williams, wunderkind of Sundance, already in demand and only twenty-three years old.

"I did."

This is still new to me, the praise from strangers. I don't tell him that I wrote the script with my friend Vanessa Cato, based on the *New York Times* bestselling novel by Arlo Ellis-Noon.

"Yeah," the guard says. "It was pretty good. I've seen it

twice. You should do a screening while you're here. You could sell some tickets. People would come from all over."

He folds his arms, leaning against the open door of the guard booth, and I paste on a wary smile.

"So, like, how accurate was it? I mean, I know it's 'fiction.'" He actually does use air quotes. "But all that stuff with the teacher, that was wild. Do you know if any of it actually happened?" He doesn't wait for me to answer. "She died there, you know. Meredith Graffam. Yeah. Fell off the edge of a cliff. Some say she jumped, that she was still devastated over the loss of this friend she had who died falling off that same cliff back in 1995 . . ."

I listen for as long as I can, and then—as the sun shifts lower in the sky—I interrupt him to say that I'm expected for dinner.

And now I am in the woods. Murton Wood. *Murder Wood.* Scarred with potholes, the road is a slender ribbon snaking its way through overgrown brush, a wall of trees on either side, everything covered in white.

A MILE LATER, I am at the Moss. It looks just as it does in my memory, perched atop the cliffs against the backdrop of trees. In the five years since I've been here, the forest seems to have grown closer, as if it is invading, and I have this sudden image of the house being consumed. Or is it the other way around? Is it the house planning to consume the forest?

There are a handful of cars parked in the drive. I pull up next to them and turn off the engine. We didn't film the movie here. Too many memories. Instead we found a place in Northern California that we convinced ourselves was a near likeness of the Moss—imposing and gloomy outside, colorful inside—with a rugged coastline that looked similar to the torturous shoreline of northeastern Massachusetts.

Gazing up at it now though, I'm struck by the fact that it's just a house. Stone and wood, brick and mortar. A spacious, rambling manor with a dozen chimneys and lots of windows. Not dark and terrifying, not a living, breathing thing at all, the way it is in my memory.

I check my reflection in the rearview mirror. The face that stares back at me looks older than it did when I lived here, but beneath my fringe—worn longer now—my eyes are brighter, relieved of the weight they used to carry. I look, for lack of a better word . . . happy.

A movement in an upstairs window catches my eye. The flutter of a curtain. A glint of light. From somewhere, I hear voices, which tells me the others are coming. Isaac from New York, where he lives with his sister and her wife. Ness from grad school at the University of Iowa, where she's majoring in poetry. Drea all the way from Madrid, where she owns a small gallery. And Arlo from the bungalow we share in the hills over Los Angeles. It's been a week since I've seen him—the book still has him touring, and I've been doing film publicity on the West Coast. As I think about him now, I feel the familiar electrical impulses flood my nervous system.

I only have a few seconds left to myself before I'm enfolded and encircled by my fellow Odds, so I walk to the cliffs. Sea grass grows up through the cracks in the rock, and a small cluster of dandelions has arrived early, fluffy white heads bent toward the sea. The air is strangely warm for January.

The day I left the Moss five years ago, I wrote a single letter to my father, agreeing to see him. We are taking things slow. Perhaps we will take things slow for the rest of our lives.

When the serial killer Dennis Rader was convicted of murdering ten people, his daughter told the press, *I had to learn how to grieve a man that was not dead, somebody I loved very much that no one else loved anymore.*

For so long, I grieved my dad, but now I'm learning to love him again. I no longer write to him—we text or talk on the phone. But I write to you, even though you're no longer here to read it.

Dear Meredith Graffam,

Did you know that Mary Shelley never called him the monster? In *Frankenstein*. "Monster" was added later by readers, playwrights, pop culture. But she never once called him that. Because the creature wasn't the monster. Victor was.

We are all monsters to someone.

I was asked recently if I would have come to the Moss five years ago if I knew what lay ahead. My answer? I can't look back. I can't change the decisions I made. I don't want to. They're what got me here. Besides, you taught me a lot about writing and about myself.

You were a person who used other people and thought that was okay. You were a person who didn't care about us but pretended to, who preyed on weakness—our deepest, darkest truths and fears—because it served a greater purpose, your purpose. Maybe that doesn't justify it. Maybe nothing justifies what we did. But sometimes we don't get a choice in who we save. And sometimes we do.

We chose to save ourselves.

Four figures emerge from the Moss, chattering, laughing, animated. Like a cloud, all thoughts of you drift away, leaving only the bluest winter sky in the fading sun. I think about who I was—who all of us were—when we first came to Brighton and Hove. How fleeting it was, even though we thought it would last forever.

Tomorrow we will welcome a new group of students, filled with hope and excitement and wonder, their entire lives before them. We will teach them that it takes more than soul stamina to achieve success. It takes fortitude, determination, and fidelity to yourself and those who believe in you. And sometimes, for better or worse, it means committing acts you wouldn't think you're capable of.

We will teach them to stand out, face their fears, shine in their own way, and plan all the way to the end. And if they don't have a story, to create one. These are things you taught us.

The philosopher Jean-Paul Sartre once wrote that who we

are is defined by our actions, and that we are all just as capable of bad things as good ones. In the end, it's the choices we make that define who we are. Turn right. Turn left. Stay home. Get in the car. Drink and drive. Send the application. Write the story. Kiss the boy. Play a game. Go to the woods. Go to the water. Dive in. Take the risk. Just look up. Live.

The breeze ruffles my hair. For the briefest second, I close my eyes and root myself in this moment. Then I reach down and pluck a dandelion. I glance toward the house.

In the early-evening sunlight, the features of the four figures start to fill in. Flesh and blood and bone and tissue. But so much more. Arlo. Ness. Drea. Isaac.

I think of a quote from Sartre, one that feels right for here and now: *There may be more beautiful times, but this one is ours.*

I turn back toward the horizon, Brighton's Woe a silhouette in the distance, and make a wish. With a single breath, I blow the seeds, watching them flutter away like snowflakes until they disappear into the sea.

Acknowledgments

When I was growing up, I read voraciously. Of the many, many books I devoured, I gravitated most to those by Lois Duncan, the Brontë sisters, and Shirley Jackson. They pulled back the curtain on humanity and revealed what lurked in the shadows. They kept me in a constant state of chilled, delicious unease.

It was my love for them that inspired some of my earliest childhood stories—prison mysteries that usually included a crumbling old estate, a dark forest, a group of disparate strangers thrown together in extraordinary circumstances, and at least one murder. After the release of my eleventh book, when I, as reader, was consuming yet another twisted mystery, I thought, *How have I never written the type of story I used to most love reading?* I have, after all, crossed genres multiple times in my career—but never once crossed into the genre I'm drawn to most.

As readers, we like to put ourselves in the shoes of the characters we read about, to ask ourselves what we might do in the same situations. I think it's normal to be fascinated by the darker side of humanity. As with true crime stories, it can be riveting to delve into the events and circumstances that might turn a good person into a monster or, at the very least, make them commit monstrous acts. And to ask ourselves, *Could this be me? Am I capable of this too?*

I also think there's something wonderfully atmospheric about dark academia. I personally love to slip into any book set on a hallowed campus surrounded by woods and mystery, inhabited by ivy-covered buildings, storied tradition, dark lore, and murder—anything to send a shiver down my spine.

I wrote *When We Were Monsters* for my teenage self, who loved ABBA and Shirley Jackson in equal measure, and who hid the scary books behind the bookcase so she would be safe at night. How quickly I learned, though, that *reading* dark academia and mysteries and thrillers hadn't prepared me for actually *writing* one of my own. The book you are holding is a genuine labor of love. As always, I could not have done it alone.

Kerry Sparks is not just the world's most brilliant literary agent—she is the greatest creative partner I have ever known. Without her energy, insight, humor, and heart, I would feel as remote as Brighton's Woe and as unmoored as the little boat that someone (no spoilers) cuts loose. Big, grateful, eternal love to her and to everyone at Levine Greenberg Rostan Literary Agency. And bouquets of thanks to the amazing Sylvie Rabineau. I still can't believe I'm fortunate enough to work with you.

My husband, Justin Conway, is my heart. I met him years

ago on a wild, remote island where we drove, no headlights, through a primeval forest by the light of fireflies. Walked barefoot through the mud to look for treasure. Escaped a locked and very haunted basement. And fell in love at first sight. Because when you meet your person, you know.

My editor, Katherine Harrison, is one of the very best editors I've ever had the good fortune to work with. She is so fully invested, so thorough and smart and savvy. She is a true partner, and this book and I could not have been in better hands. I've learned so much about my own writing from her, and I am a better writer now than I was before we started working together. Added bonus, she's a warm and wonderful human as well. I hope to write 10,000 more books with her.

Special, heartfelt thank-yous to: Melanie Nolan, who encouraged me to make this story more murdery. Oh, what a happy day that was! And for years of insightful, thoughtful, genius editing and nurturing my creativity. Gianna Lakenauth, for everything, and I mean everything, she does. I'm so honored to be working with you.

And speaking of honored—what an honor it has been to work with Barbara Marcus these past ten-plus years. Barbara is not only a force of nature, she's who I want to be—except that, even if I tried my hardest, I could never be that fabulous. Thank you with my whole heart for all you are and all you do, and for all you mean to my books and me.

Enormous thanks, too, to the fantastic team at Knopf and Penguin Random House. Production editor Melinda Ackell and proofreader Amy Schroeder. Designers Trisha Previte (cover), who created the world's most gorgeous cover, and

Michelle Canoni (interior). And the amazing artist Alexis Franklin for the cover portrait of Effy, which leaves me speechless every time I look at it. Thank you to my incomparable publicists, Dominique Cimina and Joey Ho, and the incredible marketing department—Andrea Baird, Gabriella Murdoch, Jenn Inzetta, Erica Trotta, Katie Halata, and Adrienne Waintraub. Huge thanks to John Adamo, Jackie Hornberger, Alison Kolani, Jake Eldred, Natalia Dextre, Hannah Babcock, and Claire Rivkin.

I send my love and gratitude across the pond to Penguin Random House UK and to the entire brilliant team there. With an extra-special shout-out to my extraordinary editor, Ben Horslen, who is an utter joy to work with. Harriet Venn, my phenomenal publicist. And Michael Bedo, for all his marketing wizardry.

Beauport, the Sleeper-McCann House, provided my inspiration for the Moss. If you're ever in Gloucester, Massachusetts, you must go see its enchanting beauty for yourself. While you're there, you can visit Rafe's Chasm, which is the real-life Stray's Chasm. From there, you can see Norman's Woe, the actual Brighton's Woe. And, if you're lucky, you just might spot the Gloucester sea serpent.

Thank you, E. Lockhart and Kathleen Glasgow, for your much-appreciated, much-cried-over blurbs. And to all my inspiring author friends for laughter, camaraderie, commiseration, and unconditional love.

Thank you to the magnificently lovely Holly Thomson for research, admin assistance, cat photos, love, and support.

Thank you to the fierce and fabulous women of Salon

EllaPar, especially Stacy Monticello, Kayla Clark, and Julie Gladden.

Thank you to the teachers who got me here through all your own hard work and encouragement.

Thank you to the readers who have grown up with me and the readers who are reading my words for the first time. I hope you stick around for more.

Thank you to my friends Vanessa Cato, Drea Garcia, and Scott Booker for lending me your names for this story. While real-life Vanessa (aka VCPoetry) wasn't adopted like the Ness in the book, she is a gifted poet with a warm, loving family, and—as Effy observes—she radiates lightness and joy. Real-life Drea is a brilliant artist and passionate advocate in the body positive movement who sent me my very own Petunia when I began writing this book. And the wonderful Scott—along with his brother Steve—is a dear, cherished friend from high school days. Thank you, too, to the readers who lent their names in cameos throughout.

Thank you to my friends and family, most of all my wonderful parents, Penelope Niven and Jack F. McJunkin. I miss you more than I can ever say.

And last, but not least, thank you to the literary kitties who fill our home and our hearts. I probably could have written this a little faster if you hadn't been lying on my keyboard, sitting between the monitor and me, or yelling for food. But I wouldn't have it any other way.